P9-DFH-551

# WAYWARD SON

ALSO BY
RAINBOW ROWELL

CARRY ON

LANDLINE

FANGIRL

ELEANOR & PARK

ATTACHMENTS

# RAINBOW ROWELL

# WAYWARD SON

WEDNESDAY BOOKS
NEW YORK

This is a work of fiction. All of the characters,
organizations, and events portrayed in this novel are
either products of the author's imagination or are used fictitiously.

First published in the United States by Wednesday Books, an imprint of
St. Martin's Publishing Group

WAYWARD SON. Copyright © 2019 by Rainbow Rowell. All rights
reserved. Printed in the United States of America. For information, address
St. Martin's Publishing Group, 120 Broadway, New York, NY 10271.

www.wednesdaybooks.com

Designed by Anna Gorovoy

Interior and endpaper illustrations by Jim Tierney

The Library of Congress Cataloging-in-Publication Data
is available upon request.

ISBN 978-1-250-14607-6 (hardcover)
ISBN 978-1-250-25802-1 (international, sold outside the U.S.,
subject to rights availability)
ISBN 978-1-250-61831-3 (signed)
ISBN 978-1-250-14609-0 (e-book)

Our books may be purchased in bulk for promotional, educational,
or business use. Please contact your local bookseller or the Macmillan
Corporate and Premium Sales Department at 1-800-221-7945, extension
5442, or by email at MacmillanSpecialMarkets@macmillan.com.

First U.S. Edition: September 2019
First International Edition: September 2019

10  9  8  7  6  5  4  3  2  1

*For Rosey and Laddie*
*May you know that you're loved,*
*even when you're lost*

# WAYWARD SON

# EPILOGUE

Simon Snow did what he came to do.

What they all said he would do someday. He found the big baddie—he found *two*—and he finished them off.

He didn't expect to live through it. And he *hadn't*.

Baz once told him that everything was a story, and that Simon was the hero. They'd been dancing at the time. Touching. Baz was looking at Simon like anything was possible for them now, like love was inevitable.

Everything *was* a story. And Simon *was* the hero. He saved the day. That's when stories end—with everyone looking ahead to "happily ever after."

*This* is what happens if you try to hang on after the end. When your time has come and passed. When you've done the thing you were meant to do.

The theatre goes dark, the pages go blank.

Everything is a story, and Simon Snow's is over.

# 1

## BAZ

Simon Snow is lying on the sofa.

Simon Snow is pretty much always lying on the sofa these days. With his leathery red wings tucked up behind him like a pillow and a can of cheap cider hanging off his hand.

He used to hold a sword like that. Like it was attached.

It's finally summer in London. I've been studying all day—exams next week; Bunce and I are buried in books. We both pretend that Snow is studying for his exams, too. He hasn't been at uni in weeks, I'd wager. He hasn't been off the sofa unless it's to go down to the corner to buy chips and cider; he ties his tail around his waist and hides his wings under a dreadful tan mackintosh—he looks like Quasimodo. Or a flasher. He looks like three kids in a trench coat pretending to be a complete wanker.

The last time I saw Snow without wings and a tail, Bunce had just got home from a lecture. She cast a concealment spell his way without even thinking about it—and he went feral on her. *"For fuck's sake, Penny, I'll tell you if I want your magic!"*

Her magic.

My magic.

It wasn't very long ago that all the magic was *his*.

He was the One, wasn't he? The most. The magic-est.

Bunce and I never leave him alone now if we can help it. We go to lectures, we study. (That's what Bunce and I *do*. That's who we *are*.) But there's always one of us around—making Snow tea he won't drink, sharing vegetables he won't eat, asking questions he won't answer . . .

I think he hates the sight of us most days.

I think he hates the sight of *me*. Maybe I should take the hint. . . .

But Simon Snow has always hated the sight of me—with a few recent and bittersweet exceptions. In a way, that face he makes when I walk in the room (like he's just remembered something awful) is the only thing that still feels familiar.

I've loved him through worse. I've loved him hopelessly. . . .

So what's a little less hope?

"I think I'm going to get a curry," I say. "Do you want anything?"

He doesn't turn away from the television.

I try again. "Do you want anything, Snow?"

A month ago, I would have walked to the sofa and touched his shoulder. Three months ago, I would have dropped a kiss on his cheek. Last September, when he and Bunce first moved into this flat, I would have had to pull my mouth away from his to ask the question, and he might not have let me finish.

He shakes his head.

# 2

## SIMON

Maya Angelou said that when someone shows you who they are, you should believe them.

I heard that on an inspirational television show. It came on after *Law & Order*, and I didn't change the channel.

*When someone shows you who they are, believe them.*

That's what I'm going to say when I break up with Baz.

I'm doing it so that he doesn't have to.

I can tell he wants to end this. I can see it in the way he looks at me. Or in the way he *doesn't* look at me—because if he did, he'd have to face what a tosser he's saddled himself with. What an absolute loser.

Baz is at uni now. Thriving.

And he's as handsome as ever. (*More* handsome than ever. Taller, bolder, with a beard now anytime he wants one. Like adolescence isn't quite done dealing him aces.)

Everything that happened last year . . .

Everything that happened with the Mage and the Humdrum just made Baz more of who he was meant to be. He avenged his mother. He solved the mystery that's hung over him since he was 5. He proved himself as a man and a magician.

He proved himself *right:* The Mage really was evil! And I really was a fraud—"the worst Chosen One who's ever been chosen," just like Baz used to say. He was right about me all along.

*When someone shows you who they are, believe them.*

When someone fucks up absolutely everything—that person is an absolute fuckup.

I don't know how to make it any more clear to him. I lie here on the sofa. And I don't have any plans. And I don't have any promise. And this is what I *am.*

Baz fell in love with what I *was*—power and potential unchecked. Nuclear bombs are nothing but potential.

Now I'm what comes after.

Now I'm the three-headed frog. The radioactive fallout.

I think Baz would have broken up with me by now if he didn't feel so sorry for me. (And if he hadn't promised to love me. Magicians get hung up on honour.)

So I'll be the one to do it. I can do it. One time, an orc-upine shot a needle into my shoulder, and I tore it out with my own teeth—I can handle pain.

I just . . .

I wanted a few more nights of this. Of him being here in the room with me, mine on the surface at least.

I'll never have someone like Baz again. There *is* no one like Baz; it's like dating someone out of a legend. He's a heroic vampire, a gifted magician. He's dead handsome. (I used to be someone out of a legend. I was Foretold, you know? I used to be part of the oral tradition.)

I wanted a few more nights of this. . . .

But I hate watching Baz suffer. I hate being the reason he suffers.

"Baz," I say. I sit up and set down my can of cider. (Baz hates cider, even the smell of it.)

He's standing at the front door. "Yes?"

I swallow. "When someone shows you who they are—"

Penny bursts in then, jamming Baz's shoulder with the door.

"For Crowley's sake, Bunce!"

"I've got it!" Penny drops her backpack. She's wearing a baggy purple T-shirt, and her dark brown hair is scraped into a messy knot at the top of her head.

"Got what?" Baz frowns.

"*We*"—she points at Baz and me both—"are going on *holiday!*"

I rub my palms into my eyes. They're crunchy with sleep, even though I've been up for hours. "Not going on holiday," I mumble.

"To America!" she persists. She pushes my feet off the sofa, and sits on the arm, facing me. "To see Agatha!"

Baz barks out a laugh. "Ha! Does Agatha know we're coming?"

"It'll be a surprise!" Penny says.

"*Surprise!*" Baz singsongs. "*It's your ex-boyfriend and his boyfriend and that girl you never liked very much!*"

"Agatha likes me fine!" Penny sounds offended. "She's just not an effusive person."

Baz snorts. "She seemed pretty effusive about getting the fuck out of England and away from magic."

"I'm worried about her, if you must know. She hasn't been returning my texts."

"Because she doesn't *like* you, Bunce."

I look up at Penelope. "When did you last hear from Agatha?"

"A few weeks ago. Normally she'd have texted me back by now. Even if it's just to tell me to leave her alone. And she hasn't been posting as many photos of Lucy"—Agatha's little dog—"on Instagram. I think she might be lonely. Depressed."

"Depressed," I say.

"So, is this a holiday?" Baz asks. "Or an intervention?" He's leaning against the door with his arms crossed and his shirt-sleeves pushed up. Baz always looks like he's in an ad for expensive watches. Even when he isn't wearing one.

"Why can't it be both?" Penny says. "We've always wanted to take a road trip across America."

Baz tilts his head. "Have we?"

Penny looks at me and smiles. "Simon and I have."

She's right, we have. And for a moment, I can see it: The three of us, speeding down some abandoned motorway—no, *highway*—in an old convertible. I'm driving. We're all wearing sunglasses. We're listening to The Doors, and Baz is complaining about it. But he's got his shirt unbuttoned to his navel, so I'm not complaining about anything. The sky is huge and blue and full of lens flare. *America* . . .

My wings shudder. That happens now when I'm uncomfortable. "We can't go to America."

Penny kicks me. "Why not?"

"Because I'll never make it through airport security." My tail is mostly squashed beneath me at the moment, but I flick the end up around my thigh to remind her it's there.

"I'll *coat* you with spells," she says.

"I don't want to be coated with spells."

"I've been working on a new one, Simon, it's a thing of beauty—"

"Eight hours on an aeroplane with my wings bunched up . . ."

"The new spell makes them disappear," she grins.

I look up at her, startled. "I don't want them to disappear."

That's a lie; I want them *gone*. I want to be myself again. I want to be free. But . . . I can't. Yet. I can't explain why not. (Even to myself.)

"Temporarily," Penny says. "I think it will just make them go away for a while, until the spell wears off."

"What about this?" I flick my tail again.

"We'll have to use another spell. Or you can tuck it."

*America* . . .

I never really thought I'd get to America—unless I had to chase the Humdrum there.

"The thing is . . ." Penny bites her bottom lip and wrinkles her nose, like she's both ashamed and excited. "I've already bought the tickets!"

"Penelope!" It's a bad idea. I have *wings*. And no money. And I don't want to get dumped by my boyfriend at the Statue of Liberty. I'd rather get dumped right here, thanks. Also I don't know how to drive. "We can't just—"

She starts singing "Don't Stop Believing." Which is hardly the United States' national anthem, but it was our favourite song in third year, when we first said we were going to take this road trip, someday, when we'd won the war.

Well . . . we have won the war, haven't we? (Never thought that would mean killing the Mage and sacrificing my own magic, but it's still, technically, a win.)

Penny is telling me to "*hold on to that feel-layy-anng.*" Baz is watching us from the door.

"If you've already bought the tickets . . ." I say.

Penny jumps to her feet on the sofa. "Yes! We're going on holiday!" She stops and looks at Baz. "Are you in?"

Baz is still looking at me. "If you think I'm letting you traipse around a foreign country by yourselves, especially in this political climate—"

Penelope is jumping again. "America!"

# 3

## PENELOPE

All right, so, yes, things haven't been going so well. And *I* should have been the one to see it coming.

Was *Simon* supposed to see it coming? He doesn't see anything coming! He's taken aback by Tuesdays!

Was Baz supposed to see it coming? All Baz has been able to focus on for the last year is Simon; he can't see past the hearts in his own eyes.

No, it should have been me.

But I was just so happy to be *through* everything. The Humdrum vanquished, the Mage revealed, most of us still alive to talk about it . . . Simon, all in one piece! Simon with extra pieces, yes, but hale and whole, with a future!

Simon Snow, in no grave danger—my most ardent prayer answered.

I just wanted to *enjoy* it.

I wanted to get a flat and go to university, and just be a normal teenager for once, before we left our teens behind us. I didn't want to do anything radical—I didn't fuck off to California and leave my magic wand behind, for example. But I wanted to relax.

Lesson learned: Relaxation is the *most* insidious humdrum.

We all moved to London last year and started uni, as if our world hadn't just been turned upside down and shaken. As if Simon hadn't just been turned inside out.

I mean—he killed *the Mage*, the closest thing he'd ever had to a father. It was an accident, but still.

And the Mage killed Ebb, who wasn't exactly Simon's mother figure, but who was definitely like his weird aunt. Ebb *loved* Simon. She treated him like he was one of her little goats.

So, yes, I knew that Simon had suffered—but I thought winning would make up for it. I thought victory would be enough. That relief would fill in all those holes.

I think Baz believed love would do the trick. . . .

It really is a miracle that the two of them ended up together in the end. (Star-cross'd lovers. "From forth the fatal loins of these two foes." The whole shebang.)

But it was a mistake thinking of that as an end. There is no end. Bad things happen, and then they stop, but they keep on wreaking havoc inside of people.

I know perfectly well that going on holiday isn't going to magickally fix everything. (If there were a way to *magickally* fix this, I swear to Stevie I'd have figured it out by now.) But we could all use a change of scenery.

Maybe it'll do Simon good to see himself in a new context. There are no bad memories waiting for him in America. No good ones either—but anything's a win that gets him off the sofa.

# 4

## AGATHA

I never call Penelope back.

Who even *calls* people anyway? Who leaves voicemails?

Penelope Bunce. That's who.

I've told her to text me like a normal person. (I texted her to tell her.)

*"But you don't reply to my texts!"* she replied.

*"Yes, but at least I read them, Penny. When you leave a voicemail, I just recoil in horror."*

*"Well, then tell me what I need to do to get a reply, Agatha."*

I didn't reply to that.

Because there's nothing I could say that would satisfy her.

And because I've left that world behind! Including Penelope!

There's no way to leave the World of Mages behind and hold on to Penelope Bunce—she's the mage-iest mage of them all. She lives and breathes magic. You can't even eat toast without Penelope magickally melting the butter.

One time, I turned my phone off to get a break from her, and it *still* beeped when she sent a text.

*"No more magickal texts!"* I texted her.

*"Agatha!"* she texted back. *"Are you coming home for Christ-mas?"*

I didn't answer. I didn't go home.

My parents were relieved, I think.

The World of Mages slipped into chaos when Simon killed the Mage. (Or when Penelope did. Or Baz. I still don't get how it went down.)

I was nearly killed that day, too—and it wasn't the first time. I think my parents feel partly responsible (as they *should*), for ever inviting Simon "the Chosen One" Snow into our lives.

Would my life have been different if I hadn't grown up with Simon like a brother? If I hadn't become his placeholder girl-friend?

I still would have ended up at Watford, learning magic tricks. But I wouldn't have been standing at ground zero, year after year after year.

*"When are you coming home?"* Penelope texts.

*I'm not,* I'm tempted to reply. *And why do you even care?*

She and I were never best friends. I was always too posh for Penny—too shallow, too frivolous. She just wants me in her life now because I was always there before, and she's holding on to the past as desperately as I'm trying to run from it.

I was there before things fell apart.

But my coming home won't put anything back together.


"I can't believe you're drinking that," Ginger says.

We've just sat down to lunch and I've ordered the only black tea on the menu. "I can't believe it either," I say. *"Vanilla Mint Earl Grey.* My father would be appalled."

"Stimulants," Ginger says, shaking her head.

I add some skimmed milk to my tea. Full-fat is never an option here.

"And *dairy*," Ginger groans.

All she drinks is beetroot juice. It looks exactly like blood, smells like dirt, and sometimes, like now, leaves a bright red moustache on her upper lip.

"You look like a vampire," I say. Though she looks nothing like the only vampire I've ever met. Ginger has springy brown hair and freckled brown skin. Her mom is Thai and Brazilian, and her dad is from Barbados, and she's got the brightest eyes and rosiest cheeks of anyone I've ever met. Maybe it's the beetroot.

"I feel activated," she says, spreading her fingers in the air.

"How activated?"

"At least eighty per cent. What about you?"

"Holding steady at fifteen," I say. A waitress sets down Ginger's quinoa bowl and my plate of avocado toast.

"Agatha," she says, "you always say fifteen. We've been working the programme for three months. You've got to be at least sixteen per cent activated by now."

I don't feel any different. "Maybe some people are born inactive."

She tuts at me. "Don't say that! I would never have befriended an inert organism."

I smile at Ginger. But the truth is, we were both feeling rather inert when we met. That's how we became friends, I think—travelling in the same scene, drifting at the edge of it. I kept ending up next to Ginger in the kitchen at parties, or sitting near her on the dark part of the beach at bonfires.

San Diego has been better for me than the Watford School

of Magicks ever was. I don't miss my wand. I don't miss the war. I don't miss the everyday pretending that I cared about being a good mage.

But I'll never be *of* this place.

I'm not like my classmates here. Or my neighbours. Or the people I meet at parties. I've always had Normal friends, but I never paid attention to all the small and subconscious ways people are Normal.

Like, I realized when I got here that I didn't know how to tie my shoes. I never learned! I learned how to *spell* them tied instead. Which I can't do now because I left my wand at home.

I mean, it's fine—I just leave my shoes tied or wear sandals—but there are loads of things like that. I have to be careful about what I say out loud. To strangers. To friends. It's too easy to blurt out something weird or ignorant. (Fortunately, I usually get a pass for being British.)

Ginger doesn't seem to mind when I say weird things. Maybe because she's constantly saying something a little weird. Ginger's into neurofeedback and cupping and emotional acupressure. I mean, beyond just the "I'm from California" way. She's a *believer.*

"I don't really fit in here," she said to me one night. We were sitting on the sand, with our toes in the surf. At the edge of the party again. Ginger was wearing a peach tank top and holding a red plastic cup. "But I don't fit in any better anywhere else."

It was like she'd pulled the feeling right out of my heart. I could have kissed her. (I still wish sometimes that I wanted to.) (That would feel like an answer to . . . the question of me. Then I could say, *"Oh,* that's *who I am. That's why I've been so confused."*)

"Same," I said.

The next time a party moved on without us, Ginger and I left and got tacos.

And the next time, we skipped the party and went straight to tacos.

We still felt strange and lost, I think, but it was good to be strange and lost together.

It was good to be lost with a friend.

Ginger's phone chimes, reminding me that she isn't lost anymore.

She picks it up and grins, which means *Josh,* and starts texting him back. I eat my avocado toast.

My phone vibrates. I take it out of my bag, then groan. Penny has finally cracked how to get me to reply to her:

*"Agatha! We're coming to see you! On holiday!"*

*"What?"* I text back. *"When?"* And then—I should have said this first—*"NO."*

*"In two weeks!"* Penny sends. *"YES."*

*"Penelope, no. I won't be home."* It's true. Ginger and I are going to the Burning Lad Festival.

*"You're lying,"* Penny replies.

"Ahhhh!" Ginger is saying. It turns into "Ahhhh-gatha!"

I look up. Ginger is shaking her phone at me like it's a lottery ticket.

"What?"

"Josh got us into that NowNext retreat!"

"Ginger, nooo. . . ."

"He said he'd cover our room and everything." Josh is 32. He invented something that lets you use your phone as a thermometer. Or he was on a team that invented it. Anyway. He's always covering something. The room, the check, the concert. Ginger never gets over it.

"Ginger, we're going to Burning Lad that week!"

"We can go to Burning Lad next year; the desert will still be there."

"And Josh won't?"

She frowns at me. "You know how exclusive this retreat is."

I stir my tea. "Not really. . . ."

"Only vested members get to bring guests. And usually only one guest. I begged Josh to get you in, too."

"Ginger . . ."

"Agatha—" She pauses to bite her bottom lip and squish up her nose, like she's about to tell me something big. "—I think I'm going to level up. At the retreat. And I really want you to be there."

Crowley, of course. *Level up.* Josh and his friends are obsessed with "levelling up" and "maximizing potential." If you suggest brunch, they'll be like, "Let's change the world instead!"

"Let's climb a mountain!" "Let's get VIP seats for the U2 concert!"

NowNext is their social club. It's like Weight Watchers for rich men. They go to meetings and take turns saying how "activated" they are. I've gone to a few meetings with Ginger; they were mostly a bore. (Though there are always first-rate nibbles.) At the end of every meeting, the vested members go into a locked room and do their secret handshake or whatever.

Ginger can't believe her luck with Josh. He's successful, he's ambitious, he's fit.

(*"My last boyfriend was a barista, Agatha!"*

*"You are also a barista, Ginger. That's how you met."*)

She doesn't know what Josh sees in her. I'm a little worried that he doesn't see anything *in* her. That all he sees is what there is to see. That she's young, that she's beautiful. That she looks good on his arm.

But what do I know? Maybe they're good for each other.

They both seem to like talking about phytonutrients. And, like, meridian tapping. And Ginger really does seem at least 80 per cent activated these days.

I don't think I'll ever level up.

But if that's what Ginger wants, I guess I can go along for it. She's the best friend I've made here. She'll be my friend even if I'm only ever 15 per cent activated (and less than 15 per cent magic). I sigh. "Fine. I'll go."

Ginger squeals. "Yes! It's going to be so good!"

My phone vibrates, and I look down at it. Penelope, again: *"I'm going to call you, so we can discuss details."*

I slip the phone into my purse without replying.

# 5

## BAZ

We're meeting at the airport, and Snow's already there when I arrive. At first I don't recognize him—or it's more like I recognize him from another time. He's wearing jeans and Agatha's old Watford Lacrosse sweatshirt. (I need to casually leave one of my old football shirts at his flat; he'll wear anything he finds on the floor.) The sweatshirt is slit down the back for his wings, but there's nothing there. Really nothing. Other spells only hide Simon's wings; you can still see a shimmer or a shadow. Today, there's *nothing*. I reach up to touch the space between his shoulder blades, but he spins around before I can.

"Hey," he says when he sees me. He's pulling on his hair, nervous.

My hand's still stretched out, so I pat his shoulder. "Hey."

"Penny's checking us in. Or something. I didn't have a passport." He leans closer and whispers: "She stole someone else's passport and magicked it."

As if Bunce wasn't already in deep water; we all know she used magic to buy these plane tickets. It's one of the only laws we live by in the World of Mages—no magickal counterfeiting. We'd throw the world economy into chaos if we used magic for money. Everyone bends the rules now and then, but Bunce's mother is on the Coven. "I hope she realizes her mother will happily surrender her to the authorities."

Snow's anxious: "Do you think we'll get caught? This whole thing is stupid."

"No." My hand's still on his arm, and I squeeze it. "No. It will be fine. If somebody looks suspicious, I'll distract them by being a vampire."

He doesn't try to pull away from me. Perhaps because he's out of his element, away from his worst habits. Bunce might be on to something with this change-of-scenery idea. . . .

"Speaking of," Simon says, "will you be okay on the flight?"

"Do you mean, will I lose myself to bloodlust somewhere over the Atlantic?"

He shrugs.

"I'll be fine, Snow. It's only eight hours. I get through every day without slaughtering people." I've got through fifteen years, as a matter of fact. Not a single (vampire-related) casualty.

"What about when we get there?"

"No worries, I've heard that America is overrun with rats. And other animals. Grizzly bears, show dogs."

He smiles at that, and it's so good to see that I sling my arm around his shoulders and think about hugging him. There's a woman standing in line near us, giving us her most aggrieved *"don't be gay"* face, but I don't care—easy moments with Simon are miserably few and far between.

Simon cares. He notices the woman, then leans over to mess

with his bag—the same duffel he used to carry back at Watford. When he stands up, he's pulled away from me.

He pats his thigh, nervously checking his tail.

I'm still not sure why Snow gave himself a tail. . . .

The wings, I understand. They were a necessity, he needed to escape. But why the tail? It's long and red and ropey, with a black spade at the tip. If the tail has a use, I haven't figured it out. He isn't putting it to one, anyway.

Bunce thinks that in the moment, Simon was actually turning *into* a dragon, not just wishing for wings.

Which doesn't explain why he still has them, more than a year later. Snow gave up his magic—all of it—to defeat the Insidious Humdrum. So it's not like he's using magic to maintain his dragon parts, and most spells would have worn off by now.

*"But it wasn't a spell,"* Bunce said the last time we talked about this. *"He transformed himself."*

Simon's still touching his thigh, smoothing down the back of his jeans. I try to reassure him. "No one can see it," I say.

"I'm just nervous. I've never flown before."

I laugh. (I mean, he does have *wings.*)

"In a *plane,*" he says.

"It'll be fine. And if it isn't—say, if the engines die—will you save me? Will you fly me out the nearest exit?"

His face falls. "Do the engines do that? Just die?"

I bump my shoulder against his. "Promise you'll save me first even if there are women and children."

"If the engines die," he says, "you and Penny better fix them. Have you been practicing the spells?"

"I don't know any plane-engine-preserving spells, do you, Bunce?"

Bunce has walked up with our boarding passes. "Plane-engine-preserving?" she repeats.

"You know, in case of critical engine failure."

"Simon can save me," she says.

"He's already saving *me*."

"I'm saving the women and children!" Snow says.

"Technically," I say, "you won't have wings."

# 6

## SIMON

I half expect to get stopped when I go through the security scanner. *"Sir, we just need to pat down your tail."* But it's all fine, just like Baz and Penny said it would be. I wouldn't be surprised if Penelope jammed the machine. As soon as we're through security, Penny buys me a bag of jelly babies and a Coke. (I'm skint; she and Baz are covering the whole trip.)

I've never been in an airport before. I spend an hour pacing and rolling my shoulders; they feel too light. There's really nothing back there. I keep leaning back against walls to check. I go to the men's room and pull up my shirt, looking over my shoulder at the mirror. Nothing but freckles.

When I come out, Baz and Penny are queued up to get on the plane, and Penelope is motioning for me to hurry up. I squeeze behind her, jostling no one with my wings. I'm thinking of everything I could do like this. Get on the tube. See a film. Stand next to someone at a urinal without knocking him over.

I would never have fit on the plane with my wings. I couldn't have got down the aisle without clipping everyone who was already sitting.

Baz moans when we get to our seats—in the middle of a row, in the back of the plane. "For snake's sake, Bunce, you couldn't spring for first class when you were stealing our tickets?"

"We're keeping a low profile," she says.

"I could keep a low profile in first class."

I pull him down. It's a tight fit between me and the lady on the other side. (She's wearing a cross. That's handy—Baz won't be tempted to bite her.)

It feels good to sit back and push my shoulders directly against the seat. My spine pops. It feels good to sit this close to Baz. And the lady with the cross can't get mad at us because we *have* to sit this close. It's sitting in economy that's making us gay.

Not that she *will* get mad at us necessarily. . . . You just never know when someone's going to make you feel bad about what you are. The last time Baz and I held hands in public, some girl with a nose ring took offense. If you can't trust people with nose rings to be open-minded, who's left?

Baz said the girl wasn't looking at us funny—he said her face just looked like that. *"That woman has a miserable aspect. She put that hoop through her septum to distract from it."* He also says I can't assume that everyone who frowns at me is frowning because I'm with a boy. *"Some people just won't like you, Simon. I didn't like you for years."*

That was . . . months ago. The girl with the nose ring. Us holding hands. It was snowing.

I think about taking Baz's hand now—I reach out, but he picks up a magazine and starts flipping through it.

Eight hours in the air. Penny says we can watch films. And that they'll bring us food constantly. She says we'll forget we're over the ocean after a few minutes, and it'll just be boring.

We're flying into Chicago, so that Penny can see Micah. She's hoping he'll decide to come along with us on our road trip. *"He says he has to work. But maybe he'll change his mind."*

Baz's knees are pressed up against the seat ahead of him. (All his height's in his legs. Torso-to-torso, we're the same height. I might even be taller.) The person sitting there pushes her seat back, and Baz yelps.

"You could magic yourself more space," I say.

"Can't. I'm saving my magic." He angles his knees towards mine. "Just in case I have to 'Float like a butterfly' this entire plane."

# 7

## PENELOPE

I've been dating Micah since he came to Watford as an American exchange student our fourth year.

America doesn't have magickal schools of its own. Most countries don't. Sometimes foreign families send their kids to Watford for a year for the cultural experience. *"And because no one offers the magickal foundation we do,"* Mum likes to say. *"No one."* (She's Watford's headmaster now, and she's very proud.) American children go to Normal schools and learn their magic at home. *"Imagine learning only the spells your parents can teach you. No elocution, no linguistics, no forensics."*

Micah's elocution is very good—and he's bilingual, so he can cast in Spanish. (That only works in Spanish-speaking areas, but Spanish is a growing language!)

I know everyone at Watford thought that Micah was basically my imaginary boyfriend all these years, but for us, it was very real. We communicated by letter and email. We Skyped. And then we FaceTimed. We even talked on the phone sometimes.

We went three years without seeing each other in person. Then, two years ago, I spent the summer with Micah's family in Chicago, and as real as our relationship was before, it became *more* real.

I would have gone back to visit him after we finished school; I was going to. But we were all in a state of shock, with the Humdrum gone and the Mage dead. (I didn't even go back to Watford our final term. Miss Possibelf came to London to give me my exams.) Simon was shattered. I couldn't bugger off to Chicago and leave him alone—he was already more alone than ever.

Anyway, Micah was cool about it all. He agreed that my staying in London was the best thing for the time being. The plan was, I'd come visit him, just as soon as things got better. We both agreed.

We didn't have a plan for if they got worse.

# 8

## AGATHA

I thought the retreat would be at a hotel. But Josh drives us to a gated house inside a gated community. He's got a sports car that doesn't make any noise and doesn't use any fuel and doesn't have much of a back seat.

"This neighbourhood is almost all NowNext members," he says. "Most of the founders live here."

Ginger looks impressed. I try to look polite.

We're greeted by a competent young woman, covered in tattoos and thoroughly pierced. She's the most decorative thing in the house. All of the NowNext meetings are in places like this: cavernous homes, minimally adorned. This one is the most cavernous, most minimal yet—like someone's making a real show of how much space they have to fill with nothing. My mum would go blind from the lack of upholstery and wall decor.

Personally, I'd rather be at a hotel than this big, empty house; when Ginger and I get to our room, the door doesn't have a lock.

"I don't know why you're unpacking," I say to her. "I know you'll be staying with Josh."

"Nope," she says. "It's members-only in that wing of the house. You're stuck with me every night."

Ginger doesn't want to miss a minute of the retreat's programming. She drags me to the welcome party out on the deck. We drink champagne cocktails, and no one asks me if I'm 21. (I'm four months shy.) It's mostly men here. A few women. All the vested members wear gold pins—little figure eights. (The pins remind me of a relic my parents keep in our bathroom, a silver snake eating its tail, that's supposed to keep basilisks from coming up the pipes.)

After the welcome party, there's meditation in one room and an investing seminar in another. Ginger and Josh and I choose to meditate. I like meditation. It's quiet, at least.

Then we're all supposed to gather for a big keynote talk—"The Myth of Mortality"—in one of the ballroom-sized sitting rooms. Whoever lives here must own fifty sofas, all of them black or white or creamy nothing-coloured. And all so sleek that they keep their shape even when you're sitting on them.

I spend twenty minutes fidgeting. It's practically like being at church. The guy talking says that Normals—well, human beings—were put on this earth to live forever, and it's only sin and shame and environmental factors that got in the way. He has Ginger at "environmental factors."

It sounds like crap to me. Even magicians can't live forever, and we've got thousands of spells on our side. *"Living is dying,"* my father says. He's the best magickal doctor in England. He can cure anything that can be cured. But he can't cure death. Or as he says, *"I can't cure life."*

I try to be bored by the talk, but I'm irritated. I'm irritated by everyone nodding along to this nonsense. Do they really think they can cheat death with tropical juices and positive thinking? It reminds me of the Mage.

Which reminds me of that night on the Tower.

And Ebb.

I stand up. I tell Ginger that I'm going to find a bathroom, but I just want to get away. I end up in an empty room on the other side of the main floor, a library with a big window overlooking a golf course.

I was supposed to be at a *festival* this week. I bought body paint and sewed feathers onto my bikini. It was going to be ridiculous and brilliant. Not like this—ridiculous and sad.

I dig around for the emergency fag I keep in my purse. I never really smoked back in England. Simon and Penny hated it, and, like I said, my dad's a doctor. But then I moved to California, where literally no one smokes, and having a cigarette now and then feels like toasting the Queen.

I'll bet whoever owns this house would flip their shit if I lit up.

I hold the cig between my fingers and cast, **"Fire burn and cauldron bubble!"**—one of three spells I can manage without a wand, and the only one I can cast under my breath. (A rare talent I carefully avoided cultivating once I saw how much it pleased my mother.) The tip lights up. I inhale, then blow the smoke directly onto a shelf of books.

"Got one of those I could bum?"

I look back at the door. There's a man standing there. Wearing a stupid figure-eight pin.

"Sorry," I say, "it's my last one."

He steps into the library. He's a little older than me—a little young by NowNext standards, but as clean-cut and cross-trained as the rest. I like the idea of befouling one of them. A cigarette could ruin his whole programme for the week. He'll have to confess and cleanse and maybe even fast.

"You can have a drag," I say.

He leaves the door open, which I appreciate. (Fucking men, always trying to trap you alone.) And comes over to lean against the shelves next to me. I hand him the cigarette, and he takes a deep inhale.

"You'll never be immortal now," I say.

He laughs, choking a little on the smoke. Some leaks out his nose. "Damn," he says. "I had so many plans."

"Tell me one."

"To cure cancer with gene therapy." He's being sincere, I think.

"Sorry, darling, you've got the wrong room. Your lot's next door."

"You're not buying it?" he asks.

"I'm not."

"Then why are you here?"

"Because I heard there would be lymphatic massages and vegan cupcakes."

"There will be," he says. He's smiling.

I sigh, blowing smoke just past his face. "I'm here with a friend."

He nods, looking at me. He's admiring my hair. Which happens. My hair is long and light blond. "Butter blond," Simon used to call it. No one I know here eats butter.

"*You're* buying it," I say, looking at his pin. "Or bought it."

"Founded it," he says.

"Really?" He can't be more than 25. "Huh. Were you a teenage phenomenon?"

"Sort of."

I glance at the bookshelves around me. They're all modern books, lots of paperbacks. Nothing leather-bound just for show.

"You don't seem impressed," he says.

I shrug. "I know the type."

My fag has burned down to the filter. I look around for someplace to stub it out. He lifts a bronze dish off the desk; it's some sort of award. "Here."

"I'm disrespectful," I say, "but I'm not rude."

He laughs. He's a bit good-looking when he laughs. "It's okay. It's mine."

I stub out my cigarette. "This is *your* house?"

"Uh-huh. Does that impress you?"

"Morgana, no. What does someone your age need a golf course for?"

"I like golf," he says. "And I like having a big house. For weekends like this."

"It takes all kinds, I suppose."

"You can be cynical if you want."

"I am."

"But cynicism doesn't accomplish anything."

"Untrue," I say. "Cynicism saves lives."

"Never."

"There are so many things that will never kill me because I wouldn't be caught dead doing them."

"Like what?"

I brush an ash off my dress. "Mountain climbing."

"Is that cynicism or cowardice?"

"Honestly—" I pause. "What's your name?"

"Braden."

"Of course it is . . ." I mumble, taking him in. "Honestly, Braden, I'm too cynical to care."

He takes a step closer. "I'd like to change your mind."

"Thanks, but I've just got out of a cult. I'm not looking for a rebound cult."

He smiles. He's flirting with me now. "We aren't a cult."

"You are, I think." I'm not *quite* flirting back.

"Is the Catholic Church a cult?"

"Yes. Are you actually comparing yourself to Catholicism?"

He pulls his head back. "Wait, you think the Church is a *cult*?"

We look in each other's eyes. He's thinking that mine are an unusual shade of brown. I'm relieved when he doesn't say so.

"We just want to help people," he says.

"You want to help yourselves," I correct.

"One, we count as people, and two, why *not* help ourselves? We're the difference-makers."

"That sounds like a made-up word, Braden." Braden is a made-up name.

"I'm okay with making up words," he says. "I want to re-make the world. The people in the next room? They're *already* changing the world. I'm here to nourish and encourage them, so that they can maximise their impact."

"That's why I left that room," I say. "The last thing I want is to make a difference."

# 9

## BAZ

None of us sleep on the flight. Bunce does logic puzzles, and Snow watches films where people kick each other. Every two hours, he says, "Well, that was crap," and starts another one. I would sleep, but I can't get comfortable. My knees are cramped, and there are at least three people wearing crosses sitting near me. One of them must be silver; my nose won't stop running.

I'm crowding Snow, using the tight quarters as an excuse to be close to him. I've forgotten how warm he is. We're touching from shoulder to knee; it's like lying in the sun, without the sting.

Simon's changed since we left school. Physically. He's softer, fuller. Like the butter (more like the cider) is catching up with him. Being the Chosen One was good cardio, I suppose. And being a magickal reactor must have given him a hell of a metabolism. . . .

Snow looks like he hasn't been plugged into the charger for a while. His skin's gone pale. His toffee-brown hair has lost its shimmer. He's grown it out—in neglect, I think. He's got a headful of loose curls now. They bounce when he walks, and he's constantly pulling at them.

"Crap," Snow says to the tiny screen in the seat ahead of him. "Absolute crap. I'll be damned if that bloke's ever picked up a sword." He shakes his head, and his curls wobble.

He's lovely. A bit of a sad mess. Dull and pale and rough round the edges. But still so lovely.

I close my eyes and pretend to fall asleep on his shoulder.

# SIMON

We spend an hour in the queue at Immigration.

The American border agents are dead scary, but my wings stay gone, and my passport holds. Penny says she has more to worry about as a brown person than I do as a winged person. (She's half Indian, half white. English on both sides.)

But we get through.

We're in America. *I'm* in America. Across the ocean. Me. If the kids from the care homes could see me now . . .

Well, really, I wouldn't want them to see me because then I'd have to see them. And I don't have many good memories of my childhood outside of Watford.

My therapist (the one I was seeing last summer) always wanted me to talk about that—what my life was like as a kid, how I felt, who took care of me. I tried to tell her that I can't remember—and I really can't. It's all sort of spotty. I vaguely remember where I lived before my magic kicked in, what school I was in, what I watched on the telly . . . I can remember that things were *bad,* but not specifically *why.* Trauma affects memory, my therapist said. Your brain closes off painful corridors.

*"That sounds good to me,"* I told her. *"Thank you, brain."*

I don't see why I should go looking for pain and trouble in my childhood, especially things my head has already taped off. I've got enough pain and trouble on my plate.

The therapist said I needed to work *through* the past to keep it from undermining the present. And I said—

Well, I didn't say anything. I skipped my next appointment and didn't make any more.

Penny hired us a car, but we've got to walk half a mile to get to it. Baz looks completely wiped, even though he slept on my shoulder through most of the flight. (I needed a piss for the last four hours, but I didn't want to wake him.)

When we get to the car, it stops me in my tracks. Baz walks right into me.

*"Penelope . . ."* I'm actually holding my head, like someone who's just seen their renovated living room on a DIY show. "You've got to be kidding me!"

Penny laughs. "Nope."

Crowley, it's beautiful—sleek, saltwater blue. With a nose like a Doberman pinscher. "A classic Mustang! Are you *kidding* me?! Just like Steve McQueen!"

"Well, we can't drive across America in a Ford Fiesta."

Baz is frowning at the bonnet. "Nineteen sixty-eight . . . Tahoe Turquoise."

I climb into the driver's seat, even though I can't drive—I wish I could. The seats are sky-blue vinyl and shorter than any car I've been in.

"Room for your wings," Baz comments.

"Oh, speaking of," Penny says. "Let me freshen you up." She holds up her ring hand. She's got a bell hanging from her middle finger. ***"Every time a bell rings, an angel gets its wings!"*** she casts. Then she spins her hand around, ringing the bell and hissing, ***"I put my thing down, flip it and reverse it!"***

I hear Baz take a sharp breath just as the magic hits me—with a much bigger oomph than it had back in our flat, when Penny tried this spell on me the first time. An icy feeling blooms between my shoulders.

"Great snakes, Bunce, that's genius." Baz's eyebrows are at maximum up and down positions.

Penny shakes out her hand. "That was far more powerful than back home," she says excitedly. "Do you think it's because the phrases are of American origin? This could affect our whole vocabulary!"

"Does the second spell work as a blanket reversal?" Baz wants to know.

"I'm not sure yet," she says. "It's a pop song, so it's unstable."

"I can't believe you tested an unstable spell on your best friend. . . ."

"Simon said I could!"

". . . and I can't believe he was angelic enough for it to work!"

"He's sufficiently angelic for the purposes of the spell," Penny says. "Magic understands metaphor."

"Thank you, Bunce, I also completed first-year Magickal Theory."

They keep talking, but I ignore them. Too busy pretending I'm Steve McQueen. I generally don't go around thinking about how cool I look (I'm not Baz), but I feel like I must look *very* cool right now.

Penny is fiddling with the windscreen. "Watch!" She reaches over me to flip a switch on the dash. An engine whines, and the top of the car folds out of sight. "Magic," she grins.

I'm grinning right back. This is *brilliant*. If I were by myself, I'd be making *vroom, vroom* noises.

Baz puts our bags in the boot, then comes around to the driver's side; he's the only one of us who can drive. "Shotgun," I say, making my way into the passenger seat. I'll get carsick if I ride in the back.

Penny practically crawls over me to get to the back seat, and Baz settles in, clicking his seat belt.

"Come on, Snow. Let's see America."

If I thought I looked cool behind the wheel, I wasn't prepared for Baz.

I wouldn't be able to look away from him, if there wasn't so much else to take in. We're headed out to the Chicago suburbs, where Micah lives. Nothing here is like anything I've ever seen before.

The roads are staggering—five lanes across, and full of massive vehicles. Everyone in America seems to drive a military transport. And there's advertising everywhere, giant posters along the road, for just about everything. Pizza and lawyers and hair-growth supplements.

Baz acts like he does this every day. He's completely relaxed, with one long, pale hand resting on the steering wheel and the other firmly managing the gear stick. He's wearing light grey trousers, a white shirt cuffed just below his elbows, and a pair of sunglasses I've never seen before. His hair has got longer since we left school, and the wind is bringing it to life.

I still feel manky from the plane. I know I sweated through my T-shirt (sour, sitting-still sweat), and my jeans are too hot for Chicago in June. My hair's longer these days, too, but only because I haven't cared enough to get a haircut. I'm exactly the sort of thing Baz doesn't bother with.

Penny climbs up between our seats to fuss with the radio. "Where's the plug?"

Baz tries to elbow her back. "Put on your seat belt!"

"But I made a road trip playlist!"

"Are you trying to kill us all before we can listen to it?"

I turn on the stereo. It looks like it came with the car. "I think it's just got a radio," I say, fiddling with the dial. It makes a staticky *wow-wow* sound, just like in the movies. Maybe everything in America is just like in the movies.

"Can't I plug in?" She's still hanging between us.

"I don't think so. I'll try to find some music." It takes me a second—you have to turn the dial really slowly and kind of trap the signal. I twist past people talking about politics and baseball, and find a station playing classic rock. "I think this is the best I can do."

Penny sighs and flops back into her seat.

"Fasten your seat belt!" Baz shouts. He's changing lanes now, and it's a whole complicated dance—twisting in his seat, changing gears, and pumping one of the pedals. I'm glad we haven't broken up yet, because then I never would have got to see it.

# 10

## PENELOPE

We'll be at Micah's house soon.

I told him I was coming.

I called him last week—I said I was worried about Agatha and that Simon needed a holiday. And I told him that I miss him. "We'll stop in Chicago first," I said. "On the way."

And then Micah said that probably wasn't a good idea. That we should talk about it more.

"There's no time to talk about it—Agatha might be in trouble!" I wasn't planning on saying this, but then I did, and it wasn't a lie. She really might be. Historically, she has been.

Then Micah said, "It is a day ending with '-day,' isn't it?"

"What's that supposed to mean? Do you not believe that Agatha's in danger?"

"No, I believe it. Agatha's in danger. And Simon's hit a rough patch. And Baz has a dark secret. And there's probably some conspiracy that you can't tell me about. The whole World of Mages is probably at stake!"

I decided to pretend Micah wasn't angry. So that he could

stop *being* angry at any moment without it being a big thing. I said—"Well, I don't know that there's *not* a shadow conspiracy. . . ."

And he said, "Whatever, Penelope. Do what you want to do. You will anyway."

"I'll do what I *have* to do," I said, "not what I want to do."

And then Micah didn't say anything.

"Micah? Micah, are you still there?"

"I'm here."

"Do you think I'm making all this up?" (There's a difference, I think, between making something up and exaggerating.)

"No."

"*Micah* . . ." I tried to make my voice softer, smaller. "Maybe you could go to California with us. We could use your help."

"I have my internship."

"Well, we're flying into Chicago anyway. If you change your mind—"

"Agatha might be in danger, right? You should fly straight there."

"I suppose that's true. . . ."

"And we'll talk when you get back," he said. "When things settle down for you."

And then he hung up.

And that convinced me that I was *right* to plan this trip. It's been far too long since Micah and I have touched base. Whatever we need to talk about, it will be better to do it in person.

# 11

## BAZ

Bunce's boyfriend lives in a subdivision inside a suburb.

"The houses are so far apart," Snow says. Now that we're off the motorway, we can hear each other speak again. "It seems a bit greedy, doesn't it? Just to take up as much space as you can?"

"They're not *that* far apart," I say.

"Not to you; you grew up in a mansion."

"I grew up at the top of a tower," I say. "With you."

"It's that one!" Bunce says, pointing.

I park in the driveway and start to get out of the car, but Bunce pushes me down and climbs over me. "You guys wait here."

"I want to see Micah!" Snow says. "Are you embarrassed by us?"

"Yes," she says, "but I'll come back for you anyway. I just want to see him alone for a moment."

She smooths down her T-shirt, but she still looks like she spent the night on a plane—and Bunce tends to look a *bit* absurd, even at her freshest. She dresses like she's still in Watford uniform, or wishes she was. Short, tartan skirts. Knee socks. Mary Janes or brogues. The only concession she's made to civilian life is a series of oversized T-shirts. I wonder if she even realizes she still wears so much purple and green.

Bunce gets halfway up the driveway, then turns back, holding out her hands and mouthing, *"Stay there!"*

"We get it!" Snow shouts. "We embarrass you!"

She throws her hands in the air, and runs up to the house.

Snow and I are alone. He reaches out and touches the gear stick. "It's still warm."

I nod.

"Does it feel different?" he asks. "Than your car at home?"

"Hulkier," I say. "Harder to control. . . . Do you want to try it?"

Snow's still holding on to the gear stick. "I can't even drive an automatic."

"I—" I shrug. "I could teach you?"

"Here?"

"Why not here? No one will notice. There's no traffic."

Snow looks very young, his eyebrows scrunched down, like he isn't sure he's *allowed* to try this. I open my car door. "Come on."

I get out, and he climbs across to the driver's side, rubbing his hands on his jeans. (Simon Snow in America: jeans and a white T-shirt, skin already pinking up from the sun.)

I take his place in the passenger seat. "All right," I say, sounding a bit like Coach Mac, "the handbrake is on, so we're not going anywhere."

"Right."

"Now, press down on the clutch. It's the pedal on the—"

"I know, I've played *Gran Turismo*."

"Fine. So, the clutch is always down when you start and when you change gears. Feel it out for a minute."

He pumps the clutch harder than he needs to, but I don't correct him. *Easy does it* isn't in Snow's behavioural vocabulary.

"Now put your hand on the gear stick."

Snow grabs it. I lay my hand over his and try to shake his wrist loose. "Relax. We're just practising. The car is off, and the brake is on. We're just seeing how it feels. . . ." I move the gear stick back and forth. "This is neutral." I push his hand over and then down. "And this is reverse."

Up, over, up. "First." Down. "Second."

Up, over, up. "Third." Down. "Fourth."

Snow nods his head, looking down at our hands. "There's a diagram on the knob," he says.

"Right. But you can't look at it when you're driving. Just feel. . . ." I move through the gears again.

"Got it," he says.

I take my hand away. "So, get back into neutral. . . ."

Snow lifts his hand to peek at the knob, then moves it over.

"It can be a lot to manage all at once—it's frustrating at first."

"Who taught you how to drive?" he asks.

"My stepmother."

"And she got frustrated?"

"No," I say. "She was lovely. *I* got frustrated. Go ahead and release the handbrake—it's just there." I put my left hand on his shoulder, then reach across his lap with my right, pointing.

"Did she use magic?"

"To teach me to drive?"

Snow fiddles with the brake. "Yeah."

"No. You've met Daphne. She hardly uses magic for any-thing."

"But you *could* use magic to drive?"

"I suppose, but then you wouldn't learn." I nudge him with my elbow. "Go on, James Dean, start it up."

"Just turn the key?"

"Yeah, and give it some gas."

He turns the key, and the car lurches forward and dies. I catch myself on the dash. "Good."

"That wasn't good, Baz."

"It was fine," I say. "It's normal. I should have double-checked that we were in neutral. Try again: Clutch. Neutral. Ignition. Accelerator."

The car starts fine this time. Simon revs the engine and looks at me, laughing with delight.

I give him a moment to enjoy it. "We're going to move now. This is where it gets tricky."

"It's already tricky."

"You're going to keep the clutch in, change into first, then gently press the accelerator as you ease up on the clutch."

He shakes his head, like I'm talking nonsense.

"The clutch allows you to switch gears," I say. "And you need to be in gear to move forward. The accelerator makes you go."

"So clutch, then first—" His hand wobbles, but he gets there. "—then accelerator." We jolt forward.

"Excellent."

"Yeah?"

"Yeah . . . but we're gonna hit that mailbox."

Simon looks up from the gear stick. "What do I do?!"

"Steer away."

"Oh. Right." He jerks the wheel. "Agh. Sorry."

"It's fine. You're doing really well."

"Why are you being so nice to me? Back when I was genuinely good at things, you were never this nice. But now that I'm fucking up—"

"You're just learning. Keep steering."

"Right, right. Just down the street?"

"Just down the street."

"Get your wand out," he says.

"Why?"

"Worst-case scenario."

"We won't need it." I put my hand on his shoulder. Every muscle in his torso is clenched. "You're going a bit faster now—"

"Sorry."

"No, it's fine—just, can you feel it? It wants to change up."

"What does?"

"The engine. It's straining."

"Oh, right. Yeah. So I—"

He changes smoothly into second.

"Crowley, that was excellent, Snow."

"Let me try—" And he's in third. Which is too fast for a residential neighbourhood, but well done, all the same.

"Smashing, Simon. You're a natural."

"That was okay?"

"Yeah, very."

"It's easier when I don't think."

"As you've often told me."

"Baz?"

"Yeah."

"There's a car—*there's a car*! I don't know how to stop!"

# 12

## PENELOPE

Micah's mother answers the door, and she seems confused to see me. Which makes sense. I do live in London.

"Mrs. Cordero," I say, "hello."

"Penelope . . . it's so good to see you. Micah didn't tell me you were coming."

"Oh, it's sort of a surprise," I say. "It all came together really quickly. Is he here?"

"Yeah, come in, of course."

I step into their house. I love this house. I stayed in the spare bedroom when I came to see Micah two summers ago. All the rooms are huge, and only the bedrooms and bathrooms (there are *four* bathrooms) have doors. And everything—all the walls and furniture and the two dozen kitchen cabinets—is in peaceful shades of cream and tan.

There are at least *three* tan leather sofas.

There are *two* beige sitting rooms.

There's wall-to-wall carpeting exactly the shade of porridge.

Ugh, it's so comforting. My house is every colour, none of

them planned. And our furniture is whatever colour it was when my father spotted it at a yard sale. Also, our house has stuff everywhere. Micah's family must have stuff *somewhere*, but you never see it. The only things on the coffee tables (how many coffee tables are there? easily nine) are cream-coloured vases with cream-coloured flowers and tan, marble lamps.

"I'll just—" Mrs. Cordero looks nervous. She must know Micah and I have been arguing. "I'll go get Micah."

I sit on one of the leather sofas, and a cream-coloured Pomeranian wanders up to me.

Micah's parents are both magicians, which isn't always true in America. They have no standards for these things here, and some magicians go their entire lives without meeting a mage who isn't a relative. When magicians hook up with Normals, their kids usually have magic, but not always, and most people believe that diluted mages aren't as powerful. But that might be because they get less training. There's almost no scholarship on the matter, Mum says.

Micah thinks English magicians get too hung up on magic. "*My family* uses *magic*," he says, "*but it's just* part *of our identity.*"

Utter nonsense. If you can speak with magic, you are a magician first and foremost—bother the rest of it.

Micah's parents both work for health insurance companies. They use their magic mostly at home, for housework.

The Pomeranian is trying to jump into my lap, but she's too small. I pick her up because I feel sorry for her, not because I feel like holding a dog.

I *really* think this is all going to be okay. If Micah and I can just talk face-to-face. The last time I was here, everything clicked. We felt like a real couple for the first time.

"Penelope?"

"Micah!" I stand up, bringing the dog with me. *Micah!*

"Penny. What are you doing here?" He isn't smiling. I wish he was smiling.

"I told you I was coming."

"And I told you that you shouldn't."

"But I was going to be here anyway—"

"California isn't here."

"You said we needed to talk, Micah. And I agreed. We should talk."

"I've been saying that for six months, Penny, and you've been putting me off."

"I haven't—"

Micah's arms are folded. He looks so different from the last time I saw him. He's growing one of those awful moustache/chin-beard combos. When was the last time we Skyped?

"Micah? I just don't understand why you wouldn't *want* me here. I'm your girlfriend."

He looks like I've just said something ridiculous. (Something like, *"I'm going to grow a moustache/chin-beard thingy, what do you think?"*) "Penelope . . . we've hardly talked in a year."

"Because we're both busy."

"And we talked even less the year before that."

"Well, those were extreme circumstances, you know that."

"You can't avoid me for two years and still think we have a *relationship*."

"Micah, I wasn't ever avoiding you, why would you say that?"

"You weren't *anything* about me! *We* weren't anything. I talked to my grandmother more than you."

"Am I competing with your grandmother now?"

"Not like I was competing with Simon Snow."

The Pomeranian barks.

"You know that Simon and I aren't like that."

He rolls his eyes. "I do. Actually. But I know that he matters to you—in a way I never have."

"Why didn't you ever tell me you felt this way?"

"Ha," Micah says. Like I'm being the worst kind of funny. "I tried. I'd have better luck talking to a tornado. You *are* a tornado."

I'm so confused. "We don't really have tornadoes in England. . . ."

"Well, you're a gale-force wind, Penelope Bunce. You just do what you want as forcefully as possible, and nothing else matters. I've tried to talk to you about this so many times, but you just blow right past me."

"That's not fair!" I say. I'm losing my cool.

He isn't. "It's more than fair—it's *true*. You. Don't. Listen. To me."

"I certainly do."

"Really? I told you I was tired of being in a long-distance relationship—"

"And I agreed that it was tiring!" I say.

"I told you that I thought we'd grown apart—"

"And I said that was natural!" I half shout.

He's still looking at me like nothing about me makes sense. "What does it even mean to you to be in a relationship, Penny?"

"It—it means that we love each other. And that we have this part of our lives figured out. That we know who we're going to be with in the end."

"No," he says, sounding—for the first time in this conversation—more sad than fed up. "A relationship isn't about the end. It's about being together every step of the way."

"Micah?" A girl steps into the living room. "I heard shouting, and your mom said it was fine, but—"

"It is fine," he says softly. "I'll be back down in a few minutes."

The girl keeps looking at me. She has long dark hair and wide hips. She's wearing a flowered sundress. "You're Penelope," she says.

"I am."

"I'm Erin. It's so nice to meet you." She comes at me with her hand out, but I act like it's taking all I've got to hold on to the dog.

"I just need a few minutes," Micah says. "I can explain—"

"Good," I say.

He looks back at me, like I'm still being unbelievably foolish. "I wasn't talking to you, Penny. For God's sake."

"Micah, what is this? Are you breaking up with me?"

"*No,*" he says. "I already have, half a dozen times. And you just won't hear it!"

"I'm certain you never said, *'Penelope, I'm breaking up with you.'* "

"I said it every other way! We went two months without talking, and you didn't even notice!"

"I'm sure I was working on something very important!"

"I'm sure you were, too! Something much more important than me!"

At this point, I'm very tempted to say, *"No, Micah, you're wrong. This is a mistake, and I don't accept it."*

And maybe I would if this Erin person weren't standing right there. I think she's a Normal, unless she's got a wand up the back of her dress—nothing she's wearing could hold magic. Cheap bangles and flip-flop sandals. If it weren't for her, I'd announce, *"I'm leaving now. Call me when you're feeling reasonable."*

Instead I say, "My mother set eyes on my father in third year and knew immediately that they'd be married someday."

"That's not us," he says. "That's practically nobody."

He's right. . . .

. . .

. . . How mortifying.

I walk out of the house then, without saying good-bye to him or Erin or Mrs. Cordero. I'm halfway down the walk when Micah catches up with me.

"Penelope!"

"I don't want to talk to you anymore!"

"No, you—you've got my mom's dog." He takes the Pomeranian from my arms, and it barks like it wants to come back to me. Micah jogs back into the house.

I'm crying, and I can't believe I have to face Simon and Baz now. I can't believe I have to explain this to them. . . .

The car is gone.

They're not here.

# 13

## SIMON

I'm driving, I'm actually driving. I mean, it's a housing development called Havenbrook, not the autobahn, but I'm behind the wheel and operating multiple pedals, and if I think too hard about it, I push the brake instead of the clutch, and the car shakes and dies—but that's only happened twice, and Baz is acting like I'm some sort of natural-born talent. "Perfect, Snow," he keeps saying. And I wish he was saying, "Perfect, Simon," but I'll take "perfect." He's got his hand on my shoulder, and I feel like there's nothing I'm doing in this moment to let him down.

"I think you're ready for an actual street," Baz says.

"I'm not ready for other cars."

"The only way to be ready is to do it. There's no practice traffic."

We're driving past the Havenbrook Estates entrance. I can see the main road. "Should I try it?"

"Yeah. Do it, Snow. Live dangerously." Says the vampire teaching me how to drive.

"What about Penny?" I say. I'm stalling.

"I can't imagine she's missing us, but I suppose we could check."

"Do you remember the address?"

We both look up. Every house in Havenbrook Estates looks like the same house, slightly rearranged, and painted one of five muted shades.

"I think it was light brown," Baz says.

"This light brown," I say, pointing at a house, "or that light-light brown?" I point at another.

"That's not light brown, that's a warm grey."

"They're all sort of a warm grey," I say, "even that green one."

"I don't see a green one."

"That one there."

"Surely, that's tan."

We never would have found the house again if Penny weren't sitting out on the kerb in front of it. She stands up when she sees us and climbs into the car before we've fully stopped or opened the door, falling flat into the back seat.

"Sorry, Bunce. Snow was driving in circles."

"All the streets in this neighbourhood are circles!"

Penny's covering her face. "Let's go."

I crank around in my seat. "But I want to meet Micah!"

"You've met Micah."

"Also I have to use the loo."

"Just drive, Simon!"

"I should probably drive," Baz says.

He gets out, and I crawl over, leaning into the back seat to look at Penny. "Are you okay?"

She rolls onto her stomach.

"I'm sorry we left you sitting outside," I say. "Was he not there?"

Her voice is muffled. "I don't want to talk about it, Simon."

Baz drives us out of the cul-de-sac. "Let's talk about where we're going instead."

"To the loo," I say.

"San Diego," Penny says.

Baz takes me to a Starbucks to use the facilities, and when I come out—with a massive rainbow-striped Frappuccino—he's shouting at Penny: "Thirty-one hours to San Diego?!"

"That can't be right," Penny says. "That's like driving from London to Moscow. Let me see." Baz has been looking at her phone, and she takes it back. "But it's the same country," she says.

"I thought we *wanted* a road trip," I say, getting in the car.

"Three hours is a road trip," Baz says. "With a nice picnic break in the middle. This is three *days* of driving—and we only have seven days left before we fly home." He sneers at Penny. " *'We'll just stop in Chicago on the way to San Diego,'* she said."

Penny is still looking at her phone. "How was I to know that all these middle states are each the size of France? I've never even heard of Nebraska."

"Well, we're going to spend a full day there," Baz says, "so you'll know it now."

Three days on the road doesn't sound so bad to me. These trips always take a long time in films—time for people to have adventures along the way. You can't have an adventure in three hours. (I mean, *I* have. But I'm a pretty extreme case.)

Baz has stopped glaring at Penelope and started glaring at me. "What on earth are you drinking, Snow?"

"A Unicorn Frappuccino."

He frowns. "Why's it called that—does it taste like lavender?"

"It tastes like strawberry Dip Dab," I say.

Penny's grimacing at Baz. "For heaven's snakes, Basil, I can't believe you know what unicorns taste like."

"Shut up, Bunce, it was sustainably farmed."

"Unicorns can *talk*!"

"They're only capable of small talk; it's not like eating a dolphin."

Baz takes my Frappuccino and sucks down a huge gulp. "Disgusting." He hands it back to me. "Not like unicorn at all."

He pushes up his sunglasses to rub his eyes. They look sunken and shadowed.

"Are you thirsty?" I ask.

"Yeah," he says. "I'll run in and get a cup of tea."

"That's not what I meant."

"I know what you meant. But I'm not going hunting in the suburbs at midday."

"We could get a sandwich," I say.

"I'm *fine*, Snow."

"All right, but I'd still like a sandwich."


Baz says it's safe for me to drive on the motorway. "It's easier than driving in town." He's right—though merging into traffic at fifty miles per hour is fairly terrifying, and I do something that makes the engine whine like a dog.

But then we're out on the road, and it's cracking. With the top down, driving feels almost like flying, warm wind in our hair and against our skin. My T-shirt is flapping, and Baz's black hair whips around his face like a flame.

Penelope is still lying across the back seat. I can tell something's wrong and also that she doesn't want to talk about it. She hasn't touched her sandwich. I can only guess that she and Micah got into a row.

# 14

## BAZ

Something is very wrong with Bunce. She's collapsed in the back seat like a dead rabbit. But I can't really focus on it because of *the sun* and also *the wind* and because I'm very busy making a list.

**Things I hate, a list:**

1. The sun.

2. The wind.

3. Penelope Bunce, when she hasn't got a plan.

4. American sandwiches.

5. America.

6. The band, America. Which I didn't know about an hour ago.

7. Kansas, also a band I've recently become acquainted with.

8. Kansas, the state. Which isn't that far from Illinois, so it must be wretched.

9. The State of Illinois, for fucking certain.

10. The *sun*. In my *eyes*.

11. The *wind* in my *hair*.

12. Convertible automobiles.

13. Myself, most of all.

14. My soft heart.

15. My foolish optimism.

16. The words "road" and "trip," when said together with any enthusiasm.

17. Being a vampire, if we're being honest.

18. Being a vampire in a fucking convertible.

19. A deliriously thirsty vampire in a convertible at midday. In Illinois, which is apparently the brightest place on the planet.

20. The sun. Which hangs *miles* closer to Minooka, Illinois, than it does over London blessed England.

21. Minooka, Illinois. Which seems dreadful.

22. These sunglasses. Rubbish.

23. The fucking sun! We get it—you're very fucking bright!

24. Penelope Bunce, who came up with this idea. An idea not accompanied by a *plan*. Because all she cared about was seeing her rubbish boyfriend, who clearly cocked it all up. Which we all should have expected from someone from Illinois, land of the damned—a place that manages to be both hot *and* humid at the same time. You might well expect hell to be hot, but you don't expect it to *also* be humid. That's what makes it hell, the surprise twist! The devil is clever!

25. Penelope "Girl Genius" Bunce.

26. And all of her stupid ideas. *"Good for us all,"* she said; all I heard was *"good for Simon."* Crowley . . . Maybe she was right . . . Look at him. He's as happy as a pig in mud. As happy as someone who's suffering under the "A pig in mud" spell—which I've considered casting on him *numerous* times over the last six months. Because I'm just so *tired,* and I don't how to—I mean, there's nothing— There's no *fixing* him.

27. The Mage. May he rest in pain.

28. Penelope—for maybe being right, about Simon. And America. And this wretched convertible. Because just look at him. . . .
    Off the sofa, out of the flat. Over the ocean, under the sun.
    Simon Snow, it hurts to look at you when you're this happy.
    And it hurts to look at you when you're depressed.

There's no safe time for me to see you, nothing about you that doesn't tear my heart from my chest and leave it breakable outside my body.

Simon looks over at me. "What?"

"Nothing," I say.

"What?!" he shouts. He can't hear a thing I'm saying over the wind and the engine and the classic rock.

"I hate this fucking car!" I shout back. "The sun is burning me! I might actually catch fire, at any moment!"

The wind is blowing Simon's hair straight, and he's squinting—from the sun and from all the smiling. "*What!*" he shouts at me again.

"You're so beautiful!" I shout back.

He turns the radio down, so now there's just the wind and the engine noise to shout over. "What'd you say?!"

"Nothing!"

"Are you okay? You look peaky!"

"I'm fine, Snow—watch the road!"

"Do you want me to put the top up?!"

"No!"

"I'm putting the top up!" He reaches for the lever.

"Wait!"

There's a metallic creak. I look back—the convertible hood has risen about six inches, then stopped.

"We'll do it manually!" Simon shouts. "When we pull over!"

The top of the car is well and truly stuck.

Simon is kneeling in the back seat, yanking at it, and it won't budge.

"I don't think you're supposed to raise it while you're driving," I say.

"But they always do it in music videos"—he yanks at the other side—"and Bond films."

I'm exhausted and sunburnt and starving. And about to walk into a shopping mall full of potential blood donors. One single upside of the convertible is that I can't really smell Simon and Penny when we're on the road. . . .

Though I'm well accustomed to how they both smell when I'm thirsty. Simon smells like the kitchen after you pop popcorn and melt butter. There's a singe to it, with a round, yellow, fatty feeling that sticks to the roof of your mouth. Bunce is sharper and sweeter—vinegar and treacle. She skinned her knee once, and my sinuses burned for hours.

They probably wouldn't like it if they knew I've thought about how they'd taste, but I just *really* believe I'm doing them service enough by not actually draining them. By not actually draining *anyone*. I am so thirsty right now, but I can't do any hunting till the sun sets. So instead I'll go and have dinner in a shopping mall, and everyone will live.

"Come on, Snow," I say. "The cheesecake awaits." Bunce is already inside. She went straight into the restaurant, as soon as we parked the car.

"We can't just leave the top down," he says. "Can you magic it up?"

"Sure, I've got a dozen convertible-repair spells."

"Good."

"I'm *joking*. There's not a spell for everything—did you forget them mentioning that every day at Watford?"

Simon climbs out of the car. "Yeah, I really wish I would've paid more attention at magic school—maybe I could have *been* somebody." I can hear the resentment in his voice, but when he turns to me, he starts to laugh.

"What."

He looks away from me, covering his mouth.

"What are you laughing at."

He looks down, but waves his hand at me. "You—your—"

I refuse to look down at myself. "My what, Snow?"

"Your hair."

I refuse to touch my hair.

"You look like that guy, with the wig—" He mimes playing the piano. "Duh, duh, duh, duhhh."

"Beethoven?"

"I don't know his name. With the big wig. There was a film about him."

"Mozart. You're saying I look like Mozart."

"You've got to look, Baz, it's a scream."

I will not look. I turn towards the mall. I assume Snow follows.


I look like Mozart. I look like I'm in one of those hair metal bands. (I also look deeply, strangely sunburnt, but I don't want to risk making that worse with magic.) I point my wand at my hair and cast, *"Tidy up!"* When that doesn't do it, I dip my head in the sink.

Fortunately I have the Cheesecake Factory men's room to myself.

I'd wanted to find a real restaurant for dinner. Surely, Des Moines, Iowa, has real restaurants. But Simon wanted something he'd heard of, something "famously American." Once he spotted the Cheesecake Factory sign, there was no more discussion.

By the time I leave the loo, I still look like I'm in an '80s band—but something less metal. Bucks Fizz or Wham!. (My mum was a fiend for Wham!.)

I find Snow and Bunce in a giant vinyl booth. Simon is hogging the breadbasket and paging through a menu so lengthy, it's spiral-bound. Penny is sitting across from him; I've seen zombies with more spirit.

"This menu's staggering," Simon says. "There's a whole page of taco salads. They've got macaroni and cheese, regular or fried. And every kind of chicken—look, *orange chicken*."

I sit next to him. "What's orange chicken?"

"Does what it says on the tin, I assume."

When the waitress comes, I order a steak as raw as they'll allow it. Snow orders the "American Burger." Bunce says she'll have "what they're having."

"The burger or the steak?" the waitress asks.

"Penny," Simon says, "you don't eat beef."

"Oh," she says. "Then I'll have the . . . I'll have whatever people have."

"People like the Buffalo Blasts," the waitress says.

"Isn't buffalo still beef?" Simon asks me.

I shrug. I don't know the first thing about buffalo.

"They're chicken," the waitress says. "With buffalo sauce."

"Fine," Penny agrees.

"I suppose she can skip the sauce. . . ." Simon mutters after the waitress has walked away.

I get that Bunce is in a catatonic state, but we really need to talk about our plan now. I need the old Bunce back. With the chalkboards and the diagrams. "So, about tonight," I say, "I assume we don't have a place to sleep."

Snow and I wait for her to answer. She's staring at a spot between the breadbasket and Simon's shoulder.

"Right," I say. "Hand over your mobile, Bunce, I'll find us a hotel. . . . Bunce? . . . *Penelope.*" She looks up. "Your phone?"

"It died in the car," she says. "And I couldn't charge it."

"Where's *your* phone?" Simon asks me.

"It doesn't work out of the country."

"Why didn't you switch it over?"

Because I'm on my parents' plan, and I didn't want them to know I was leaving the country, which I don't want to tell Simon. "Did you switch yours?" I say instead.

"No. I figured you and Penny would."

Bunce is staring at her lap now.

"Penelope?" Simon asks. "Are you okay?"

"Clearly not," I whisper.

"Penelope?"

"I want to go home," she says abruptly.

Simon sits back. "What?"

"This was a mistake." She's looking more like her usual bold self, but with a manic edge I don't like. "I didn't think this through. I'm sorry."

"Can we do that?" I ask. "Our tickets—"

"There's got to be a spell to change them," she says.

"There isn't a spell for everything," Simon says unpleasantly.

She shrugs. "Then we'll buy new tickets."

I huff. "We already stole these!"

Bunce won't be discouraged: "Then *you* can buy us new ones, Baz—you're rich."

It's not like her to throw my money in my face. "I'm on an allowance," I say, "and I can't use my Visa. My parents don't even know I'm here."

"Well," she says, "*my* parents don't know *I'm* here."

Simon looks hurt. "Why didn't you guys tell your parents?"

"Because this was a terrible idea, Simon"—Penny's voice is breaking—"and they would have said no!"

Simon drops his elbows on the table and his forehead on his hands. "Can we even pay for dinner?"

"I'll pay for dinner," I say. "But I can't pay for airline tickets. And we can't just keep stealing. A youthful indiscretion is one thing—the Coven might overlook that. This is turning into a crime spree."

"It isn't a crime spree!" Penny retorts. "We're not robbing banks and murdering people."

"Yet!" I say.

"I just—" Her chin is wobbling now. "I really thought this would work out. I thought—" She closes her eyes and opens her mouth, taking a deep breath, then sucks in her lips and exhales through her nose. It takes me a second to realize she's trying not to cry. "I thought it would be different if I talked to him face-to-face. And it *was.* It was so different."

"You mean Micah?" Snow asks.

"Of course she means Micah," I say.

Simon keeps prodding at her. "Did he break up with you?"

"Uh, no." Bunce's voice is thready. "Apparently he'd already done that. And I just hadn't got the message."

"Damn," Simon whispers. We've both leaned back in the booth, like we're trying to back away from the horror of this news. Like Bunce is suddenly contagious.

And I know this makes me a shit, but my first thought is that Simon and I have been given a reprieve. Like the Grim Relationship Reaper came and accidentally took Penelope and Micah instead of us.

# 15

## SIMON

Penelope and Micah are going to get married, and Penny's going to move to America and leave me alone—I've been bracing for it since sixth year.

Penelope and Micah are sure of each other.

I've never heard Penelope worry over whether Micah still loved her or loved her in the right way. I've never seen her crying about him in the hallway with her girlfriends. (Penny doesn't really have girlfriends. She has Agatha, sort of. And her mum. She has me. . . .) Penelope and Micah never fight. He never forgets their anniversary. I don't think Penny cares about anniversaries.

When Penelope talks about Micah, she seems stronger, more rooted to the ground. She doesn't blink. She doesn't doubt. I've never heard her snipe at him, the way people do, for saying something harmless. I've never heard her say, "*What does* that *mean?*" Or "*Why are you using that tone of voice?*" I've never seen her roll her eyes when he's talking—or breathe passive-aggressively, that breathing that means, *"I'm so tired of you. Shut up shut up shut up."*

I suppose I haven't actually seen them together since fourth year. And they weren't really in love then, they were just kids. Micah was a massive swot. All he wanted to do was study and talk about video games. Penelope liked him immediately— which is unheard of. I don't think Penny liked *me* immediately. It was more like she took charge of me immediately. Like I was an easy mark. Maybe Micah was an easy mark, too. He followed Penny around Watford, practicing spells and catching Pokémon and eating sesame seed sweets that his mum got from Puerto Rico and sent from Illinois. (They weren't bad. Chewy.)

There was no Internet at Watford, so Penny and Micah wrote each other actual letters during the term. I have so many memories of Penelope running out onto the Great Lawn with a letter from Micah that they've become one memory—Penny in her pleated skirt and knee socks, smiling, a white envelope in her hand.

Penelope and Micah were going to get *married*.

And now . . . Merlin, what now?

Baz and I aren't saying anything, but Penny is nodding as if we were.

"Are you sure—" I try.

"Very," she says.

"You probably both need to sleep on it."

"No."

"Maybe—"

"No! Simon! He's dating someone else."

"Bastard," Baz hisses.

"No," Penny laughs. "He's not a bastard, he's just—" She looks up at me. "—not in love with me." Her shoulders start shaking, and a second later, she's crying. "I think it was all in my head, all along."

"Buffalo Blasts?" A different waiter is at our table. Baz takes the plates, then waves the man away while he's asking whether we need any ketchup or ranch dressing. Crowley, this burger is gorgeous. It has hash browns on it. Baz's steak is so rare, it looks like strawberry jelly.

"It wasn't all in your head," I say. "He wrote you letters." *Are we eating,* I wonder. *Or is this too tragic for eating?*

"We were pen pals," Penny says.

"You Skyped. He told you he loved you, I've heard him."

That makes her cry some more. "Well, apparently he didn't mean it!" She picks up a Buffalo Blast and takes a big, tearful bite. *(Hurrah—we* are *eating!)*

"He said it was my fault," she says with her mouth full, "that I didn't want a real relationship. He said I just wanted to have a boyfriend, so that I could check it off and worry about more important things."

Baz picks up his knife and fork, and carefully starts cutting his steak.

"I can see what you're thinking, Basilton. I know you agree with him."

"I don't agree with him, Bunce."

"But?"

"I don't agree with him. And I don't know anything about relationships."

"But I *had* checked him off," she says. "I thought we were going to get married." She's crying hard now.

Baz drops his cutlery and swings over to Penny's side of the table, helping her set her Blast down, putting his arm around her. "Please don't choke to death, Bunce. Imagine the humiliation of dying at The Cheesecake Factory."

Penny turns in to his shoulder and cries some more. "Micah's right," she sobs. "I took him for granted."

"Maybe," Baz says, "but that doesn't excuse what he did. He's a coward."

"He said it's impossible to tell me something I don't want to hear!"

Baz catches my eye, and we both grimace, because that's absolutely true.

"I like that about you," I offer.

"We all do," Baz says. "If you weren't relentless, the Mage and the Humdrum would still be a plague on the whole World of Mages."

"But you wouldn't want to date me," she says.

"I would *never* want to date you," he earnestly replies, "but it's not because you're muleheaded. That's practically my type."

"I'm such a fool, Baz!"

Baz rubs her back and lets her cry into his shirt. I love him so much, and I want to tell him so. But I've never managed to say it, and now is definitely not the time.

He looks up at me, his eyes urgent. "Switch places with me, Snow. I'm about to drain her dry."

Penelope sits up—not as urgently as she should, I reckon—and Baz extricates himself from her arms and her hair and the booth.

He shakes his head, trying to clear it. "I think I'll step outside. For a moment." He's white as a sheet, though his cheeks and nose look sort of flushed with black. He wheels around and heads for the exit, dipping towards the hostess on his way out, then backing out the door.

I sit down next to Penny and pull my plate over. "I know you don't eat beef," I say, "but this burger tastes like America."

She takes one of my chips.

I put my arm around her. "I'm sorry."

"Don't be," she says.

"I feel like this is my fault."

"Did you introduce Micah to a girl named Erin?"

"No, but I—" My voice drops, I'm embarrassed to say this. "—I know you stayed in England, for university, because of me."

"Don't be stupid," she says.

"I'm *not*." I look in her brown eyes. "Penny, I'm not stupid."

She looks right back at me. "Simon, I think I would have come to America for university if I really wanted to. I could have brought you with me."

"Would you have?"

"No. Baz would never have allowed it." She looks down at her plate. "Anyway. I was happy. The way things were with Micah. Apart. It was enough for me."

# 16

## BAZ

It's still broad daylight, but I can't wait anymore—I have to kill something. Or find something dead. . . .

I wander around to the back of the mall, behind some skips. I have no idea what sort of wildlife can be found in West Des Moines. Rats, probably—but I'd need a boatload of them at this point.

There are some houses over the hill. I hate to use this spell unless I'm desperate, but I am desperate. I crouch low and hold my wand out over the ground, pouring in as much magic as I have available.

*"Here, kitty-kitty!"*


When I get back to our booth, the waitress is putting three monstrous slices of cheesecake on the table.

Simon's sitting next to Penny, and I'm flushed with warm feelings for both of them. (A side effect of being flushed with

the blood of nine cats, probably.) I go to their side of the booth—
"Scoot over"—and pick up a fork.

Simon points at the plates of cheesecake: "This one's Out-
rageous, this one's Ultimate, and this one's Extreme."

"No, *this* one's Extreme," Bunce says, taking a giant bite.
"With the Oreos."

I take a bite of the same piece and cover my mouth. "Oof,
thas good."

"It is The Cheesecake *Factory*," Simon says. "Does what it
says on the tin."

After dinner, we're all shattered. We'd meant to keep pushing
on through Iowa, but we're jetlagged and full of cream cheese,
and Bunce still looks like someone blew out her pilot light.

We end up at an inn near the motorway. It's cheap, but the
room is huge with two big beds. Bunce falls onto one. I nudge
her foot. "Plug in your mobile."

Snow and I are still holding our bags. We *could* take the
other bed. We've shared a bed before. A few times. We've . . .

Being with Simon hasn't meant what I thought it would.

It seemed at first that all my dreams were coming true, that
he was finally mine. Mine to love, mine to live with—to walk
with—to have. I'd never been in a relationship before. *"I want
to be your terrible boyfriend,"* Snow said, and I couldn't wait
for it.

Maybe I should have taken him at his word.

For we are indeed terrible at being boyfriends.

We're very good at *this*, though—standing uncomfortably in
the same space, absolutely not saying what we're both thinking, squeezing through a room full of elephants. We're cham-
pions.

"I'll take the sofa." Snow brushes past me and drops his bag near a brown settee. "My wings'll pop in the middle of the night."

I take the bed.

I'm the only one who takes a shower. But I'm also the only one who spent half an hour behind a skip, wrestling tabby cats. I have a nasty scratch on my chest, plus my nose is still charred from the sun. (That's never happened before, and I'm not wholly confident that it will heal. Maybe *this* is how you disfigure a vampire.) I'm glad I brought my toiletries from home. The hotel soap smells like marshmallows.

When I get out of the bathroom, the lights are out, and I can't tell if the others are asleep.

I lie in bed for a while, watching the ceiling fan spin in the dark. I think Bunce might be crying.

I don't blame her. I don't have half the security she had, and I can't bear the thought of losing it.

# 17

## SIMON

It's freezing in this hotel room.

Penny's crying.

Baz is clean. He opens the door to the bathroom, and steam and cedar and bergamot roll out. It takes me back to our room at Watford. To every morning that he stepped out of the shower, and I pretended not to care—no, I wasn't pretending. I just didn't know.

I genuinely didn't know how I felt.

I thought I hated him. I thought about him all the time. I missed him so much in the summer. (I thought I was just lonely. I thought I was hungry. I thought I was bored.)

Baz stepping out of the shower with his hair slicked back. Baz tying his school tie in the mirror—I could never take my eyes off him.

We used to spend every night together and wake up together every morning.

How long has it been since I fell asleep listening to him breathe?

If I wait, tonight, could I sit up and watch him sleep? (I used to be that shameless.)

It wasn't supposed to be like this—Baz and I were supposed to kill each other.

And then it wasn't supposed to be like this—we were supposed to *be* together.

I'm the one who fucked it up (*I am fucking it up*) by being too fucked up in the first place. By not wanting to talk to him. And never wanting him to spend the night. By not wanting him to look at me. (By not wanting him to see me, actually.)

*"How can you expect me to do this?"* I said one night. When he— When we—

*"I thought you wanted this,"* he said.

And I *did*. But then I *didn't*.

*"It's just a lot,"* I said. *"You're pushing me."*

*"I'm not pushing you. I won't push you. Just tell me what you want."*

*"I don't know,"* I said. *"I'm not the same anymore."*

*"What do you mean?"*

*"I don't* know—*stop* pushing *me."*

*"Are you talking about sex?"*

*"No!"*

*"Okay."*

*"Yes, maybe."*

*"Okay. I don't know what you want, Simon."*

*"It's just too much."*

That's the last time I tried to explain how I felt, and the last time he asked me to. I still don't have any answers. What do I want?

Baz is the only person I've *ever* wanted. The only person I've ever loved, like this.

But when I think about him touching me, I want to run. When I think about kissing him—

You can't hide from someone who's kissing you, even if you close your eyes.

I hear Baz getting up and moving around again in the dark. I wonder if he's cold. Or thirsty. Then, in a rush of warmth and cedar and bergamot, he kisses my cheek. "Good night, Snow," he says.

And then I hear him climb back into bed.

# 18

## AGATHA

Ginger slips into our room, trying not to wake me.

I came back to the room hours ago. I didn't have the stomach for evening cryotherapy. Or the singalong out on the deck. (Which I could still hear from our room. I swear these guys only know two songs—"Everybody Wants to Rule the World" and that Queen song about wanting to live forever. It's like being in the car with my dad.)

"I'm not asleep," I say.

"You should be!" Ginger whispers. "Tomorrow's a big day."

"You're the one up late, fooling around in somebody else's mansion."

She giggles, but doesn't argue.

"Why is tomorrow a big day?" I ask. "Are you levelling up?"

"No, that happens on the last night. It's a ceremony, I think."

"What does it even mean, Ging? Do you get a pin and a key to the clubhouse?"

"It means I'll be one of them. Like, I'm one of the people who's going to lead humanity *forward*. Toward the light."

"Ginger, please don't follow anyone into the light."

"It's not a joke, Agatha. It's like they see me for who I am. My spirit."

"I just . . . what does that even *mean*? The rest of them invented the Internet and work in pharmaceuticals."

"Are you saying I'm not successful enough to level up?" She sounds hurt, and I don't blame her. That is basically what I'm saying.

"I just worry," I say. "You should think about what it is they want from you."

"Should I think about what it is *you* want from me?"

"Ginger, you know what I want from you. I want to go to Burning Lad with you. I want to hang out at your apartment and watch shitty TV."

"We'll still be able to do that after I level up!"

"Oh, I'm sure. Hanging out with me will definitely lead humanity forward."

Ginger is propping herself up on an elbow to look at me. "Are you jealous? Is that what this is? Agatha, you know I want to bring you with me."

"Hmmm," I say flatly.

"And I'm not the only one. You made quite an impression on Braden tonight."

"Despite my best efforts."

"I'm serious. He says you have a 'singular energy.' "

"Ginger, that just means 'blond.' "

"It's more than that. He's going to invite you to his office tomorrow."

"I never go to a man's office on the first date."

"Agatha!" Ginger is sitting up now. "I'm being serious. This could be so good for you. Braden has a huge destiny—his aura is *golden*."

"Can you see it?"

"You know that I feel them. . . ."

"You said my aura was gold."

"Yours is more like ginger ale. It has bubbles in it."

"Hmmm." I roll away from her.

"You should give him a chance. Even if he is just hitting on you. He's, like, *iconic*. He's vacationed with the Obamas. He's got an Hermès bag named after him. Imagine dating a legend."

That's the trouble.

I don't have to.


Braden finds me at the cupcake table.

I should have expected this, I suppose.

I bailed on today's NowNext programming. I tried to go to a seminar on genetically engineered grain, but I couldn't tell if the speaker was for or against it, and anyway, I was exhausted. I can't sleep in an unlocked room. Not since fourth year, when the Humdrum sent a harmadillo into our dormitory. (Harmadillos don't even live in the UK; Penny got very fired up about it being an invasive species. "*Well, its invading days are over,*" Simon said, disposing of the corpse.)

"Hi," Braden says. He's wearing khaki pants and a navy jacket. It looks like a school uniform. He *is* cute, isn't he. In a blandly symmetrical, perfectly groomed, very, very wealthy way.

"Hello," I say.

"I told you there'd be cupcakes."

"I think *I* told *you*. . . ." I pick out a pink one.

He grins at me. "Agatha—"

"I did *not* tell you my name. . . ."

"Ginger told me," he says, looking caught out but not a bit ashamed. "I was hoping we'd get a chance to talk today."

I try to cut this off before it becomes a scene: "Look, Ginger told *me* that you think I have some sort of special energy. But I know that's all bullshit. So maybe you could not try that line on me, okay? Just spare me."

Braden's eyes are bright. "It isn't a line. You are special."

I snort, but continue taking a bite of cupcake. "Literally everyone in your club is some sort of nerd-bro supreme. I just met two guys who have *been to space*. Actual space. Do you think I've somehow missed the fact that most of the men here are people like you and Josh? And that most of the women, few as we are, are like Ginger and me? I'm not fooled. I know what's 'special' about us."

"Your friend Ginger is incredibly special," he says. "I'm surprised you don't see that."

"No, I do see it. That's not—"

"Do you know she can see auras?"

"It's more like she feels them," I mutter.

"She read my palm. It was extraordinary. She said my lifeline is completely unbroken."

"No, I know." I don't know how I ended up arguing that Ginger isn't special. That wasn't my point.

"And she's the most organically activated person I've ever met."

"I know!" It comes out too loud. "Ginger's like nobody else. She's my best friend."

Braden is smiling at me again. "You're right," he says, "this is sort of a boys' club. But we're trying to change that."

"I don't actually care. I don't even know why we're arguing about this."

He steps closer to me. We're about the same height. That bothers some boys, but it doesn't seem to bother him.

"Because you don't believe I see something rare in you,"

he says. "You think that I'm interested in you because you're beautiful. And you're right—I am, you are. But beauty is cheap, Agatha. Cheap and bountiful. In my position, beauty is a faucet that never stops running. . . ."

His eyes are locked on mine. I finish eating the cupcake, because it seems like the best way to show I'm not bothered, but my mouth has gone dry.

"There's something about *you*," he says.

I wipe my hands on a cloth napkin.

"Can I give you a tour of the grounds?"

I sigh. "All right, fine. Show me the grounds. Because I'm so special."

"Exactly right," he says, offering me his arm.

# 19

## PENELOPE

I wake up in an empty hotel room. It's already noon, and someone's knocking on the door.

"Housekeeping!" A small woman has keyed in.

"Just a minute!" I say. "Can I have a few minutes?"

"Ten minutes!" she calls, and closes the door.

My eyes are so swollen that they won't fully open. I slept in my clothes last night, even though I was coated in North America. I've got dust up my skirt, in my ears. When I push down my knee sock, there's a line of grime at the border. Also, my hands smell like Buffalo Blasts.

I decide to take a very fast shower. The room really is empty; Baz and Simon must have taken their stuff out to the car already. I glance out the window. The Mustang is still in the car park. Baz is standing beside it, not so discreetly casting spells at the broken top. Simon is sitting in the front seat, possibly pretending to drive.

Right. Shower first. Then decide where we're going. Then decide what to do with the rest of my life.

Not much has changed, I suppose: All those things I was going to do with Micah waiting at home for me? Now I'll do them with no one waiting.

If I'm being *rational*, nothing has changed. I hadn't seen Micah for a year. Who knows when I would have seen him again? Would I have even pushed for this insane trip if I hadn't felt like something was wrong between us?

(For a cheap hotel, this shower is massive.)

If I'm being rational, if I'm being *honest*, I never wanted to move to America. I didn't want to go to university here. I couldn't see myself living here—or maybe I should say that I couldn't see myself living anywhere but England.

So what *did* I see?

Micah coming around eventually. Seeing things my way . . .

Is that so wrong? Is that such a fatal flaw? Simon's never said it, but Baz has: *"You think you're always right, Bunce."*

So what if I do? I usually *am* right. It's just good sense to go through life assuming that I am. It's the law of averages. Better to assume I'm always right and occasionally be wrong than to fiddle about doubting myself all the time, saying to everyone, *"Yes, but what do* you *think?"*

I'm very good at thinking!

Would things have been so bad for Micah if he'd just followed my lead?

My dad does exactly what my mum tells him to, and he's happy. They're both very happy! My mum makes all the decisions, they're mostly correct, and it's an incredibly efficient operation all around.

Micah could have had a good life with me. I'm intelligent, I'm interesting, I'm *at least* as attractive as Micah is. I would have given him very bright children! I'm a genetic upgrade in most ways; both of my parents are geniuses, I have very straight teeth—

He never would have been *bored* with me.

I might have been bored with him. It's something I've considered. But I'd have my work! And I'd have Simon, I'm never bored with Simon.

Micah was supposed to be the stable element in the equation. The constant.

He's right. I'd ticked off the boyfriend box; I thought I'd got it settled early. Everyone around me wasted years trying to fall in love. I wasted nothing! I'd crossed it off my list.

Now I suppose I've wasted everything. And the worst part is—

The worst part is . . .

The worst part.

Is that he doesn't want me.

I put my hand on the shower wall. There's that cold feeling washing through my middle again.

I'm not being rational.

"Housekeeping!"


The boys are leaning on the car when I get down there. Simon's eating a banana. Baz is wearing his giant sunglasses and a beautiful floral shirt. (White with blue and purple flowers and fat striped bumblebees. It probably cost as much as my tuition.) He's tying a pale blue scarf around his hair.

"You can't wear that," Simon grins.

"Shut it, Snow."

"Where did that even come from? Do you just carry a ladies' scarf around with you?"

"It was my mother's," Baz says.

"Oh," Simon says. "Sorry. Wait—do you carry your mother's scarf around with you?"

"I wrap my sunglasses in it when I'm travelling."

"Are those your mother's sunglasses, too?"

Baz is rolling his eyes, but then he sees me, and his face goes gentle. It's intolerable. "Good morning, Bunce."

"Hey, Penny," Simon says, just as kindly, "how are you?"

"Fine," I say. "Right as rain."

Baz looks doubtful, but busies himself rubbing sunblock onto his nose.

"You slept through breakfast," Simon says, "but it was awful."

"Snow was very excited about continental breakfast," Baz says.

"It's not what you think." Simon frowns. "It's not French stuff. It's just really sad pastries and bad tea. Oh and you missed Baz eating a squirrel."

"I didn't eat the squirrel."

"Oh, sorry, you *drank* it, and threw its little squirrel body in the ditch. Do you think there are *any* magickal creatures or magicians here, Penny? Everything seems so mundane."

Baz turns to me. "Snow needs you to cast your angel spell on him. I hid his wings for breakfast, but they're still there."

"Um," I say. "What are we going to do now?"

"What do you mean?" Simon asks. "Our plane tickets are from San Diego, right? We press on."

"Yeah, but—" I don't feel like pressing on. I feel like pressing off. "Agatha isn't expecting us. She might not be happy to see us. I was wrong about surprising Micah. . . ."

"It won't be that bad," Simon says. "It's not like Agatha's planning to dump us."

Baz elbows him. Like I can't be reminded that I've just been dumped. Like I might have forgotten.

"I mean," Simon says, chagrined, "we may as well see the country. The mountains. The ocean. Maybe the Grand Canyon. Or that rock with all the guys' faces on it."

I don't know. I wasn't thinking clearly when I got us into this. I'm still not. "What do *you* think, Baz?"

Baz is rubbing sunblock on his hands. He looks like my grandmother in that scarf. He glances over at Simon. "Yeah," he says, "we may as well finish our road trip."

# 20

## SIMON

Iowa is beautiful. It's all gentle green hills and fields of maize. It reminds me of England. But with fewer people in it.

## BAZ

Iowa looks exactly like Illinois. I'm not sure why they bothered to separate them. Just an endless stretch of motorway and pig farms. (There's the distinction: Iowa smells more like pig shit than Illinois.)

The sun is relentless.

The radio is blaring.

I haven't had any tea at all today. None.

And I've decided not to let my nose smoulder off, so I'm re-applying sunscreen like an addict.

*And* I think my magic's gone wonky. I tried a few spells on the car top that should have fixed it. I put all the magic I had into *"Shipshape and Bristol fashion!"*—and nothing! My wand shot out *sparks*.

## SIMON

Baz coached me through traffic today, then onto the motorway. I feel like I'm really doing this, I'm driving. I need to get some sunglasses now. Wayfarers.

Baz's sunglasses are as big as his head. And that scarf. It should make him look like a mad old bat, but I'll be damned if he doesn't look half glamourous. Like a boy Marilyn Monroe. . . .

My brain gets kind of stuck on "boy Marilyn Monroe" for a while.

Then my favourite song comes on again.

## BAZ

Apparently there aren't enough golden oldies to fill out a whole station, because this is the fourth time we've heard this song since we left Chicago. Why would you go through the desert on a horse with no name? Why wouldn't you name the fucking horse at some point?

Snow goes to turn the stereo up, but the sixty-year-old volume knob is already cranked all the way to the right.

I slide my wand out of my pocket and point it at the radio. *"Keep schtum!"*

Nothing happens!

## SIMON

*"In the desert, you can remember your name, 'cause there ain't no one for to give you no pain. . . ."*

## BAZ

" *'Welcome to Nebraska . . . the good life'*—I wonder if that's a spell. . . ."

It's the first thing Bunce has said since we left Des Moines. She's been lying in the back seat with her arms over her face. I've envied her.

We whiz past the sign and into the first city we've seen in two hours. I'm encouraged that most Americans seem to realize this part of the country is blighted and have settled elsewhere.

"I'm hungry!" Penny shouts. Snow doesn't hear her. She leans between us to turn down the radio.

"Hey!" Snow grins at her. "You're up! Are you hungry!? I'm hungry!"

She gives him a thumbs-up, hanging between our seats.

"Belt up!" I shout at her. She lifts her arse in the air and wiggles it, just to bug me. I point my wand at her and say it with magic—***"Belt up!"*** But, again, nothing happens! That spell should have made her sit down *and* shut up *and* buckle her seat belt—but nothing!

You're never supposed to point your wand at your own face, but I do. *Is something wrong with it?*

"What do people eat in Nebraska?!" Snow asks.

"Their dreams!" I shout at him.

"Hey, look—" He points at another sign at the side of the road. Middle America is papered in signs. EXOTIC DANCERS! WHOLE WHEAT BREAD! VERY COLD BEER!

This one says, OMAHA RENAISSANCE FAIRE & FESTIVAL! JOUST DO IT.

"Nooooooo," I say.

"It's this weekend!" Snow shouts. "How lucky are we?!"

"Desperately unlucky," I say.

"Penelope?!" He looks at her in the rearview mirror and shouts. I'm sure she can't hear him. "Are you in?! It's a festival!"

She gives him another thumbs-up.


We follow the signs to the Renaissance Festival and eventually pull into a long gravel field filled with hundreds of cars. The Mustang kicks up a load of dust (which then settles on us). Snow finds a parking spot, then looks very pleased with himself for managing it. "I think I'm going to get a car when we get home," he says.

"Where will you park it?"

"In the magickal parking spot you'll manage for me."

He doesn't usually talk like that—about magic. About us. About the future. I can't help but smile at him. I hate everything about this road trip, but if it's going to keep drawing Simon out of his shell, I'd gladly drive to Hawaii.

Bunce climbs out of the car; it's like she's forgotten how to use doors. I untie my scarf and shake my hair out, pulling the rearview mirror towards me to check it. The scarf's worked like a charm.

When I look away, Simon is standing next to the car watching me, his head tipped slightly to the side. I can just see his tongue in the corner of his lips.

My eyebrows drop, in suspicion, then I slowly raise the left one. Maybe Nebraska *is* the good life. . . .

He lifts his chin—"Come on. Festival!"—and starts to walk backwards.

I hurry out of the car to follow him. "Oh, wait—Bunce!"

Penny turns back to me.

"You'll have to spell an umbrella over the car, in case it rains. My wand's gone wonky."

She comes back. "What do you mean?"

"I mean I've been casting spells all day, and nothing's happening."

"Are you sure it's the wand?" She holds out her hand. "Let's see."

I give it to her. "Are you suggesting that *I've* gone wonky?"

"Anything's possible." She sniffs at the wand. "May I?"

I shrug. Your own wand will work for someone else, just usually not as well. Bunce slides off her own magickal instrument, a gaudy purple ring, and hands it to me. Then she points my wand at the ground and murmurs, ***"Light of day!"*** Light shines out of it, weakly, but definitely there.

"Damn it," I say, taking the wand back. I look around. There are a few Normals walking by, inexplicably dressed like fairies. (Not like real fairies; they're not wearing cobwebs. They're dressed like fairies from Normal fantasies. With costume-shop wings and glitter on their faces.) I wait for them to pass, then point at an empty water bottle. ***"A glass and a half!"*** The bottle should fill with milk, it's a child's spell, but—nothing!

Bunce starts giggling. She still looks ghastly from no sleep and all the crying, so the overall effect is ghoulish.

"What?" I demand. Very tired of these two laughing at me on foreign soil.

"What were the other spells you cast, Basil?"

"I don't know—'Bristol fashion,' 'Keep schtum,' 'Exceedingly good cakes.'"

She laughs harder. Snow is frowning at her, like he doesn't get it either.

"Baz," she says. "Those are all spells from back home. They're British idiom—useless here."

Oh. Crowley. She's right.

"Wait," Simon says, "why?"

"Because there aren't enough Normal people here using those phrases," I say. "It's the Normals who give words magic—"

Simon rolls his eyes and starts quoting Miss Possibelf. "*'The more that they're said and read and written, in specific, consistent combinations'*—right, I know. So your magic's fine?"

"Yes," I say, tucking my wand away, feeling like a pillock. "It's my syntax that's buggered. Come on."

As we get to the festival entrance, a man dressed like a mediaeval peasant steps up, ringing a bell. Without any warning, Simon's wings explode from his back and spread out completely, in all their red-leather glory.

Simon freezes. Bunce holds out her ring hand. But the people in the queue don't seem fazed—some of them even start clapping.

"Excellent cos," a teenage girl says, stepping up to inspect the wings. "Did you build these yourself?"

"Yes?" Simon says.

"So cool—do they move?"

He tentatively folds his wings back.

"Wow!" she says. "I can't even hear the motor. Are they on strings?"

"A magician never reveals his secrets," I say (which is also a spell, though Crowley knows whether it works here).

Penny takes Simon's elbow and muscles him to the end of the queue.

"What is this place?" I murmur. The person in front of us is dressed as a Viking. There's also a genie, a pirate, and three women dressed like Disney princesses. "Is it fancy dress?"

"Five dollars off for cosplay," the ticket seller says to Simon. "You, too," she says to me.

I look down at myself. "This is a very expensive shirt."

"Come on," Simon says, taking my hand. He's laughing. He turns towards me and pulls me into the festival—and for a moment, everything feels almost magickal. Simon with his wings spread wide, a row of hanging lanterns behind him. There's smoked meat on the air. And somewhere, someone is playing a dulcimer. (My aunt plays the dulcimer; all the women in my family learn.)

Then Simon swings over to my side, and the fair itself stretches before us.

"What in the curs-ed fuck?" I say.

Bunce and Snow are similarly gobsmacked.

The festival is set up like a tiny village, with hastily built shacks and hand-painted hanging signs. Nearly everyone is dressed like—Crowley, I don't know. It's like *Monty Python and the Holy Grail* crossed with *The Princess Bride* crossed with *Peter Pan*. . . .

Crossed with some film where all the women wear push-up bras and extremely low-cut dresses. Every other woman here, maid or matron, is laced into a ridiculously tight bodice and spilling out the top. I've never seen so much and so many breasts in my life—and we're only five feet into the festival.

"Crikey," Simon says.

A nearly topless woman catches his eye and wheels around him. "Good morrow, my lord."

I wave her away—"Right, right, move along."

"Fare-thee-well!" she calls to Simon.

"What on earth is the theme?" Bunce has her hands on her hips, properly puzzling it out.

"The Renaissance?" Simon suggests.

"That's Galileo and da Vinci," she says. "Not . . ."

Frodo Baggins waddles by.

"Look," Simon says, "turkey legs!"

I half expect to see someone wearing turkey legs, but it's another shack with a large drumstick-shaped sign hanging over the window—SMOKED FOWL.

Bunce and I follow Simon to the shack. "It's so strange," he says, grinning. "Nobody's looking at me."

Two children have stopped in their tracks to stare at him. Their mother is taking a mobile-phone photo.

"Everyone is looking at you," I say.

"Yeah, but not like it's any big deal. They think it's a costume." He spreads his wings out wide. Everyone in the turkey-leg line says, "Ohhhh." A few more people point their phones at him.

Bunce covers her eyes. "My mum's gonna kill me."

There's another bosomy woman behind the cash register. "Well met, my lord, what dost thou require this bonny afternoon?"

"Uh, yeah," Simon says. "I'll have a turkey leg and"—he looks at the menu—"a tankard of ale."

"I'll be needing to see your papers, young master."

"My papers?"

Bunce speaks up. "Our passports?"

The serving wench leans forward, practically depositing her

breasts in Simon's arms. "Ye look a little green around the ears, I hazard."

"Crowley, Snow," I say. "She sounds like Ebb."

"I'm twenty," Simon tells her. "It's fine."

"I admire thine accent and thine courage, lad, but I must obey the king's law. Mayhap thou wouldst enjoy a tankard of Coca-Cola instead?"

"Sure . . ." Simon says.

"Really though," the woman whispers. "*Great accents.*"

We get our food and walk away from the shack right into a parade. "Hear ye, hear ye!" a man in homemade chain mail is calling. "Make way for the queen!" I start to bow my head, and I notice Bunce begin to curtsy (which is absurd on both our parts, but there you are). A horse, carrying a woman dressed as Elizabeth I, trots by.

"Pardon me, chap." Another woman, dressed as Sherlock, pushes past us.

Bunce waves her turkey leg at the whole preposterous scene. "Is the theme *British*?" she asks, suddenly indignant. "Is it just weird and British?"

"If so, Bunce, you've got the best costume."

"But there are also Vikings," Simon says. "And people dressed up like big furry animals."

"And handsome young men with dragon wings," I add, earning another rare smile from him.

"That shop over there sells magic wands!" Penny says. "It's like they're mocking *us,* specifically."

"They're just having fun," Simon says. "Let's find a table."

"The young master hath a fine idea," I say. "He is fair in aspect and sharp in mind."

"How'd you do that?" Simon asks. "Did you flip a switch?"

"I'm just pretending to be in a Shakespeare play. Lay on, my boy."

"I'm not your boy," he says, laughing, but also laying on.

" '*He's gone,*' " I lament. " '*I am abused, and my relief must be to loathe him.*' "

"*Othello,*" Bunce says. "Very nice, Basilton."

I twirl my turkey leg and bow.

"You're having fun," Simon accuses.

"Fie!"

# 21

## SIMON

Renaissance Faires are brilliant.

I had a turkey leg and a big sticky Coke and then something called funnel cake, which is just a mess of fried dough with powdered sugar, and is A-plus-plus in my book. The woman who sold it to me gave me free chocolate sauce. "Angels get upgrades," she said.

Everyone here is *so* friendly. I don't know if that's a Nebraska thing or just a part of their Olde English act.

Penelope has decided to take umbrage at all the bad English accents. (And bad Scottish accents and bad Irish accents and some that sound like very bad Australian accents.) But Baz has taken to it like a fish to water. He can out-thine the best of them.

I beg them both to walk around for a bit. "You're not supposed to stay in the car the whole time on a road trip," I say. "You're supposed to get out and see things, meet strange people—lotus-eaters and sirens."

"That's not a road trip," Baz says, "that's the *Odyssey*. When did you read the *Odyssey*, Snow?"

"The Mage made me read it—I think he wanted it to rub off on me—and it is so a road trip!"

Baz smiles at me. Like he hasn't in a while. Like he almost never has, in public—like it's easy. "You're right, Snow. Better tie you to the mast."

He's wearing a shirt with a whole field of flowers on it. I didn't know how to dress once we didn't have to wear uniforms every day, but Baz was apparently spoiling for it. He almost never wears the same thing, the same way, twice.

He's coming into himself. And I'm coming apart.

But not today. Today I'm someone else entirely. Today I'm just a bloke with fake red wings.

There's a shop selling crystals and magickal artefacts down the way. Penny wants to stop and make sure nothing actually magickal has snuck in. Across the path is a sword shop—so many people are selling swords here!

Baz follows me into the sword tent. (LONG & BROAD, the sign says.) "You can't pick up every sword, Snow."

"I can't hear you," I say, trying out a poorly balanced sabre.

"Pray, my lord, my light—thy cannot test every blade in the kingdom."

That makes me laugh, and him, too. I toss him the sabre, and he catches it.

"I don't know anything about swords," he says.

"More's the pity," I say. "We could spar." I look back at the racks. "We could have, I mean." I suppose I don't have a sword of my own anymore. The Sword of Mages used to hang at my hip, there whenever I called it. I can't call it now. I can't say the spell to summon it. Or—I can say it, but nothing happens.

Baz tried once—held his wand over my left hip and said the incantation: *"In justice. In courage. In defence of the weak. In the face of the mighty. Through magic and wisdom and good."*

It didn't appear.

*"I suppose it only works for the Mage's Heir,"* he'd said.

*"That's nobody anymore,"* I said back.

Baz throws another sword at me. I scramble to catch it. It's lighter than I expect, made of foam. He's holding up one just like it. "This is more my speed," he says.

"That's the Master Sword," I say.

"Perfect for me then."

"From *The Legend of Zelda*?"

He still doesn't get it. Baz isn't into games. He holds out the foam blade. "En garde, you knave. You reprobate scapegrace."

I tap his blade with mine. He tries to parry. He's terrible at this.

I can't think of anything else Baz is terrible at. He's someone else here, too.

"You breaketh, you buyeth!" a man shouts at us.

We ignore him, banging our swords and shuffling out into the road. I'm going easy on Baz. Just batting him back. He's trying to look fierce, but he keeps laughing.

He breaks through my cover just once to tap my leg. "You're losing it, Snow! Is this how you defeated the hobgoblin horde?"

"You're more distracting than a hobgoblin," I say. "Your hair is shinier."

" '*You have witchcraft in your lips,*' " Baz says.

"Is that more Shakespeare?"

"Yeah, sorry. I know you prefer Homer."

He's pushing me back into a wooden post. I'm totally letting him. I hold my foam sword up in front of my chest. His is pressed against it. "Check. Mate," he says.

"That's completely wrong," I say.

"I win."

"I'm letting you win."

"That's still a win, Snow. That might even be a more conclusive win."

Baz's grey eyes are shining. He smells like sunblock. I'm trying to think of an insult. I'm wondering if I could kiss him. If the other person I am today could kiss the other person he is. Is that legal in Nebraska? Is it allowed at the Faire?

Baz hisses, turning his head and body away from me, like he smells blood.

I turn after him. "What . . ."

He's staring at a pack of people coming our way—six or seven of them dressed like vampires, plus a few of the busty women in corsets that you see everywhere. (I still haven't sorted whether I'm still attracted to women or whether I ever was, or whether I'm some kind of Baz-only-sexual. But the cleavage at this place is abundant, and I'm not mad about it.)

"Look," I say, trying to draw his attention away from the fake vampires, "I know this is—whatever Penny called it, appropriation—but don't let it get your back up."

Baz's lip is curled. The band of vampires swaggers closer. They're dressed like various bloodsucking stereotypes. A couple of them have capes. One's a girl, dressed like Captain Hook or something. There's fake blood splattered all over their costumes. Only their mirrored sunglasses are ruining the effect.

Whatever they're selling, the wenches are buying it. One of the vampires has already got a girl in his arms, her legs wrapped around his hips. He must be wicked strong. Baz turns away, just as the guy nearest us pulls down his sunglasses to look at me. His skin is pale as ash, and his cheeks look too full. He winks.

I shudder. "*Baz.*"

"I know." Baz's fangs are popped. He's turned back to watch them again.

"They're—"

"Simon, I know."

"Where's Penny?"

"We'll find her when we're done."

"Done what?"

He takes a determined breath. "Slaying these vampires."

"We can't just kill them," I say. (I can't, anyway. I'm not the sort of person who picks fights with monsters anymore.)

"We bloody well can. As long as we get the drop."

"But they haven't done anything wrong!" (Now I'm the sort of person who gives vampires the benefit of the doubt.)

"*Yet*, Snow. They're probably opening those harlots like cans of lager while we argue about it."

"We should get Penelope," I say. "We're outnumbered."

"They're outnumbered. Two magicians to none."

"Like I said—we should get Penelope."

"Where'd they go?"

I look. The vampires have disappeared.

"Damn it." Baz is already following their trail.

"*Baz—*"

"*Simon.* They're going to murder those girls!"

"Not immediately. Not in broad daylight."

"Do you think there's a Vampire Code of Conduct?"

The sword seller yells at Baz. "Hey! Cometh back and pay-eth for that!"

"We'll be right back," I say, dropping my Master Sword on a table—then decide to grab a broadsword. "Right back!"

I catch up with Baz as he ducks between two shacks. "Do you see them?"

"I smell them," he whispers. "Quiet."

This part of the festival is set up along a stand of shade trees. There's no business happening behind the sheds and tents; it's like being backstage.

I hear giggling. It takes a second before I see them, hidden in the trees: The vampires have surrounded the women, and they're all . . . making out, it seems like.

"Christ, you people are perverts."

"These are not my people," Baz says. "And be quiet. Vampire ears."

"They still haven't done anything wrong. We can't kill them for copping off."

Then one of the women shrieks. And not in a copping-off way. In an *"I'm dying"* way. Another woman joins her.

Baz snarls—just as Penelope shouts, ***"Burn, baby, burn!"***

One of the vampire's legs is suddenly on fire. He tries to stamp it out, but . . . vampires are very flammable. The other six jump back and take off after Penny. Baz and I take off after them.

The vampires are unbelievably fast. But then, so is Baz. I run after them all for a minute before I remember I can fly. I flap up over the tents, looking for Penny. The vampires are chasing her through the crowd. She's got her ring hand out, but no clear shot at them.

I settle down near her. People make room for me, clapping—which lets the vampires through as well. Penny takes aim. ***"Off with your head!"*** she shouts at one of them, and isn't that just what happens. (Penelope's never been one to pull punches.) His head rolls backwards, and his body falls forward—and his mates rush towards us, enraged.

I charge one of them, swinging my sword. My extremely shit sword. Which buckles over the bastard's shoulder.

I shuffle back, directly into another sword stall. (Which doesn't take as much luck as you'd think; at least half of these shops sell weaponry.) I grab a claymore and swing. The blade hits the vampire, then separates from its hilt.

This vamp's got shaggy blond hair and a Count Chocula cape with a big collar. I grab another sword and hold him back for a moment, before he pulls it out of my hands by the blade. I hook my tail around his leg and yank him to the ground—which gives me a second to grab a scimitar with my left hand and a battle axe with my right.

He's already recovered. I step back, onto the main thorough-fare. All the fairgoers have lined the dirt pathway like they're watching a parade. I can't see Penny. She won't have enough magic left in her for another decapitation. But she's clever, I tell myself. And Baz is an even match for any three of these creeps. I hope.

The vampire lunges towards me—and I bash the scimitar into his chest. It breaks like a matchstick, and the vampire gets hold of my hand. This is very bad news. He could bite me like this. Or break me in two. If I still had magic, I'd be trying and failing to think of a good vampire spell about now. (Imagine how much I'd miss magic if I'd ever properly mastered it.)

I try to fly up and away from the vampire, but he holds on tight. I've still got a battle axe in my other hand, so I take one last desperate swing at him—

The head of the axe snaps off when it hits his neck.

# 22

## BAZ

Penelope Bunce has decapitated one vampire and set two more on fire. She's my mother's daughter.

*Where is Simon?*

I keep looking for a way to contain the vampires. (Contain them, for what? For who? The authorities? Does America even have magickal authorities?)

*Where are you, Snow?*

He's not with Bunce. She's still fighting one of the vampires.

I'm keeping two more at bay: a guy in a polyester cape and a woman dressed like Tom Cruise's Lestat. (Of course I've read Anne Rice. I was a 15-year-old closet case whose parents pretended they didn't notice when the family dog disappeared.)

And I'm trying to find Simon. He's usually impossible to ignore in a fight.

None of my spells are doing much damage. I try **"Guts for garters!"** but it just seems to irritate them. Then I try **"Sod off!"** That should push them back a few feet and at least give me time to think. It doesn't. It doesn't do *anything*. Which

means I must be being too English again. What a time to realize I should have been watching more *Friends* reruns.

*"Bugger off!"* I shout, fruitlessly, dodging behind a tree.
*"Push off! Naff off!"* Nothing, nothing, nothing. (I would try
"Fuck off," but the magickal effect of swear words is unpre-
dictable; it depends entirely on the audience.)

"Buzz off!" someone in the crowd shouts at me—a young
black man in granny glasses. I've jumped into the tree. The
cloaked vampire is tearing at the branches below me. "Buzz
off!" the man in the crowd shouts again.

I point my wand at the vampire. *"Buzz off!"*

It works. He jumps back like he's been shocked.

I cast it at Lestat de Lioncourt, too. *"Kindly buzz off!"*
The adverb doesn't give the spell the extra zing I'm hoping for.
But it still works: She falls back.

I drop out of the tree. What's my plan here. . . . (*And where
is Simon?*)

And why am I holding back? I'm casting schoolyard spells
at coldblooded murderers—at no-blooded murderers.

When I first realized what they were, I told myself I had to
*act*. That I had to *do* something. My mother's murderer might
be gone, but her death isn't avenged. That's what my aunt is
doing now. Hunting vampires. Repaying them for my mother's
death, one by one.

We *saw* these vampires attack those girls. If we let them go
now, they'll kill more people. *That's what vampires do.*

There's no point in trying to be covert. They've already
chased us into the middle of a crowd. We're all going to be Internet famous after today. The Mage himself wouldn't be able
to clean up this mess.

And there's no point trying to be humane. Penny's on the
right track: We can't lock them up, and we can't let them go.

And it's not like I have an opportunity to convert them to rat-drinking. *"Have you heard the good news about small mammals?"*

I can't just keep pushing these two back. I've been trying to keep my distance from them, casting instead of punching. (I couldn't take them both in a fistfight.) But Lestat has her eye on my ivory wand—she'll grab it as soon as she's close enough.

I hear a familiar bellow and spin around.

He's at the other side of the square, swashbuckling out of a sword shop like the illegitimate grandson of Indiana Jones and Robin Hood.

*There you are, Simon Snow.*

With a blade in each hand and a fair-haired vampire on his tail.

Simon's beautiful in battle: He never stops. You never see him plan his next move. He doesn't plan, he just *moves*.

But he's running out of options. His sword has already cracked in half. He's got an axe in the other hand, and—it breaks against the vampire's rock-hard neck. *Crowley, no.* Simon's no match for him now, not without magic.

"Snow!" I shout, forgetting my two opponents—

Just as Simon takes the broken axe handle and stakes the vampire right through the heart.


# SIMON

I hear Baz call my name. When I look up, two vampires have grabbed him by the arms.

The vampire impaled on my axe handle has already started to wither. Like it was the magic in his heart holding him together. I pull back the stake, and he falls—a man-shaped pile of blood and boots and ashes.

I'm already in the air, flying towards Baz as fast as I can manage. The vampires have pushed him to the ground—bollocks! One of them has his wand!

I beat her over the back with my axe handle; I'm at the wrong angle to stake her. She turns on me, waving Baz's ivory wand as if a spell is just going to fall out of it.

Baz uses the distraction to get back on his feet and throw a punch at the other vampire, the guy. It's a messy punch. Baz has never learned to fight with his body, even though he's made of steel. But the vampire he's fighting is the same—all power, no skill. They're trading hits like clumsy steam engines.

I hook my tail around the girl vampire's leg, but the trick doesn't work this time. She holds her ground, then jerks her leg back, pulling me into her arms. Then she goes for my face with the wand—she's given up on casting spells and is just going to stab me with it—but I wrap a wing around her, holding her so close she can't move.

I forgot about her fangs. She opens her mouth wide.

I whip my wing open, flinging her away.

It gives me a moment to deck the guy Baz is fighting squarely in the jaw. (It has almost no effect on him—vampires are nigh invulnerable—but it feels good to land a punch.)

The girl's on my back faster than I thought possible. I was wrong to turn away from her. I beat my wings, but she hangs on.

"Simon!" Baz yells, and I want to tell him not to get distracted.

I crash my skull back, trying to keep her fangs off me. My wings are still flapping, and I've lifted a few feet off the ground, but it's not enough to take off.

Baz staggers back from his opponent, then stands tall,

making two fists at his hips. His eyes go hooded and dark. *That's a very attractive way to die,* I think. But then Baz opens his palms, and he's holding two balls of fire.

He shoves one in the boy vampire's face, then hurls the other at the beast on my back—she bursts into flames.

And so do I.

I fall to the ground, rolling—as the crowd around us erupts into applause.

Baz reaches for my hand to help me up. I take it, snagging his wand from the ground. I hand it to him. "Penny," I say.

We both turn to the other end of the square, where Penny has just vaporized the last vampire. He's there, and then he isn't. Once he's gone, she sees us. She gives me a hesitant thumbs-up, then steps around the vampire's meagre remains.

We all start walking then, almost like we agreed to do it. Slowly. Towards the exit.

The Normals are still applauding. Baz turns and waves at the crowd. He elbows me, so I wave, too.

Penny catches up with us and grabs our arms. "We've got to get out of here."

"If we run," Baz says through his smile, "they'll follow us." He bows and waves with both hands.

Penny and I try to imitate him.

"Thank you!" Baz shouts. "We'll be back with shows at six and nine!"

We back slowly through the edge of the audience. People are taking our photo and grabbing at my wings.

"Keep going," Baz says.

Queen Elizabeth and her court watch us go by, clapping genteelly.

Baz takes a deep bow.

Then we all start walking faster, as fast as we can without breaking into a run, trying to stay ahead of the dispersing crowd. As soon as we get through the exit, we do run. Down the steps. Past the queue. Past the fairies and the peasants and the vaping warlords. I can't stop laughing. I haven't felt this good in a year.

# BAZ

We run through the gravel towards the Mustang, and Penny actually leaps into the back seat.

Simon catches up with me and traps me against the car. He's kissing me before I see it coming, bending me back over the boot. "You were amazing," he says, taking a breath. "You didn't even need a wand."

I hold on to his shoulders. "I'm a little disturbed that you find slaying vampires this exciting."

He kisses me so hard, my head tips.

"Guys!" Bunce shrieks. "We are literally fleeing a crime. And also still in Middle America."

She's right. I give him a push.

"So hot," Simon says. "Got to see you fight without picking a fight with you myself."

Bunce throws a plastic bottle over my shoulder, and it smacks Simon in the wing. "I swear to Stevie I'll leave without you both!"

I look past him. There are a dozen or so people headed our way.

"I promise to be just as hot later," I say. "I'll start fires all the way across the Midwest."

Simon breaks away from me, still with that strange light in his eyes, and jumps into the passenger seat.

I'm not going to be the only one who fusses with a door—I hop into the driver's seat and start the car, and we roar out of the car park, kicking up a thundercloud of dust and rock.

# 23

## PENELOPE

My mother is going to kill me. She's going to throw me in a witch's hole herself; she won't even call the Coven. We have broken every rule today. The World of Mages doesn't have many, but we've shattered them all:

*Don't pester the Normals.*

*Don't interfere with the Normals.*

*Don't steal from the Normals.*

*Above all, don't let the Normals know that magic exists.*

*Above even that, don't let the Normals know that we exist.*

Magicians have to live amongst Normals because their language is the key to our magic. But if they knew about us . . . *If Normal people knew that magic existed, and that someone else had it . . .*

We'd never be free.

My mother is going to take away my ring. She's going to lock me in a tower.

In the old days, magicians would magickally alter their faces if they'd been witnessed doing magic in public. You can only erase memories one at a time (and the ethics are dodgy)—you can't mindwipe a whole crowd.

Your only options after a big, unfixable scene are, one, to disappear or, two, commit to the sin wholeheartedly: Put on a cape and top hat and go on the road. Once you tell Normals that it's all a *trick,* you can do anything in front of them. You can make the Statue of Liberty disappear.

Baz was clever. To pretend it was all part of some show.

I'm not that sort of clever. I can't pretend.

I killed those vampires in front of hundreds of Normals. Mum won't care about the vampires; you can get a medal for slaying vampires. But I used so much magic, right out in the open.

I can only imagine what Simon and Baz did. They have wings and fangs and superstrength between them. Baz has an actual magic wand.

Hopefully it was all so obvious and over the top that no one will believe it was real. No *real* magicians would be so careless.

Morgana the mighty, *everyone's* going to see this. All our friends. Our teachers.

Micah's going to think I went directly off the deep end as soon as he dumped me.

I suppose I did.

# 24

## BAZ

I should be very upset right now.

Bunce is a wreck in the back seat; you can see the waves of guilt and fear and shock rolling through her. Appropriately! Our parents are going to *cut out our tongues* when we get home. We're definitely facing a trial before the Coven. Undoubtedly. The moment we're back on British soil.

But we're very much not on British soil now, are we?

And Simon Snow doesn't have any parents.

His euphoria is contagious. Beyond contagious—enchanting.

I can still feel his mouth on mine, his arms around me. For the first time in so long. Maybe for the first time ever like that. So heady and carefree.

It's like the day we turned back the dragon on the Watford lawn—but on that day, I had to pretend I wasn't soaring inside. That I wasn't absolutely shimmering from his magic and attention.

Simon's still grinning—a half hour out of Omaha—letting the wind whip his hair into his eyes. Penny finally spelled his wings away so that he could put on his seat belt. (We got a few odd looks on the freeway.)

He keeps reaching over to squeeze my shoulder or my arm. And it isn't a question. There's no hesitation. He's just touching me because he's happy. Because he's high. And because I was there, I'm part of it, what's making him happy.

He grabs the back of my neck and squeezes, shaking me gently back and forth. When I look over, he's laughing.

They're going to stone us when we get home. They're going to strike our names from the Book.

But not until we get home.

If we get home.

America is endless. We may never run out of roads.


We pull over eventually, at a motorway service station. To use the loo and buy more terrible sandwiches.

Bunce and I are the first ones back to the car. "We must need petrol," I say. "We haven't filled up once."

"I've been charming the tank," she replies, frowning at her dinner. "How do Americans mess up *sandwiches*?"

"They're dry *and* soggy," I say, taking a bite. "At once."

"How much trouble do you think we're in?" She looks up at me, closing one eye against the setting sun.

"All of it," I say.

"Maybe no one will see."

"More people were videoing us than not videoing us."

"I've been trying to think of a spell. . . ."

"To erase the Internet?" I set my sandwich on the car bonnet and start wrapping my scarf around my hair again. "You'd have to cast a holy book and sacrifice seven dragons."

"So it's not *impossible*. . . ."

"Give it up, Bunce. We are well and truly fucked."

"Then why aren't you more upset?"

Simon swaggers out of the shop, holding a bag. "I've found a way around the sandwich problem," he says. "Beef jerky! This place sells at least thirty different kinds."

He reaches into my jeans pocket for the keys. "My turn to drive."

I spin away from his hand. "Is it?"

He holds my hips against the car and digs the keys out. We're both laughing.

Bunce is watching us.

Simon gets into the driver's seat, and Penny steps closer to me. I still haven't managed this scarf. "We'll be home in less than a week," she says. "We have to think of something."

The car starts. The radio is already blaring.

"Where are we sleeping tonight?" Simon asks.

I slide past Penny and get in the car. "We'll know it when we see it."

I was being poetic earlier, when I said that America was endless. But Nebraska really *is* endless. As big as England and as empty as the moon. I've never seen the sky look so black.

Cornfields give way to scrubby grasslands and rocks. We think we see pixies just after dark—flashes of light in the tall grass. But when we pull over and get closer, they turn out to be little phosphorescent beetles. "Fireflies," Simon says. "I think."

He and I wade into the grass, watching the bugs slowly blink on and off. They're so sluggish in the air, it seems like you could almost catch one—and then Snow does catch one. He holds it out to me in his cupped palms, and I put my hands around his and look.

"Are they magic?" I ask.

Simon shakes his head. "I don't think so."

The firefly gets bored of inspecting Simon's palms and flits up between our bowed heads—we both jump. Then we try to catch another one, chasing each other as much as the blinking lights.

Even Bunce stops brooding long enough to join us. She squeals when she catches a beetle, dancing around like a pony. "*Wolla-la-laggh!* I've got it! I can feel its wings!"

"Don't crush it!" Simon says. "Let's see!" He opens her fist, and the firefly flies out and lands in his hair. Simon freezes, a smile hanging off the edge of his lips, the light blinking slowly on and off over his ear.

I move in to kiss him, trying not to startle the firefly. I can do it, I'm vampire-stealthy. Snow sees me coming and doesn't move. But when my lips brush his, he pulls his face to the side. The firefly takes off.

Back to this then. Whatever was making him bold earlier has burned away.

"Come on," he says. He's still smiling, at least.

I want to take his hand and keep him here with me, in the weeds. "*Are you still mine?*" I'd ask him. "*Do you still want this?*"

But I don't.

Because I don't want to hear him say no.


We do see actual pixies an hour later. Spinning in a tall field, a dozen in a circle, with clouds of fireflies in their hair. "*Those* are magic," I say.

All Simon can see are the lights.

# 25

## SIMON

I notice the silver truck about an hour before I really *notice* it.

The same pair of headlights lingering in the rearview mirror. The same smiling silver grille. Never passing us, never getting off the motorway. I suppose there's not much to get off for out here, is there?

The truck should have passed us when we stopped to catch fireflies. Or when we stopped to watch the pixie circle. (I couldn't quite see the pixies. Because I'm Normal again, obviously, though no one will just say so.)

But it's still behind us.

I suppose it could be a *different* silver truck. Or maybe it's the same truck, and they made a stop, too, and they're just now, coincidentally, catching up with us.

Maybe.

I get off at the next exit. Baz raises an eyebrow at me, but doesn't say anything.

"We're not stopping for any more pixies!" Penny shouts.

"Unless they're running a hotel. I'm tired, and my bladder is bursting!"

I watch the mirror. After a minute, I see the same pair of wide-set lights. I turn down the radio. "We're being followed."

"What?" Penny shouts back. "By who?!"

"Don't look!" I say.

She turns to look. Baz looks at the mirror instead. "For how long?" he asks.

"At least an hour, closer to two. Before the fireflies."

He pulls out his wand.

I've been followed before. Ambushed. By goblins. By werewolves. By down-on-their-luck magicians with a grudge against the Mage. But I was armed then. I had a legendary sword and a belly full of magic. I was never good with a wand, but my magic would annihilate anything that came too close to killing me.

I've got nothing now.

But two very powerful friends.

Penny unbuckles and leans between us. "I'll spell them!"

Baz puts his hand on her ring arm. "Don't hurt anyone!"

"I'm more worried about *them* hurting *us*!" I shout. We're all shouting over the wind.

Baz is still holding Penny's arm. "We can't spell every Normal who looks at us wrong!"

She shrugs him off. "It's not like we can get into any *more* trouble!"

"That isn't the point, Bonnie and Clyde!"

Penny has already turned away from us. She's kneeling against the back seat, her short skirt flying up in the wind. She holds her right hand out and shouts, ***"Get lost!"***

The headlights don't waver.

"Give it a moment to set in," Baz says.

We wait for the truck to stop or turn. We pass two crossroads, then three. At the fourth, I abruptly turn from a two-lane motorway onto a gravel road. The tyres grind on the gravel, and we can feel rocks battering the undercarriage.

Baz and Penny watch the darkness behind us. I stare at the mirror.

The headlights appear again.

"Fuck," Baz says.

Penny spits out another spell—**"*Freeze!*"** Nothing happens. She spreads her fingers—

"No!" Baz says. "You'll wear yourself out."

"It could be vampires!" she says.

"It could be anything!" I say. A wraith, a leach, a ghoul. Something specifically American: a gun demon, a prairie mog, one of those sirens who live in wells. Can coyotes drive cars? I know they can play poker, the Mage told me.

*"Know your enemy before he knows you"* was one of the Mage's favourite lessons. He drilled me on every potential threat, no matter how improbable. He told me to avoid America at all costs: *"Every kind of magician and magickal creature has made its way there. There's old magic and new. Hybrids and twists you can't anticipate. It's the most dangerous place in the world."* I was 13 and thought America mostly sounded really cool. Every kind of magic, every kind of spell, all in one place.

"Stop at the next town," Baz says. "We're safer with an audience."

But there is no next town.

I turn from one gravel road to another. The headlights follow.

Baz never sets down his wand. Penny watches the headlights for a while, then sinks down below the seat, so that whatever she's been watching can't watch her back. The gravel bangs against all the car's metal parts.

Thirty minutes pass like this.

I shout over my shoulder to Penny: "Do you still have to pee?"

"Yes!" she says.

"Should I stop?"

"No!"

There's no next town. There are no lights. I can only see the road a few feet ahead of us and a few feet behind us. Baz and Penny are shadows.

The truck tailing us slips in and out of view.

I tell Penny to find a town on her phone. But she doesn't have any bars.

The lights in the rearview mirror flash off, then on again.

"What's that supposed to mean?!" Penny shouts.

"Pull over," I say.

Baz turns to me. "Don't you dare!"

The lights flash on, then off. It's slow. Deliberate.

"Is it Morse code?" Penny asks, huddled between our seats.

"I think it's basic code for 'Pull over,' " I say.

"Don't!" Baz says again.

"I won't, all right?"

"We need a plan," Penny says.

"We have a plan!" Baz is firm. "We wait for a town."

"There *are* no towns!" I say.

Penny: "We need a battle plan!"

Me: "Agreed!"

"Listen to yourselves!" Baz shouts almost soundlessly. (We can hardly hear our own voices.) "We can't afford to fight!"

"There are three of us," Penny argues.

"There might be three of them!" he says. "And even if we've got more power, we can't afford another scene!"

"Look around—" She waves her arm at the dark nothingness around us. "There are no witnesses!"

"They could be recording us right now, Bunce!"

"Well, we can't just go on like this," I say. I'm going mad, waiting for something to happen. I've never waited this long for a fight.

"This is safe!" Baz says. "This is de-escalation. No one is being hurt."

The truck moves closer to us than it's come before, its headlamps whitening Baz's pale skin. He blocks his eyes with his hand. The lights blink off again, dark for a few beats, then on.

"Fuck this." I change gears and press the accelerator to the floor.

The noise is monstrous. Penny and Baz hold on with both hands.

# BAZ

I used to admire these two for getting out of so many tight spots.

Now I know firsthand that they make so many great escapes because they walk into so many traps! This is the behaviour that drove Wellbelove to California.

The Mustang sounds like a bat on its way out of hell. And Simon is its getaway driver. Fourth gear on a gravel road, his blue eyes narrowed to slits. My mother's scarf catches the wind and slips off my head. Snow whips out his hand to rescue it. He glances over at me, for just a second, holding it like a banner.

# SIMON

The silver truck falls back again, but it keeps up with us.

I take another ninety-degree turn. We're back on pavement

and picking up speed. Probably too much speed. I couldn't stop now if I had to—the road is coming at me before I'm ready for it.

Baz has his wand out, and Penny has her right hand raised.

"Slow down!" Baz screams.

But I don't. I don't want to. I'm tired of this standoff. I'm tired of being *chased*.

Suddenly my wings explode out of my back—I don't know why, a bell didn't ring. The force pushes me into the steering wheel, and the convertible careens back and forth.

Baz is casting a spell, but I can't hear it. Then he's shouting at Penny. She tries a spell, too.

"There's no magic!" Baz shouts.

"It's a dead spot!" Penny hits my shoulder. "We can't stop here!"

"I'm not stopping!" I say, but just then, the engine starts to sputter. "What did you do?" I yell at Baz.

"Nothing," he says. "Not this!"

The engine flags. I pump the accelerator. I try to change gears. The truck behind us is gaining too fast. A driveway comes up on my right. I yank the wheel at the last minute, and we spin into a gravel lot.

The Mustang rolls to a stop at the foot of Stonehenge.

# PENNY

When our car leaves the road, I close my eyes and cover my head. Every spell I've tried has failed. There's nothing left to do but think about all the modern automobiles with airbags I failed to hire—and brace for impact. . . .

But there is none.

When we eventually stop moving, I open my eyes, and I swear I see Stonehenge just a few feet away. And all I can think is, *We're home, somehow, Morgana be praised.*

But it isn't Stonehenge. It can't be. First of all, there's no magic here—it's a dead spot. *(Has the Humdrum been to western Nebraska? Is there an American Humdrum? Is this one Simon's fault, too?)*

Second of all, the standing stones aren't *stones*. They're . . . *cars*. Huge old cars, painted grey and arranged just like the stones in Wiltshire. Some of them are tipped on their ends and sunk into the ground, and some of them are stacked on top of the others. What *is* this place?

We don't have magic.

We don't have mobile service.

We need a *plan*.

Simon's leaning over the back of his seat, touching my arm. "Are you okay?"

"We still have Baz," I say. "We still have your wings. We fight like orcs if we have to."

Baz hops out of the car, taking point in the rear lights. I stand beside him with my shoulders square. I'm accustomed to fighting next to someone far more powerful than I am. "Take out their phones first," I say.

Simon stands at Baz's other side and spreads his wings.

The truck pulls into the parking lot, moving slowly now that it has us cornered. It stops in front of us. The engine and then the lights turn off.

One person gets out. A black guy, about our age. He's wearing a denim jacket and wire-rimmed glasses.

His hands are empty, and after a second, he waves. "Hi."

# 26

## SIMON

"Hi," I say back.

Penelope isn't having it. "What do you want?!"

The guy scratches his neck. He looks embarrassed. "Nothing. I saw your, uh, show, in Omaha—and I wanted to talk to you."

"So you chased us across Nebraska?"

He shakes his head. "It wasn't meant to be a chase."

"It felt a lot like a high-speed chase," I say.

"We obviously didn't want to talk," Penny says.

Baz is cold as ice. His wand is pointed at the guy. "What are you?"

"I'm nothing," the guy says. "I swear, I'm a Normal."

A chill crawls up my spine.

*Normals don't know that they're Normal.*

"What do you *want*," Baz says, stepping forward. It's a threat, not a question.

The guy is smiling. His hands are out where we can see them. "Look, I'm sorry, I really did just want to talk to you. And then I got caught up in the game of it."

Baz sneers. "This isn't a game."

"You're right, I'm sorry. I've just never seen—"

"You haven't seen anything."

"—a vampire-slaying vampire."

I feel linked through the heart to Baz and Penelope. I can feel all of us holding our breath.

"We don't know what you're talking about," Penny says, "and we don't want to talk to someone who's chased and intimidated us."

"Look"—he's still trying extra hard to seem friendly—"I get carried away sometimes. I just knew that if I lost you, I'd never see you again. This is a once-in-a-lifetime—"

"You *are* never going to see us again," Baz says. "Now get in your truck—wait." Baz stops. His wand hand dips. "I recognize you."

"I'm Shepard." The guy holds out his hand.

Baz doesn't take it. "You're the one who gave me the spell. At the Renaissance Faire."

"Buzz off," the guy says, smiling.

"If you really think we're vampires," I say, "why'd you follow us into the middle of nowhere? Aren't you afraid of us?"

"I'm Shepard," he tries again, holding his hand out to me.

I take it, and Penny groans.

"*You're* not a vampire. . . ." Shepard says. He's looking at me like I'm the Ark of the Covenant, and he's Harrison Ford. "You're something new. Or maybe something old. I'm hoping you'll tell me over a hot cup of coffee."

"A hot cup of bullshit," Penny says. "You need to leave now, Mr. Normal."

"Shepard," he says, reaching his hand out to her.

"No!" She points at the road. "Go! You're lucky we don't call the police!"

"All right." He puts his hands in his pockets. "I know I handled this all wrong. I'm sorry." He starts walking to his car. "I can call somebody, if you want, to bring you gas. You spelled the tank, right? And it died when your magic stopped?"

"Who says our magic stopped?" I flap my wings. Unintentionally.

"There's no magic out here," he says. "Not for Speakers."

"Why not?" Penny asks. She must want to know the answer more than she wants to keep our secrets. "Where did the magic go?"

"There aren't enough Normals here," he says. "There's no language to draw on. Nebraska's one of the least magickal places in the country for people like you—why'd you leave the interstate?"

Penny's furious. "To get away from you!"

I turn to Baz. "Is that even a thing?"

He raises his eyebrows like, *"Beats me."*

"So we're stuck here," Penny says.

"I could give you a ride," the Normal offers.

"Are you kidding me!" she snaps back.

"How do you know"—Baz is glaring at him—"what you think you know about us? About magic?"

Shepard smiles. (I wouldn't be smiling in this situation.) "People have told me. Other magic-Speakers."

"Pfft," Penny says. "Because you chased them into the wilderness and cornered them?"

"Because I asked," he says. "And because they knew I didn't mean any harm." He turns back to Baz. "I've never met a vampire."

"I hope your luck holds," Baz replies.

The Normal is standing near his truck, with the door open. He pushes up his glasses. "I could help you guys—"

"You're the reason we need help!" Penny shouts.

"How?" I ask. "How could you help us?"

He steps towards me. "You're lost. You clearly don't know anything about America—half your spells don't work, and you drove right into a Quiet Zone. I don't know where you're going, but I could be your guide, your Sacagawea."

Penny folds her arms. "So we can invade America and steal it from you?"

"Oh, shit, is that what you have planned?"

"Yeah," Baz scoffs, "we're off to a flying start."

The Normal isn't giving up. "Are you hunting vampires? Is that your mission?"

"No!" Penny says.

"We're on holiday," I say. "Vacation."

He pushes up his glasses again. "You came to *Nebraska*? On vacation?"

"We're just passing through," Baz says. "Listen, Shepard . . . could my magickal friends and I have a moment?"

While Shepard is saying, "Sure," Baz grabs my arm and Penny's, and pulls us back towards the ring of cars. (Someone has built *Stonehenge* out of *cars*. This is the best thing I've ever *seen*.)

"We should take his help," Baz says.

"Don't be mental, Baz."

"We're stuck here, Bunce."

"Yeah, because of *him*."

"So we take his help," Baz goes on, "then we hit him with a memory spell. He has everything to lose here: We outnumber him, and our magic will come back as soon as we get to a town."

"What if he has a gun?" I ask.

"I'll sit behind him and break his neck if I have to."

I frown at Baz—"Do you know how to break someone's neck? I should show you before we get in the car—"

We hear tyres on gravel, and for a second, I think Shepard has decided to leave without us. We all look back.

There's a new set of headlights turning off the road. Two sets. Now three.

"Who's that?" Penny asks.

Baz shakes his head. "No one good."

# 27

## BAZ

One, two, three trucks turn off the road and creep towards us, pinning us against Shepard's truck with their headlights.

We don't try to run. Simon could. He could have escaped already.

I elbow him. "Fly away, Snow. Now."

"No."

"You could get help."

"From who?"

Doors open and close. There's someone coming towards us, but with the headlights in my eyes, I can't see them.

It's something like a man . . . *Like*.

There's a clicking noise, and then a gunshot. And then whatever-it-is finally gets close enough for us to see—

It's a man-sized polecat holding a shotgun.

Black and white stripes. Beady eyes. Blue jeans. He opens the corner of his maw and shoots a stream of brown liquid at my feet. It smells like pipe tobacco.

"So the rumours are true," he says. "We got some trespassers."

Another something floats over the polecat's shoulder—a thick grey mist. With arms. It curls around Penny, hissing, "Speakers." Its hand brushes through my cheek, but I can't feel it. "And vampires."

"Are you all armed?" The polecat looks over his shoulder. "Search 'em."

A third thing steps out of the glare. Another manlike creature. This one's huge, wearing camouflage pants and a flannel shirt, and he's got a head like a goat's—not one of Ebb's goats, something fiercer, with horns that curve back over his ears then twist forward again. He reaches out to me with fleshy human fingers.

"Don't even think about it," I say.

The black-and-white polecat cocks his shotgun. "Look here, son. We don't want any of your trouble. They might put up with you deviants wherever you come from, but this is Nebraska." (He could mean literally anything by "deviants." Magicians, vampires, bird boys, queers . . . ) "You knew what you were getting yourself into when you entered the Quiet Zone."

The goat-man is patting Bunce down, looking for a wand, no doubt. She's lucky with that ring of hers; Normals and creatures don't even realize it's magic. My own wand is safe for the moment—coiled in Simon's tail and hidden behind his back.

Bunce is staring up at the goat's face, like she recognizes him from a film. "Are you one of the *Fomorians*?"

He sneers at her.

"You *are*, aren't you." She's so curious, she's forgotten to be scared. "Chaos demon," she says excitedly to Simon and me. "Droughts, blight, deaths at sea." She turns back to him. He's patting down her knee socks. In a non-pervy way, fortunately. "What are you doing out of Ireland?"

"I'm an *American*," the goat-man says. "Fourth generation. My family came here to get away from the likes of you."

"Magicians?" she asks.

"Indians?" Snow says.

"The fucking English," the goat replies.

I clear my throat. "Apologies," I say to the polecat. "We didn't realize we were entering any zone. We don't know the rules here."

The goat-man is patting me now, and being significantly more skeevy. I could probably snap his neck—I might even take the polecat down before he can shoot me, I *am* very fast—but there are other shadows lurking behind them. Who knows what sort of warped menagerie is out there? How many man-things with shotguns?

"So," I say, ignoring the goat breath, "we're terribly sorry. We'll move along now."

"Ignorance of the law is no excuse," the polecat says. "And the law is very clear on this matter: No Speakers in the Quiet Zone, not outside of the reservation or off the interstate. The Normals in these parts, few as they are, are ours."

"We don't want your Normals," Bunce says.

"Your kind never gets enough," the polecat says, spitting again. "If we let you go your merry way, that sends a message. That we're not holding up our end of the bargain." He aims his gun at Simon. "You look more like one of us than one of them. What are you? Red devil? Spite sprite? Were-adactyl?"

Simon's jaw is set. His cheeks are dark, even in the bright lights. He's watching the goat-man check my back pockets. Again.

The polecat looks over at the goat's hands. "For God's sake, Terry. Get your giggles on your own time."

And then Simon goes *off.*

He's less explosive than he used to be—but no less a spectacle.

He tosses my wand over his shoulder with his tail, catches it in his right hand, then slams it into the goat's neck. The goat falls into me like a stack of wet bricks, and I shove him off, thinking only of the gun.

Bunce had the same thought. She's lunged at the polecat. They're both on the ground, clinging to the barrel of the shotgun. I pull the polecat away from her, and his gun goes off—for the last time. I seize hold of it and break it over my knee. (It doesn't hurt.)

"Don't let him bite you!" someone shouts. "He's *were!*"

"As if I'd want the likes of you in my surfeit," the polecat snarls. He's a foot shorter than me, and he's pawing at my chest with long, sharp claws. I drop the gun and grab him by his furry wrists. I don't have a plan. I *think* I'm trying not to kill him.

I can see Simon in my peripheral vision, fighting someone/something that looks human, with hands that glow red. Simon is flapping above her, kicking her in the back, trying to avoid her red magic.

"Hey, vampire!" someone shouts. I ignore it.

Then I hear Penny yell, "Baz!"

I turn and see the Normal behind the wheel of his truck. Penny's in the passenger seat, leaning out the window. "Come on!"

When I look back down at the polecat, he's grinning. I catch a whiff of some hideous funk, and then I'm surrounded by it. I let go of his arms and shove him away from me.

"Baz!" Penny yells again. She's still got her window open. Something small and hairy is scrabbling at her door. The truck is driving away. I run after it, shouting Simon's name.

It's easy to catch up. It's easy to wrench the creature away from the cab. To leap into the truck bed. I'm standing in the back, screaming for Simon.

He's still fighting. Kicking. Flying.

There's a gunshot. Then three more. Then—

"*Simon!*"

# 28

## SIMON

I'll be damned and drawn and fucking quartered before I watch some devil-eyed goat feel up my boyfriend right in front of me.

Baz was trying to talk us out of this disaster, but it was never going to work—these creatures came for blood, they said so. Plus I recognized their vibe. They'll take anything we've got, shake us down for information, then put our heads on pikes.

I like their chances. All three of us are deeply off our game. Penny and Baz are hamstrung and blinkered without their magic. Baz is probably the most powerful being here. But he thinks like a magician, not a vampire. Without his wand, the fight's gone out of him—he wants to *talk*. Well, we'll never talk our way out of this.

We don't even know what we're dealing with; is this a posse or an army? None of us know the first thing about American magickal creatures. I'm not even sure what that animal with the rifle is—a badger?

The Mage always said America was a constant threat to

the World of Mages. America is decentralized, unorganized, magickally lawless. The magicians here don't even talk to each other if they're not related. It's every mage for himself.

"*Mavericks and terrorists,*" the Mage said. "*No sense of community, no common goals. Half of them using their magic to wash the dishes, half of them living like debauched sultans.*

"*I blame the vernacular. Wholly unstable! Too much in flux! Their dialect is like a river stripped of its natural bends and shallows—their spells expire before they ever master them.*

"*My heart is always with the rebels, Simon, in any struggle. But America is a failed experiment. A chaos country where mages have lost all sense of themselves. Where they live off the Normals like parasites—like dark creatures.*"

He'd flip if he knew I came here. If he were alive to know it.

That goat devil had his hands in Baz's back pockets. As soon as the badger took his eyes off me, I finished the goat with Baz's wand. (Maybe I'd have had more luck with my own wand if I'd wielded it this way.) Anyway, I *think* I finished him off. I don't know if goat devils have windpipes.

Baz went for the badger that was holding Penny. That should have been the end of the badger—Baz could have cracked it in half like a Kit Kat. But for some reason, he didn't.

I'm ready to do it for him when something else jumps on my back. A womanish monster with hot hands. We're properly brawling now, which was always the only way out of this. I'm flying above the red-handed thing, slapping her with my tail. Wishing I had something to swing at her.

I can't see Penny—where'd she go?

And why hasn't something shot us yet? Even toddlers in America have access to guns. Surely more of these dark creatures are armed.

I hear an engine start and spare a glance over my shoulder—it's the silver truck. The Normal must be making a run for it. Baz is chasing after him. *Let him go, Baz, we have bigger problems.*

I kick Hot Hands in the teeth. I wish I was wearing steel-toed boots. I look around for Penny—

Oh. There's the gunfire I was expecting.

# 29

## PENELOPE

*"Hey! Witch girl."*

Baz had just pulled that skunk off me, and I was still lying on the ground. I thought I might be bleeding—I'd hit the gravel hard.

*"You, in the plaid skirt!"*

I lifted my head and spotted the Normal, crouched behind a rock and hissing at me. *"Come on!"*

I looked back at Baz, still wrestling with the skunk, and Simon, fighting some sort of fire fiend, and crawled over to the Normal.

He put his hand on my shoulder and whispered, "We're going to my truck, all right?"

"I can't," I said. "My friends—"

"Are very tough customers. They'll catch up with us. Our only job here is not to get shot."

"How do I know this isn't all part of your trap?"

"Come with me or not. I'm getting out of here."

He ran towards his truck, staying low, and I followed him.

(Because he was the least of at least six evils.) Fortunately the creatures weren't paying attention to us; Baz and Simon are sufficiently distracting, in nearly every scenario.

The Normal started his truck, then we both yelled at Baz, who seemed to immediately get the drift. An animal of some sort was trying to open my door, but Baz tore it off—while running alongside the truck. Baz is *truly* frightening when he's not pretending he's not a vampire.

He's in the back of the truck now, calling for Simon—calling over the gunfire, when did that start? The Normal is hunching over the steering wheel, and I'm practically squatting on the floor. I crawl up to my window to look for Simon: He's back at the monument, still flying over the creatures. There are at least half a dozen waving guns at him.

I roll down the window and scream, "Simon!" as loud as I can, worried that he still won't hear me—but his head whips around, and then he's streaming our way, climbing higher and higher in the sky.

"Go, go, go!" I shout at the Normal, even though he's already going. The truck crunches back onto the gravel road and tears forward.

"They'll follow us," I say.

"They'll try." The Normal is grinning.

"What'd you do?"

"Slashed their tyres."

"You didn't!"

"I did. They were totally focused on you guys. I don't smell like anything interesting."

"That's . . . a bit good," I concede.

"I mean, they could catch up," he says. "They've still got magic. But the treaties work both ways. They can't touch you when you're back in Speaker territory. And most of the country belongs to the magicians, not the creatures."

"When will we get our magic back?"

"The far side of Nebraska. An hour or so."

Baz is tapping on the back window. I make eye contact with him. His eyebrow is raised. I nod to tell him I'm okay.

The Normal unlatches the window and slides it open.

I reach through. "Simon?"

Baz takes my hand. "Keeping up."

"Hang on back there," the Normal says.

Baz looks at the Normal. And then at me. And I think Baz is asking me if we can trust him. I don't have an answer. But we need the Normal now. He's getting us out of this mess— even if he's getting us into another one.

# BAZ

I lean back against the cab of the truck, looking up.

Simon is flying just above the clouds. I want him to land, I don't want to lose track of him.

I hope he isn't hurt.

I am, I think. . . . Hurt.

I don't want to look away from Simon, so I rub my fingers along the pockmarks in my chest. They sting, but they seem to have already stopped bleeding. I still don't know what kills vampires—but I suppose I can rule out a chestful of buckshot.

There are still no headlights behind us. Maybe the dark creatures don't need headlights. Maybe they don't need cars.

Bunce's face is in the window again. "We're trying to put some distance between us!" she shouts. "He slashed their tyres!"

Who did, the Normal? That was clever. Still doesn't mean we can trust him. Did he purposely herd us off the motorway? Right into their paws? What's his angle now?

There's a heavy thud.

Snow has landed in the truck bed, crouching, his fingertips down, his wings half folded behind his neck. He looks up at me. "*Baz.*"

Simon. I reach out and pull him up to me, next to me, onto me. I'm checking him for holes and wet spots. "Are you hurt?"

"I'm fine," he says. "Penny—"

"She's fine."

"And you—" His hands are on my shoulders. His mouth is over mine.

"I'm fine," I say, while he kisses me.

Crowley, if this is what it takes to keep Simon in my arms—gunshots and Quiet Zones and high-speed chases—I'm here for it. I'll swear to it. I've found my vocation.

He pulls away, petting my hair down. "Baz . . ."

"Simon?"

"You smell like a dead merwolf."

# SIMON

Worse than that.

"Like goblin intestines," I say.

"How do you even know what a goblin's—"

"*Lower* intestines." I cover my nose with my hand. "Eight snakes, Baz!"

"I know, all right?" Baz shoves at my shoulder. "I have enhanced senses."

"It's making me cry," I say. "I can taste it."

"You can get off me, Snow. Nothing's stopping you."

"No, I'm fine. I'm good."

Wild horses couldn't drag me.

# 30

## PENELOPE

My magic comes back in an hour. I've been murmuring spells to myself since we got back on the road—tapping my ring on my leg. Suddenly a *"Clean as a whistle!"* takes hold and scrapes along my skin and scalp, scrubbing me clean. I've got my hand at the Normal's throat before the spell's done.

He flinches, but that's it. I think he was expecting this. "I guess we're out of the Quiet Zone," he says.

I push my thumb into his throat. *"Is this a dagger which I see before me!"*

A pocketknife falls out of his jacket, but the Normal doesn't twitch or glow.

I try another spell to reveal his intentions—*"True colours!"*

The Normal glows a little purple, and I'm almost disappointed. Blue is safe, red is danger, but purple is the most common outcome—almost everyone wants *something* from you.

I hear Baz casting spells in the back of the truck. Making us hard to see, making us hard to follow. Deep magic. He's probably already exhausted.

"I don't want to hurt you," the Normal says. "Or expose you."

"You expose us by looking at us and knowing what we are!"

"I could *help* you." He's remarkably calm. "I could show you—"

"You pushed us away from our magic and straight into a trap!"

"That was an accident!"

"Was it?" My teeth are bared. "You knew we'd run out of magic."

The Normal looks guilty. I still have my hand at his throat. His skin is a few shades darker than mine, and he's wearing a thin gold chain around his neck. "I was just following you," he says, sounding a bit more urgent. (Good, he *should* feel urgent.) "I thought you were *leading* me off the interstate. How was I to know you didn't know what you were doing?"

"Why would you follow three monsters leading you away from civilization?"

He shrugs. "Curiosity?"

I blow air through my teeth. My grip tightens. "If it was all an accident, then how did the dark creatures know to find us there?"

"You weren't exactly lying low," the Normal says, glancing over at me. "You cast a dozen spells and killed seven vampires at a Ren Faire. Out in the open! Those places are crawling with magickal types."

"Why would anyone with magic want to go to that place?" I demand. "It's a complete farce—it was insulting!"

The Normal starts to laugh. I can feel it under my thumb.

I feel ridiculous. This whole situation is ridiculous. This whole country. I let go of him and sit back in my seat.

Simon's face is in the window behind me. He's clinging to Baz. "Where are we going?"

"There's a town ahead," the Normal says. "Scottsbluff."

"They'll expect us to stop there," Simon says.

The Normal's looking at Simon in the rearview mirror. He raises his voice to be heard: "Maybe. But we're safer in plain sight. On the road. In towns."

"All right," Simon says, "but we need to pull over for a second." He turns to me. "Baz . . ."

"Pull over," I order.

"There's a rest stop in five minutes," the Normal says. "Sanctuary."

# SIMON

It's too loud to talk in the back of the truck.

I huddle close to Baz, half in his lap, while the shock of still being alive passes. He holds me there, a little too tightly. Usually I forget Baz is so much stronger than me. He doesn't carry himself like he's that strong. He doesn't touch me that way. He never pulls or pushes me, not like that. Not any harder than I can push back.

I push in a little closer.

His voice is thick, strained. "You should be wearing your cross."

"We've been through this—I'd rather risk a bite."

His arms tighten. It's a bit hard for me to breathe.

"I would never," he says.

"I know."

After a few minutes, we pull over at some roadside services. Baz gets out to hunt, and I get out to piss. Penny charms a vending machine—it takes her a few tries—and I grab arm-fuls of crisps and cheese biscuits.

She leans, headfirst, against the glass. "I'm running on empty. I couldn't cast a truism right now."

I nod. "Baz's the same. He dumped all his magic on cloak-ing us. Can we trust Shepard?"

Penny pushes away from the vending machine, shaking her head. "My magic says yes, but my gut says no. Simon, he knows too much—how does he *know* so much? We should leave him here and steal his truck."

That feels harsh. "He did save us. And we don't even know where we're going."

"Fine," she says. "But we lose him at the next stop. Steal someone else's car, spell him stupid."

I lick my lips and nod.

Baz is steadier when he climbs back into the truck. But he still looks a shambles. His hair is as wild as I've seen it, and his fancy blouse is shredded and stained with blood. He looks like some sort of disgraced angel. (I suppose that'd be a demon.)

He drops down next to me, and I rap my knuckles on the back window. We roll out. The engine was already running.

I hand Baz some crisps. "All right?"

"I've had better holidays, Snow."

I sneak my arm around him—the mood has changed, and I'm not sure this is still okay. "*Have* you?" I say.

Baz casts his eyes down and smiles—girlishly, I would have said, but on him it's not girlish. It's, I don't know, *vulnerable.* He leans in, so I can hear him, his mouth at my ear. "Does Bunce have a plan?"

I nod. "Get to Colorado, lose the Normal, regroup."

"We need to rest," he says.

"We can rest first."

"Maybe we should go home."

I feel Baz's back under my arm. I feel his shoulder in my palm. "Yeah," I say. "Probably."

# PENELOPE

"How many hours to Denver?"

The Normal sneaks a look at me. He's been very eyes-on-the-road, lips-sealed since the rest stop. "Three."

"And we're clear of the . . . Quiet Zone?"

"Yeah. There's not that much of it. There aren't many places left without people, even around here."

"Who . . ." I think about what I want to ask him, and whether I want to encourage more conversation. "Who makes the rules?"

He looks over again and smiles. I wouldn't say it's a nice smile, but there's nothing *obviously* evil about it. I think of a few more defensive spells I could cast on him, but I don't have the magic in me. Simon used to ask me how that felt—to be empty. When Simon had magic, he never ran low.

It's like losing your voice, I'd tell him. Like knowing you only have a few words left until it gives out completely. The only way to get it back is to rest. And to wait.

Some mages never cast big spells unless they absolutely need them. That's what the Mage taught us: Save your magic for defence.

But my mother taught me to cast big spells every day. To be

bold with my magic. *"Build up your lungs,"* she'd say. *"Dig a deeper well for your reserves. Train your body to hold more magic and carry it."*

Today would have exhausted even a powerful mage. I threw everything I had at those vampires, then everything I didn't have on our Stonehenge getaway. (I did ask the Normal about the standing-stone cars. He said it was folk art. A roadside attraction.)

Anyway, the most I could do to him at the moment is irritate him.

"Tell you what," he says with his not-evil, but also not-working-on-me smile. "I'll trade you—question for a question."

"Tell you what," I say. "You answer my questions, and I won't turn you into a newt."

"That'll work, too." He shifts in his seat, making himself more comfortable. Now that we're not in immediate, apparent danger, I realize I haven't taken a good look at him. He's tall. At least as tall as Baz. And lanky. The black guys at Watford all shaved their hair close, but his is longer, taller, with tight, dense curls on top.

His clothes are a bit odd. I wonder if he was in costume for the Renaissance Festival. He's wearing green, wide-wale corduroy trousers, worn down to just stripes at the knees, and a denim jacket with a dozen different enamel pins and badges. He's got a long, lanky face, too—can a face be lanky?—and gold-rimmed John Lennon glasses. He's still covered in dust.

"I mean, I don't know everything," he says. "But, from what I can tell, the Quiet Zones happen naturally. No people? No spells. Some of these magickal creatures were the first immigrants. They had plenty to get away from back home, right? So they came to the Great Plains, and, yeah, there were native Speakers and creatures here already, but there was also a hell of a lot of *room*. It wasn't till the Irish and the German Speakers showed up that there was real trouble. At some point, everyone agreed to mostly stay out of each other's hair. The Quiet Zones were left to the creatures. The Speakers didn't want them anyway; they stayed close to the Talkers."

"What's a Talker?" I ask.

"What you'd call a Normal. Me."

"Right. So . . . we need to stay in well-populated areas?"

"As a rule, yeah. I mean there are magickal creatures everywhere these days; there are too few quiet places left to contain them. But that's good news for you. Western Nebraska is the only Quiet Zone east of the Rockies. There are a few more between here and California." He looks at me. "Is that where you're headed? West?"

I don't answer.

"I know you're not really on holiday. Is this a mission—is it a *quest*?"

"If it were a mission, we'd be better prepared."

"Are you on the run?"

"We are now," I snap.

He leans forward, hanging on to the steering wheel. "I could *help* you. It's not just the Quiet Zones you have to worry about. Like I said, there are only a few of those. But the magickal rules change every five miles around here. And the bosses. You could piss off somebody much worse than Jeff Arnold."

"Who's Jeff Arnold?"

"That were-skunk."

"His name is *Jeff*?"

"What'd you think his name was—Flower?"

"How do you know so much?" I hold my ring hand up again. "Are you really a Normal?"

He lifts up both hands, letting go of the steering wheel. "Completely. I'm the most basic bitch possible."

That makes me laugh. Just a little, I'm not sure why. I'm very tired.

He laughs, too. Probably relieved. *Don't get too relieved, Normal. I'd still stop your heart if I thought you were dangerous.*

"Then how do you *know* so much?" I repeat.

He looks at me again, like he's being serious—like he wants me to think he's serious. "By being the sort of guy who follows witches and vampires off the main road."

"That was incredibly stupid of you," I say.

"I know."

"We could have killed you."

"Right, I know."

"We could still kill you, at any moment."

"Trust me," he says. "I get it."

"Then, why? Do you work for someone?"

"Dick Blick."

"Who's that? Another skunk enforcer?"

"No. It's a shop. We sell expensive paints and pencils."

"This is so frustrating—you're not telling me *anything!*"

Baz hears me raise my voice and looks in from the back. I shake my head. Baz nudges Simon, and Simon looks in on me, too. I give him the thumbs-up, which is our personal code for *"Everything's fine."* (It's a very obvious code, but you only need a sneaky code for when you're *not* fine.)

"I'm telling you *everything*," the Normal says. "I've answered every single question."

"So—how do you know about witches and vampires?"

"Everyone knows about witches and vampires!"

"How do you know about *us?*"

"I don't know about you, Witch Girl. I want to. It is actually *killing* me not knowing. Three new Maybes show up, *practically in my backyard*, and go all Buffy the Vampire Slayer in front

of half of Sarpy County—oh my God, is that what you are—
*slayers?*"

"No, and what did you just call us—'babies'?"

"*Maybes.* Magickal beings. It's what people like me call
people like you."

I'm holding my forehead to keep it from exploding. "American Normals have a *name* for us?" For the Grace of Slick, this
is an actual catastrophe.

"Not all Normals. Normals like me."

"Like you. . . ." I purse my lips. "Do you mean irritating or
foolhardy?"

"Normals who know about *magic.* I'm part of an online community—"

"Fuuuck meee." I droop back against the seat.

"Hey." He looks over at me. "Are you all right? What's
wrong?"

"Everything, apparently. My mum was right about America.
Also the Internet."

"Did you think you could keep us in the dark forever?" The
Normal's getting passionate. Either this is coming from his
heart, or he's extremely cunning. "The world is full of magic!
Look around you, these fields are full of pixies! You expect us
to just ignore it?"

"Yes! Our safety basically depends on it!"

"Would you? If you were Normal?"

"I could never be Normal."

"You could—"

I sit up again. "No. I wouldn't be me."

"I'm saying, just *imagine*—"

"It's unimaginable! It's like asking me, '*How would you feel
if you were a frog?*' Well, I wouldn't be *me* then, would I? I'd
be a *frog.* Do frogs even *have* feelings?"

He shakes his head. Like I'm the one being ridiculous. "Normals have feelings, I can assure you. We may not be like you, but we have eyes and ears. We notice things."

"In my experience? Not usually."

"*I* notice things," he says, pointing at his chest and looking at me over the top of his glasses. He's apparently forgotten he needs to watch the road. "Look, I don't know anything about you, personally. Because you've answered exactly none of my questions. But if you didn't know about magic, if you were born Normal or just ignorant, and then you saw some magic—if you witnessed a miracle with your own eyes—would you just leave it be? If you got a glimpse into a secret world, would you pretend it hadn't happened? Or would you spend the rest of your life trying to find a doorway?"

I can't really process what he's saying. All I can think about is the danger we're in. "So that's what you do, you go looking for ways into our world?"

"Hell, yes, and I've found a few."

It's my turn to shake my head.

"Does that bother you?" he asks.

"Yes!"

"Why?"

"Because . . . it's *none of your business.* It's not your world— it's ours. You have no right to our secrets!"

"What makes it yours?"

"What do you mean? It's obvious."

"Not to me. What makes magic yours?"

I laugh. "We're magickal. And you're not."

He turns his head completely to look at me. "We are *made* of magic. Without our magic, you're worse than Normal. You're useless."

# 31

## SHEPARD

Welp. I screwed that up.

I was supposed to charm her. Some people do find me charming, believe it or not. When I was 18, I got a creek dryad to tell me her life story. She gave me mulberry cakes and dandelion wine. It's the first time I ever got drunk.

How did I learn so much about magic?

My strategy is simple: I tell the truth.

I always use my real name (even though fairy tales tell you not to). I always say exactly what I want from a situation and exactly what I mean.

These magical beings are always running a con. . . . They've been lying low for so long, they only know how to talk in tricks and riddles.

If you come in with your real face and your real name, and you tell them exactly what to make of you? It throws them off their game.

Yes, *occasionally*, they'll repay your honesty with a magical ass-kicking. (I'm probably never going to have kids, because I owe at least three imps my firstborn.) But often they find it refreshing! There's a hinkypunk in my mom's subdivision who just likes to complain to me about her migraines.

Who else will listen?

Who else wants to hear their stories?

There are trolls who've spent the last two hundred years sitting alone under a bridge. If you can get past the bluster and the wooden clubs, if you bring them a little bone broth, they're just grateful to have a sympathetic ear.

If you tell them that you *mean* no harm, and then you never *do* any harm . . .

They start to like you. They start to look forward to you coming around.

I'm not saying this approach would work for everyone. I'm not saying it isn't *dangerous*. . . .

It's not worth trying to charm something truly dark. And sometimes you can't tell if they're *truly dark*. Sometimes you give them your real name, and they never give it back.

And sometimes they just ignore you. . . .

Magicians are the worst.

They call them*selves* "magicians." Everybody else calls them "Speakers."

A jackalope broke it down for me once: *"It's like—we're all technically magicians, right? We've all got magic. But they took it for their* name. *Imagine acting like you're the only species who drinks water! Or breathes air! 'Look at us! We're the air-breathers!' "*

Magicians think they're the only ones with magic because they're the only ones who can control it. All the other spirits and creatures have rules they have to follow—true limitations. But the magicians can do anything they find words for.

Most of what I know about magicians I've heard from other

Maybes. Speakers are hard to track down. You can't just meet one by hanging out at the neighborhood watering hole. You can't plant some yarrow and valerian and wait for one to drop by.

Usually you don't even *know* when you've met one. They go out of their way to look Normal—which is such a mind-fuck because they think of *real* Normals as livestock. Beasts of jargon.

Even if you *do* find Speakers and identify them as such, they rarely feel like talking. They don't want any of their power to trickle down. They don't want anyone to learn their tricks.

I thought maybe these three were different. They *are* different. What's a vampire doing with a magic wand? What kind of devil is that Simon guy? (Is he a devil? Or just some kind of sphinx I've never seen before? There's so much I haven't seen. . . .)

But my no-scheme scheme isn't working on them.

They're going to lose me as soon as they don't need me anymore. And then I'll never know their story. . . .

We stop at a motel on the outskirts of Denver. I was worried about who we were going to send into the lobby—the black guy, the white devil, the Middle Eastern girl, or the pungent vampire. (Probably the white devil, right?)

But it's one of those dives where every room has its own external door. The witch girl picks a room, puts her hand on the doorknob, and says, ***"Open Sesame!"*** It's that easy.

Then she tries to magic the skunk funk off her friends. Both of them reeked of it when they got out of the truck.

I stand back and watch. "Do you have a tomato-soup spell? That's the only thing that works on skunk spray."

"*Skunk*..." the Simon one says. "That makes so much more sense than badger."

Once we get in the room, the girl and the vampire collapse onto one of the beds together. (Which I did not see coming, but all right.) And Winged Victory settles on the carpet, against the door. (Maybe his kind doesn't need sleep.) That's when I realize I'm their prisoner. Which ... fair enough. I've been in this situation before. I can still talk my way out of it.

Problem is, I still want to talk my way *into* it.

I sit down on a sunken brown couch. "I can take first watch," I say after a while, when I think the girl and the vampire are asleep. (I did *not* know vampires need sleep; I've never gotten this close before. Maybe this one is a hybrid. Can you be half vampire? Can you catch a mild case? Maybe he's one of the Next Blood. All the High Plains Maybes are worried about the Next Blood.)

Simon doesn't answer me.

"I may as well take first watch," I try again. "I'm still too wired to sleep."

He sighs. "How're you going to watch yourself?"

"I keep telling you guys—you can trust me."

"Why should we?"

"Because I'm a good guy. And I like to help."

"Because you're a good guy ..." he says. I can't see his eyes in the dark. "What if *we* aren't?"

That is an extremely solid question. I've guessed wrong before.

"Try again," he says. "Tell me what you want from us."

"I want to know about magic," I say.

"You already seem to know a lot."

"I want to know *everything*."

"*We* don't know everything. . . ."

I'm sitting up now. "I want to know whatever I can. Why are you here? Are you friends? Are you a team? A family? What are *you*? I've never seen something like you before."

Simon laughs, but there's no humor in it. "Like I'm gonna tell all my secrets to someone who calls me a *something*."

"Jesus," I say. "You're right. I'm sorry. I'm screwing this up. I really could help you guys. I have a vehicle, I know my way around—I know about *America*. I helped you out of that mess at Carhenge, but I could have helped you avoid it."

"You chased us into it!"

"That was an accident!"

"So we let you tag along on our holiday, and then you what, post a documentary about us on your YouTube channel?"

"I wouldn't."

He sighs again. "Go to sleep, Shepard. We're not going to hurt you."

I lie down again, trying to think of another tack. They're all going to be gone in the morning, and I'm going to have a headache.

"We're good guys," Simon says.

# 32

## BAZ

Bunce spelled that kid six ways to Sunday. (Which was a little excessive; "Six ways to Sunday" almost always is. I'd be surprised if he remembers his own name when he wakes up.) Then she cleared his mobile.

I couldn't help her with the spells. I'm still not . . . *right* from the gunshots. My skin has closed and mostly healed—I look like I was shot twenty years ago, not twenty hours—but my chest aches. And I feel listless. Like my undead body had to make some steep sacrifice to hold on to its "un."

We only slept for a few hours. Simon didn't sleep at all.

Bunce uses another spell to steal a car. Simon wants a convertible, but Penny insists on something low-profile this time—which, in America, means a giant white monstrosity called a Silverado. (*Silverado, Tahoe, Tundra.* Everyone gets it, America, you're very American.)

The Silverado makes the Normal's truck look like it hasn't hit puberty yet. This one's so high off the ground, it's got its own steps. There's a full-sized back seat and more places to set a drink down than in my sitting room back home.

(We literally have three "pickup trucks" in all of England, but here they're everywhere. What is it that Americans have to pick up that the rest of the world doesn't?)

I drive, just in case things get dicey, and Bunce tries to navigate using a map she's found in the glove compartment. Her mobile's still in the Mustang. Mine is still offline.

Our main goal is to get away. That Normal was too clever. He might be tracking us. He might even have a magickal way of tracking us. Snow has switched into full-on battle mode; I haven't seen him like this since the Mage died.

I envy what he has with Bunce. They act like this is their tenth tour of duty together. It makes me realize that Simon had a whole life I didn't know about back in school. The Mage used him to fight whatever needed fighting—even when Simon was just a kid. (Simon was always just a kid.) And even though his power's gone, Simon is still perfectly comfortable playing the boy soldier.

I suppose he isn't a boy anymore. . . .

I suppose neither of us are.

We intentionally lose ourselves in the mountains. Bunce says there are towns everywhere, so we won't have to worry about our magic dropping out—what we have left of it. We've both been casting ourselves dry. You might wonder how magicians could ever lose a battle against other magickal creatures; our advantage seems so steep. *This* is how. Exhaustion.

The sun is bright in the Rockies. I'm happy to have a roof over my head, after escaping Nebraska as cargo. But I'm tired, and I swear I can feel that we're climbing closer to the sun.

# SIMON

I don't think I've ever been anywhere prettier than this.

The mountains are every colour—grey and blue and almost purple, with slashes of dark green trees, and orange and red rocks.

We pull off the road near a stream, and Baz goes to rinse some blood out of his shirt and hair. (He must have torn the heart out of that skunk.) We left the motel before any of us could shower.

"We should summon our luggage," Baz says. He's facing away from us. His shirt is off, and his back is pale and bright, his hair wet and black, dripping down his neck.

"What if that leads them right to us?" Penny wants to know.

"I don't much care," he says. "I want my clothes. And my sunglasses. And my mother's scarf."

"I suppose I'd like my phone back," she says.

I'd like them to summon the entire classic convertible, but I don't think they'd be into the idea.

Penelope and I are sitting on the ground, eating some turkey jerky we found in the Silverado. (I quite like jerky.) Baz walks over to us, buttoning his wet and mangled shirt.

"What are you thinking?" Penny asks, holding out some jerky for him. " 'Lost and found'?"

"How would that even work?" I ask. "Is your stuff going to fly from Nebraska?"

"Maybe," she says. "I've only used 'Lost and found' for things that were close at hand, like when I've set my keys in the wrong place."

"Baz," I say, "what if your flying suitcase kills someone?"

"I don't think we could summon something that far anyway," Penny sighs. "Especially not right now. I'm clapped out."

Baz settles between us on the ground. "I've got a better idea." He holds his wand out to Penny. (He must have rinsed that off, too. Last time I saw it, it was covered in goat blood.) "Give me a hand."

Penny raises an eyebrow, but she wraps her ring hand around his wrist.

"Follow my lead, Bunce." Baz closes his eyes. His eyelids are dark grey. He takes a deep breath and then he . . . starts to sing? *"A-ma-zing grace—"*

Penny yanks her hand away. "A *hymn*, Basil?"

Baz sighs.

"We can't cast a hymn!" she says.

"Not with that attitude . . ."

"It's sacrilege!"

"Superstition, Penelope."

She shakes her head. "And it's too general. That song's more of a vibe than a spell."

"It's *old*," he says. "It's powerful. The Americans know it."

I bang my shoulder against his. "Are you guys trying to summon Jesus?"

Penny points at him. "You know I'm tone-deaf."

"Fortunately," Baz says, catching her forearm, "the goal isn't to sing well, just to sing together. Our ancestors cast in *choirs*."

He's got her attention now; Penny's a fiend for magickal history. "But we're both spent, Baz. . . ."

"Harmony is power," he says.

Penny sighs and wraps her hand back around his wrist. "If this works, my mother will be so impressed, she might grant me a last meal."

"Lean into it," he says. "And hit 'found' hard. You know intention counts."

Baz closes his eyes again. ***"Amazing grace, how sweet the*** *sound!"* His voice sounds lush when he sings. Deeper and heavier than when he talks. The last time I saw someone cast a song—the *only* time I've seen someone cast a song—it was the Mage. That day. Over Ebb.

Ebb . . .

The Mage, he—

Well, he never taught us music. How much did he leave behind when he took over Watford? There used to be a drama society, I know, and more of an emphasis on history. Was there a choir, too? It's like I never got to know the World of Mages, because my mentor turned it upside down before I got there.

I suppose it doesn't matter. I'm not a part of that world anymore.

Penny is singing now. Sort of. Her voice is flat and talky: **"I once was lost, but now am found."**

Baz sings louder, like he's trying to fill in her gaps. **"Was blind, but now I see.** Again, Bunce. **Amazing grace . . ."**

Baz hunted just outside of Denver, but he's as grey as I've ever seen him, and his nose is still sooty from those days in the sun. (He went black instead of red.) Penny tried to spell away the skunk spray, but he still smells of brimstone. All his clothes are lost or ruined. . . . It's like America is taking bites out of Baz. Taking a swing at him every time it gets a chance.

He makes Penny sing the verse three times. (Her voice gets looser every time.) Then they open their eyes and look at each other. She smiles. "All right, you win. That was cool, even if it doesn't work. . . ." She looks around. "Are we supposed to wait?"

"I don't know, maybe for a minute." He looks around. "Come on, stuff, *find* us."

The forest is quiet. Or, I suppose, it's noisy like a forest—wind and branches and moving water. This place is probably crawling with dryads.

Then we hear it—something whizzing closer.

Penelope's mobile drops between us. She laughs. "It worked!"

Her hand darts over the phone, and she casts, **"Without a trace!"** before picking it up. "Hopefully that'll keep anything from tracking us."

Baz stands and looks out in the direction that Penny's mobile came from.

Penny is checking her texts and missed calls. "No one seems to have tampered with it. I mean, who knows, maybe it's been sitting in the Mustang this whole time. Or they could have magickally hacked it. Oh—*finally*, Agatha." Penny puts the phone to her ear.

Baz is frustrated. "Be fair," he says to the forest, hands on his hips. "The hymn was *my* idea."

"Oh, no. Oh, Simon—"

Baz and I both turn to Penny, who's let her hand drop to the ground. She looks as pale as Baz.

"What's wrong?" Baz asks, as his suitcase hits him squarely on the back.


Penny puts her mobile on speaker, and plays the voicemail so we can all hear it:

*"Penelope? It's me. Agatha."*

She's whispering.

*"Sorry I haven't got back to you. I know you've called . . . a lot. I mean, I'm not that sorry because I did tell you not to call so much. I don't even like to talk on the phone. But . . ."*

Agatha's whispering, and her voice feels cornered. Like she's calling from inside a wardrobe. Or a bathroom. Maybe a car.

*"I just thought that I'd check in. I'm at a fancy retreat. I think I told you about my friend? Ginger? It was her idea. It's*

*this group—I don't know if it's a group or a programme—*
*they call themselves NowNext.*

"*I thought it was all self-help bollocks. . . . Maybe it is. . . .*

"*But maybe it isn't.*"

The way she's whispering, so close to the phone, it's like she's
right there with us.

"*There's this guy . . .*

"*Crowley. Did I really call you to talk about a boy? Never*
*mind, Penny. I'm fine.*

"*It's just . . . There are just days when I wish I had my wand*
*with me. In that security blanket way. I guess today is one of*
*them.*

"*I hope you're not on your way to San Diego. I did tell you*
*I'd be gone.*

"*Anyway—*"

A man's voice cuts her off. He's not whispering: "*Agatha?*
*Are you ready?*"

"*Braden.*" Agatha isn't whispering anymore. "*Just a second. . . .*"

There's a noise like rubbing fabric. And then the man sounds
muffled. "*Were you on your phone?*"

"*No. Of course not.*"

"*You know the rules.*" His voice is moving farther away. "*No*
*distractions.*"

Agatha is farther away, too: "*I just needed a moment to myself.*"

"*I thought I heard you talking—*"

"*I was practicing my mantras.*"

A door opens and closes, and then there's silence.

"That's it," Penny says. "The message goes on like that for
five minutes—I think Agatha's in trouble. Really!"

"It sounds like she's at some expensive yoga retreat," Baz
says. He's gone back to looking at his suitcase. His apparently
empty suitcase.

Penelope frowns. "Where she can't have her phone?"

"It's called a social-media cleanse."

"No." Penny's firm. "I know Agatha. She'd rather kiss a troll than call and talk to me on the phone."

"Then why do you ever call her, Bunce?" Baz is shaking out his suitcase.

"Because I worry! Because she's like a lamb who's wandered away from the flock."

"Is the flock England?" I ask.

"The flock is *magic*!" she says. "If one of you wandered away from magic, I wouldn't just let you go."

"I'm not a magician anymore, Penelope."

"You're still a magician, Simon. Aeroplanes don't stop being aeroplanes when they're on the ground."

Baz throws his suitcase down, in disgust.

"Agatha wouldn't call me just to talk," Penny says. "She wouldn't call me unless she was *scared*."

There's a noise from Penny's phone. The voicemail must still be playing. It sounds like there's a door opening.

*"She was talking on the phone."* It's the man's voice again. He still sounds faraway, but his voice has a harder edge. *"Find it."*

There are more noises. *"Do we have her phone number?"* a different man asks. *"We could call it."*

*"Find it and bring it to me. We'll have to move up the extraction."*

There's a rustling sound. A hand on the phone. A third man, unmuffled: *"Found it—fuck, she's still on a call."* A scuffle. The voicemail ends.

None of us move. We're all staring at Penelope's mobile.

Then Penelope jabs her hand out and powers the phone down. She looks up at me. "Agatha is in trouble."

# 33

## AGATHA

It's all perfectly fine.

I mean, I'm probably being recruited into a cult.

And seduced by its charismatic leader.

And I am stranded at their compound. . . .

But everything seems mostly *fine*?

Yes, I would rather go home than spend another minute in this place. But I can't leave Ginger (whom I haven't seen since yesterday). And I can't imagine just *leaving*.

Partly I can't imagine it because I have no idea where the door is.

I've been upgraded to the members-only wing. Which feels much more like a hospital than a nouveau riche mansion.

Like a nouveau riche mansion/hospital.

All the hallways are stainless steel, and the floors are polished concrete. And there are far fewer windows than you'd expect.

"There's a lot of innovation happening in this part of the house," Braden said when he was giving me the tour. "Security is paramount."

He showed me his perfectly ordered labs. And then a room full of computers that felt like a lab. And then a spa that looked like a lab—with white leather recliners and a whirlpool. "Do you have scientists who give pedicures?" I asked.

Braden laughed. "I spend most of my time on health science. Deep cleanses, detoxification, rejuvenation."

"My mum would love it here."

"Come on in," he said, taking my arm. I let him. I was feeling charmed by him at that moment. Maybe it *would* be okay to date a thirty-under-thirty type. I'd get lots of excuses to dress up. And he seemed to like it when I took the air out of him.

I'd never been able to tease Simon that way when we were dating. He was too fragile. Simon was like a nuclear missile with self-esteem issues; it was exhausting.

I followed Braden into his stainless-steel spa, and he sat me in one of the leather chairs.

"Grip here," he said, directing me to a handle.

I did.

"Do you know your blood type?" he asked.

"I can't remember. . . ."

He pressed a button on the chair. I expected it to start massaging my back. Instead, a touchscreen panel swung out of the side. "A-positive," he said. "Look here, that's your red blood cell count. Perfectly normal. Here's your leukocytes."

"What— How does it know all that?"

"It just took a blood sample," Braden said. "You didn't even feel it."

"No. I didn't."

"Your glucose is higher than I'd expect. I wonder what that means."

"Is this your way of making sure I don't have STDs?"

"Ha, no, of course not. You don't, though. Nothing out of the ordinary. I have a vaccine—"

"Braden, what are you doing?"

He grinned at me. "Showing you what I do." He waved his arm around the room. "This is the most advanced medical equipment in the country. I can cure almost anything here."

"Shouldn't you . . . *tell* someone?"

He laughed again, like I was being clever. I'm never being clever.

"I can't wait to get some electrodes on you," he said. "And we'll need a fasting sample, too. Maybe tomorrow morning."

"Why? Am I sick?"

"No, you're perfect. You're exquisite."

"Do you have some weird medical kink?"

He shrugged. "Maybe. A little. I just geek out over stuff like this. I like to see what makes people tick. I like to decode them."

I pictured Braden unravelling my DNA and selling it off for parts.

"This is a sales pitch, isn't it? Where you sell me juices based on my blood type? Because Ginger and I tried those. It's a pyramid scheme."

Braden picked up my hand. The one that was clenched around the chair.

"Agatha, why can't you accept that I'm exactly what I look like? A billionaire genius who can't take his eyes off you."

That was yesterday.

I spent most of the day with him and didn't see Ginger till late in the afternoon. "Where have you been?" she asked. Her whole face was shining. "Don't tell me, I already know—you *like* him, don't you?"

"Who?"

"Don't give me that. Josh saw the two of you in the members' wing. You like him!"

"I don't know," I said. "I suppose he's interesting."

"*Interesting*? He's handsome and powerful, and he eats cleaner than anyone I've ever met. No grain, no meat, no nightshades, no dairy."

"What does that leave, Ginger?"

"So much! Nut meats, plant proteins, green vegetables, algae—"

"Right," I cut her off. I gave up meat when I left England, as well as any animal by-product that isn't freely given—but these people will scrape your whole plate into the trash if you let them.

"I can't believe Braden allowed you into the members' wing," Ginger said. "I've been cleansing for weeks to prepare. I think he's going to let you skip some steps in the programme. He likes you *so* much."

"I'm not in any programme."

She grabbed my hands excitedly. "Agatha! What if we get to level up *together*?"

"I'm not levelling up," I insisted. "I'm just . . . talking to a boy."

"You're evolving before my very eyes. You're at least forty per cent activated."

I rolled my eyes.

But I still let Braden give me another VIP tour before dinner. He showed me the grounds. Gardens, golf course, greenhouse. "You're missing your retreat," I said.

"The goal of the retreat is to focus," he replied. "I feel very focused."

Normally I try not to talk about myself on dates. Most guys make that easy—they're happy to do all the talking. But Braden wanted to know everything about me. What my parents are like, where I grew up, whether I still have my tonsils and appendix.

My answers were vague. There's little of my life before now that isn't magic.

I told him my father is a doctor, and my mother attends parties. I told him that I didn't like school, that I don't miss England.

"Don't you miss your friends?" he asked.

*I don't miss being chased by monsters,* I thought, *and helping my boyfriend feel straight.*

"We were thrown together at school," I said, "and now we're not."

After the tour, Braden walked me to my room to change for dinner. But it wasn't the room I shared with Ginger; it was this suite in the members' wing. He'd had all my things moved here.

We aren't supposed to use our phones during the retreat; they asked us to check them in when we arrived. "It's a retreat from the outside world," Ginger had explained.

But I'd held on to mine. It was still in my bag. While Braden waited for me to change, I ducked into the bathroom and tried to call Penny. She didn't pick up.

When I came back after dinner, my phone was gone.

I turned off the lights then, I'm not sure why. No, I know why—in case someone was watching me.

I turned off the lights, and I slept in my clothes. There's a lock on the door to this room. But I'm sure Braden has a key.

Which is probably fine. He hasn't tried to hurt me. He hasn't even stood too much in my space. Or touched me with any disrespect.

Maybe this is how dating works when you're a pharmaceutical kingpin. You set a girl up in a stainless-steel suite and ask her how she feels about MRIs.

A woman brought me breakfast this morning. She brought me teff porridge with sultanas and a small dish of vitamins.

# 34

## PENELOPE

I used to be very good at *what's next*.

Something terrible would happen—or maybe just something strange and mysterious—and Simon would turn to me, and I'd tell him our plan. I always knew our next move, even if it wasn't necessarily the *right* move. I never got hung up on right or wrong. I trusted myself to digest the current scenario and plot the best path forward.

Sometimes we'd get into a situation where the only thing left to do was fight. And sometimes we'd get to the point where the only thing left was for Simon to blow everything up.

And then, when the dust settled, Simon would turn to me, and I'd tell him the new plan.

I haven't had a plan since we got off the plane.

Agatha's in trouble, I know she is. But we don't know where. And we keep blowing all our magic in one place. And we're leaving a *trail* of mistakes.

I can't remember the last time I made a good decision. Maybe on the flight, when I chose cheesecake over strudel.

Simon has grabbed my mobile. "Where is she?"

"We'll cast a finding spell," Baz says.

"It won't have any reach," I say. "I poured everything I had left into 'Amazing Grace.' "

Baz did, too. He kicks his empty suitcase into the creek.

"We can look it up online," Simon says. " 'NowNext.' "

"What if the people who took her phone try to call us?" Baz looks afraid. "They have our number."

"Should I throw away *my* phone?" I ask. "They could track it."

"No," Simon says. "Agatha might call."

"Right . . ." I say. "Right."

Baz is standing at the edge of the creek. His hair is lank. His skin is grey.

Simon is chewing his lip. I haven't had enough magic to hide his wings today. I tried, but they just blinked off and back on. I'm not sure I've ever been this drained. It takes so much magic to stay alive in America.

"All right," Simon says. "We have to keep moving. Shepard is probably looking for us—and the magickal creatures might be looking for us. The last we knew, Agatha was in San Diego. So we keep heading west. We keep Baz out of the sun. We keep my wings under wraps. We steal food and clothes when we can—or we magick them. And we have the Internet now. We can find these NowNext people down some rabbit hole." He glances over at me. "I mean, you think?"

I nod. "Yeah. It's a good plan."

Baz nods, too. "Good plan, Snow." He looks into the trees. "I should hunt. So we don't have to stop again."

"Not by yourself," Simon says.

"I'm not letting you watch—"

Simon spreads his wings. "Not by yourself."

I can't be alone right now. I follow along after them, from a respectful distance.

I've known about Baz's vampirism for at least a year—and Simon suspected for years before that—but Baz is still self-conscious about it. He won't ever feed in front of us. He won't even eat a sandwich if he thinks you're watching. Simon says it's because Baz's fangs pop, and he's embarrassed, so I always look away. (Though I would love to get a better look at them, for scientific purposes.)

I know Baz casts spells sometimes, to lure in his prey. But today he doesn't have to. There's a large wild cat, crouched on the ground ahead of us. I wait for Baz to strike.

Instead he stamps his feet, shouting at it. "Go! Away!"

The cat startles and runs away from us.

"What on earth?" I say. "Do you prefer it when they play hard to get?"

"I don't kill predators," he says.

"Why not? Fellow feeling?"

"They're too important to the ecosystem. Besides, there are sheep around here, of some sort. I saw tracks."

He leads us deeper into the trees. "I could manage this perfectly well on my own, you know," he mutters.

"Yeah, yeah," Simon whispers. "You're well fierce."

Baz glances back, frowning. "I *am*."

It's darker here. We're pushing through evergreen branches—and there's a fog hanging at our knees. I don't know why it didn't occur to me that even *trees* would be different in America. Simon and I have spent plenty of time wandering around in woods back home. But never woods like these.

Baz stops. He's caught a scent.

He runs forward, faster than Simon and I can keep up, and more graceful than we could dream. When we do catch up, Baz is kneeling at the edge of the stream, a horned sheep dead in his lap, both of them blanketed in mist. I think he's broken its neck.

"All right," he says. "Give me a minute."

I look down. The fog is up to my chest, and it's *so* dark. I hold up my ring.

"*Poaching . . .*" someone says. It sounds like a woman. And it feels like she's saying it inside of me. The darkness has risen up over my chin. "*Bloodeater poaching on my very back.*" The voice—I swear it's in my head—sounds English. Northern.

"We can explain!" Baz calls out. He must hear it, too.

"We didn't know!" I shout.

Simon takes my hand. "We're not from around here!"

"*No,*" the voice says. "*Can see that. Can smell that. . . . You are something different. Not just bloodeaters. Something much more foul . . .*"

I close my eyes and cast into the murk—**"Come out, come out, wherever you are!"**

"*Mages,*" the voice says, scornfully.

And then the darkness swallows me.

# 35

## BAZ

I can't move.

I try again—I can't move. My arms are tied.

I can't sit up. My legs are tied.

My face hurts. I'm lying on a rock.

I can't move.

*I can't breathe!*

No—I can. I can. My mouth is gagged, but I can still breathe.

I can't move. I can't see—

I open my eyes. . . .

I'm lying on my shoulder near a campfire. There's a woman sitting on the other side. An older woman—or perhaps a younger woman with long white hair. She's holding her hands out over the fire. There are gold rings on every finger and gold bands around her wrists. She's watching me.

"Urrrghhff." Simon is struggling, somewhere close to me— thrashing around by the sound of it. I wish I could tell him to calm down. I grunt, so that he knows I'm here.

He thrashes harder.

"*Should send you back to sleep,*" the woman says. Her mouth doesn't move. Her voice is inside my head. "*All of you. Don't need you awake to sort you out.*"

She stands and walks over to me. She *is* old, I think, though she moves like a young person. She's wearing worn jeans and a beaded red shawl that glints in the firelight. Her eyes are pale, that shade of green you only see on cats. She lifts my chin with the tip of her grey cowboy boot. "*Heard about you,*" she says. "*Didn't think they'd manage it, but here you are. You smell like blood and magic, boy. Both gone rancid.*" Her lip curls. "*Not. On. My. Mountain.*" She kicks me in the stomach.

*Fuck.*

I try to shout, but choke instead. My chest still burns from the gunshots. I need to eat. I need to drink. I am under every sort of weather.

Simon is tossing around again. The woman turns to look at him. "*Fool kitten. Gone and made a dangerous friend. You'll suffer for it.*"

What *is* she? A fairy? An elf? Does America still have those? Are these the Undying Lands? My mother would know. She could name every sort of magickal being and creature, even the lost and the dead.

The woman lifts her head. She smells something.

I smell it, too—something human. A Normal.

"Shepard!" the woman says out loud. She's smiling.

"Margaret!" It's the Normal we left in Denver. I can't yet see him, but I recognize his voice and his scent. He must have been working with this woman all along.

The Normal steps over me, and the old woman holds out her arms, ready to embrace him.

"I wasn't sure you'd be awake," he says, hugging her.

"Too warm." She's petulant. "Can't sleep. Too warm all the

time now." She's butting her head against his shoulder. Down his arm. "You've brought me something. Can smell it."

He laughs and holds out his palm.

She grabs whatever he has in it—rings—and slides them on her already crowded fingers. "Too good to me, Shepard. Good boy. Good man."

"I see you've met my friends," he says.

The woman frowns and steps away from him. "Not your friends. Now and Next."

"I thought so, too," Shepard says. "First spotted them back in Omaha. But they can't be part of the Next, Margaret. I watched these three slay half a dozen vampires in cold blood."

"No! How cold?"

"Frigid."

I can't believe the Normal's defending us. I can't even believe he recognizes us—Bunce spelled him so hard, he shouldn't recognize his own reflection.

"Have turned against their own kind, maybe." The woman looks down at me, nudging my hip with her boot. "This one is their work. Finally come. The hybrid."

"*Is* he?" Shepard goggles at me for a second. "I wondered if—" He shakes his head. "I don't know . . . I really think it's a coincidence, Maggie. I think they're just tourists."

She spits. It lands, hot, on my cheek. "Tourists?!"

"They don't know any of the rules," he says. "They drove right into the Quiet Zone just to see Carhenge."

"Supposed to be spectacular," she says. Begrudgingly. "Seen photos."

"I agreed to be their guide. We were just getting to know each other when a posse tried to round us up."

The woman crouches to look at me, stroking her chin. She has six rings on her pinkie finger. One of them is Penelope's.

"*Mages*," she sneers. "Reckless kittens, hybrids. Next Blood trouble and trash . . . *Poachers*, Shepard. This one killed my ram."

"He was probably thirsty," Shepard says. "I drank from your stream once, remember? Before we met?"

She stands up and frowns at him some more. "But you are a good boy—an innocent. Not a knight. Not a mage. Not a *blood-eater*."

"Let's hear what they have to say," Shepard says. "If you don't like it, you can still eat them."

"Wouldn't eat him," she says, glaring at me. "Rancid."


Shepard ungags Simon first. "Thank you," I hear Simon say. "I owe you one."

"Friend," Shepard says, "you owe me so many, we need to draw up a contract."

He unties my gag next and helps me sit. "No spells," he says softly. "She can shut you down from a distance."

I nod.

"Found this on him," the woman says, holding up my wand. "Probably stolen. Heffalump tusk. Extinct." She tosses it over her shoulder.

Bunce starts making demands before her gag is even off: "Who are these NowNext people? What are they up to? They have our friend!"

"Now we're talking," Shepard says, helping her sit up.

"Unhand me!" Bunce shouts. He does. She falls over. "You have to tell us—our friend is in danger!"

The white-haired woman (*is* she a woman?) sits down again on the other side of the fire. "Needn't must. You will do the telling."

"Anything," I say. "Anything you want to know." I look over at Simon. He nods at me, like he's all right. His hands are still tied. And his ankles. And his wings. But he's fine.

"Tell Maggie why you're here," Shepard says, sitting down next to the woman by the fire.

I try to take charge; I'm the only one of the three of us with any tact. "We're on holiday," I say. "We *are* tourists."

"What about this friend?" Margaret demands.

"We were coming to see her—"

Bunce interrupts me: "We wanted to check on her, we were worried about her—and then she left a message for us yesterday saying she was with the NowNext. They're going to *extract* her. You have to tell us—"

Snow has his chin thrust out. "Who are *you*?"

"It doesn't matter," I say, willing them both to shut up. "You don't have to tell us anything. We'll go. We won't come back."

"You are the Next Blood," she says to me, matter-of-factly.

"No. My blood is ancient. I'm from a very old family."

She isn't listening. "*You*. Are the hybrid."

The Normal leans forward. I hate the way he looks at me, like I'm a safe he's going to crack. "The NowNext," he says, "some people call them the Next Blood—they're trying to teach vampires to Speak. . . ."

"They're doing what?" I'm flabbergasted.

"That's an abomination!" Bunce says.

"Yes," Margaret says, pointing at me. "*You* are an abomination!"

"I'm not—*that*," I say. "I'm a mage! I was bitten by a vampire as a baby!"

"Aha!" Shepard says, snapping his fingers like he's just solved a riddle.

"No." The woman looks repulsed by the idea. "Would have cast you out, would have fed you to dragons. This is mage law."

"Yes, well, my mother was killed. The vampires killed her. There was no one strong enough to cast me out."

"Not too late," the woman says. "Dragons are still hungry."

"He's not a bad vampire," Simon cuts in. "He doesn't bite people. Just rats and deer and sheep—"

"Poacher!" she says.

"I'm sorry!" I plead. "I didn't know the sheep belonged to anyone!"

"He's sorry," Shepard says. "I believe him."

"Expects us to believe he is not the hybrid? When the whole world knows bloodeaters are mixing blood and magic?"

"*How?*" Penny asks.

The woman glares at us over the fire. "Don't know. Nothing good. Darkness."

"If the vampires can get magic," Shepard says, "nothing will stop them. They'll be the top of the food chain."

The woman hisses.

"Look"—Bunce is uncowed, even trussed up like a hog on Solstice—"I know this looks bad. But we're not part of that vampire business. And if our friend is caught up in it, she's in trouble and needs our help. You have to let us go."

The woman rolls her fingers, clacking her rings together. "What is your judgment, Shepard?"

"I believe them," he says.

"Soft," she says. "Believe everyone."

"I spent two days with them, and the only things they harmed were those vampires."

"And my ram."

"I'm sorry about that," I say again.

She waves one hand. "Let them go, bloodeater and mage. The kitten stays with me."

"What?" everyone but her says.

"Does she mean me?" Simon asks. "I'm not a kitten!"

She sighs. "Fool kitten. Lost hatchling."

The Normal is looking at Simon, as if Simon has replaced me as the best riddle. "No. . . ."

The woman walks over to Simon, to get a closer look at him. "Orphan. Must be. Flying with mages and bloodeaters—the shame of it."

"I'm not an orphan!" Simon objects. "I mean, I am. But I didn't hatch from anything."

"I thought he was a demon," Shepard marvels.

"Pfffff." The woman is circling Simon. "Red wings. Sharp tail. From the north like me. Precious hatchling. Lost."

"No, no, NOOO," Simon says, realizing what she means.

"Croowww-ley," I swear.

Penny goes for: "Fuck. Me."

"I'm not a DRAGON!" Simon shouts.

"Not yet." She pets his wing. "Are kitten. Someday dragon. Someday ferocious."

"He's not a dragon!" I say. "Those wings were spelled on."

"This one is not a dragon, and that one is not a vampire. Am blind, am I? Am foolish?" She's snarling at me again.

"No," I say. "It's not you. It's us. We're very confusing."

"I'm just a Normal with wings!" Simon insists.

"Dragon wings." She nods. "Great Red."

"Look closer," he begs.

"Smell him!" Bunce says. "Does he smell like a dragon?"

The woman frowns at Bunce. Then she reaches for the ropes around Simon's chest and pulls him to his feet. She leans in to his neck to smell him. He raises his chin. She walks behind him and presses her face into his tied-up wings.

"Smells like dragon . . . but also smells like iron. Another abomination!"

"It was just a spell," Penny says.

"Whose magic?" Margaret yanks at the ropes, heaving Simon back.

"M-mine," he stammers. "I was a magician. I cast the spell."

"Why!"

"I wanted wings," he says. "I wanted to fly."

"Why tail?"

"I wanted to be free!"

She steps away from Simon, and he falls back to the ground. She watches him try to sit up. *"Yessss. Am free,"* she says in our heads. *"Is better than this. Is best."*

She walks back to the fire.

"Do you believe us?" Bunce asks.

Margaret shrugs. "Believe you are malformed outcast tourist trash."

She's not wrong there. "So," I say carefully, "we can go?"

"You will go to the Next Blood? Fight them?"

"Yes!" Simon yells.

"Go," she says. "Tell the Next Blood they will never be top. Are the top! *Am.* Next Blood will burn, up when we wake. Up when we wake at the top."

The woman—the *dragon?*—takes the Normal's hand. "Take them away, Shepard. Don't let them hurt you. Let them hurt bloodeaters." She squeezes his hand, then walks away from us and the fire.

"Wait!" Bunce calls out. "My ring. I need my ring."

The woman turns abruptly, as if Penny has attacked her, and holds up a clenched fist. She must be wearing thirty rings and a dozen gold bracelets. *"Is mine now!"* she thunders in our heads.

Penny sounds tearful. "Please. I can't do magic without it. I can't help my friend. Or hurt bloodeaters."

The dragon—she *must* be—walks back to Penny and glares down at her. She brings her heavy hand to her mouth and closes her teeth around Penny's ring. Then she spits something—the purple stone from its centre—into the dirt.

And then she leaves.

We're still alive. And she's gone.

# 36

## SIMON

Shepard unties me first, then I free Baz. "Are you okay?"

"I've felt better, to be honest," he says. Which makes me think he must be nearly dead.

I help him stand. "We'll get you out of here and get you something to drink. More cats. A cow. Something."

My wings are flapping around, half out of control. It hurt so badly to have them tied down—I think I might have sprained something. I hope it isn't a break. It's not like I can pop in to a veterinary clinic and have it set.

Penny doesn't wait to be untied before she starts hammering Shepard with questions: "Where are these vampires? How do we find them? Where's our car?"

"The truck you stole?" He's working on the knots around her ankles. "Down the mountain, where you parked it."

"We need to leave," she says.

"You need to *take a breath*. You just barely lived through that."

"Was that really a dragon?" I ask him. My wings are convulsing. Shepard hands me a water bottle.

"Yeah." His eyes are shining. "Isn't she magnificent?"

"That depends," Baz says. "Is she listening?"

"Definitely," Shepard says. "She hears everything on this mountain."

"How?"

He grins. "Because she *is* the mountain."

We all look down at the ground.

"Dragons," he whispers. "A herd of them. Asleep since God knows when."

"We need to leave," Baz says. There's a low spinning sound, like a boomerang, and a pair of trousers hits him in the face.

Shepard looks confused. "What the—"

"Thank Crowley," Baz says, pulling the jeans free of his neck. "My kingdom for fresh pants as well."

Penny's still staring at Shepard. "The mountains are *dragons?*"

Shepard nods. "Isn't it incredible? Most of them are native. Margaret settled here a few hundred years ago, I guess. That's why she wakes up; she's used to a colder climate. But she says the others are stirring now. She's excited to meet them—and nervous, I think." His voice drops. "Don't tell her I said that."

"But she looks like a woman."

"That's just her public persona," he says. "Sort of a magickal envoy."

Penny's free of the ropes. She folds her arms. "Take us to our car."

Shepard steps back. "So you can wipe my brain again?"

"Why didn't it work the first time?"

He shrugs. "Maybe I've been given too much pixie dust over the years. Memory magic doesn't seem to stick anymore."

Penny holds out her fist—I reach out to stop her, but she's already casting. ***"That doesn't ring a bell!"***

Shepard lurches backwards, like he's been decked in the jaw. He shakes his head and lifts it, his eyes clear and unglazed. "I mean, it doesn't feel *good.*"

Her hand drops.

"I don't understand why you don't trust me," he says. "I've saved your skin twice now. I'm still your only safe way off this mountain—why can't we be friends?"

"You don't want to be *friends,*" Penny says. "It's not like we all hit it off at a pub. You're only helping us because you want information."

"And that's fine," Baz says. We all look at him. He looks at Penny. "We can't rescue Wellbelove on our own. We couldn't even rescue ourselves. We *need* a guide."

"That's what I'm talking about!" Shepard says.

Baz looks at him. "If it's knowledge you want, you can have it. You help us find our friend, and we'll let you travel with us. We'll answer some of your questions. But you can't share that knowledge with anyone else."

Shepard nods immediately. "All right."

"What's all right?" Baz asks.

"I won't tell anyone what I learn. I'll keep it to myself."

"Shake on it," Baz says.

Shepard holds out his hand. Baz holds his own palm out to Penny. She drops her purple stone into it. Then he takes Shepard's hand, pressing the stone between them. ***"Cross your heart, and hope to die!"*** Baz casts. Their hands light up.

Shepard's eyes get big. But he doesn't try to pull away. "I keep my promises."

"You'll keep this one," Baz says. "Or you'll drop dead." He slumps to the ground, exhausted from the spell. "Now, where's my wand?"

———

We all want to go help Agatha immediately, but Penny and Baz are literally spelled out. Baz looks like one of the bloodless carcasses he leaves behind. When we get to the next town, I steal a dog for him. It's not my finest moment. But it's not any of our finest moments.

We break into another hotel, and Baz and Penny collapse on the beds. Shepard offers to go get pizza. Penny gives him a weak thumbs-up.

Before he leaves, he stands in the doorway—"If you all want to leave while I'm gone, that's fine. I won't follow you this time. Just don't count on me to bail you out of your next mess."

None of us try to argue or reassure him. I'm too shagged out to care.

When the door closes behind him, Penny sits up. "We give him ten minutes, then we leave."

Baz throws a pillow at her. "Stand down, Bunce. We need help. And I need a shower." He looks a bit better since drinking the dog, but his hair is bushy and matted, and there's fresh blood on his already stained and shredded shirt. Huh. It's not like him to spill blood when he's drinking. . . .

"Baz—" He's walking past me on his way to the bathroom. I catch his arm. "Are you *bleeding*?"

"No."

"You are so," I say. I start to unbutton his shirt.

Baz looks away from me. "Snow," he says, his voice quiet but stern, "please don't—"

"*Baz*." His chest is covered in raised, round bumps. The skin is broken in places, and bloody. I touch him—the bumps feel like pebbles. A couple of them break open under my fingers, and little pieces of black metal push through his pale skin. "What happened?"

"Buckshot," he says. "From last night. My body seems to be rejecting it."

"Does it hurt?"

"Not really."

I look up at his face, my fingertips still on his breast. His eyes are narrow and shadowed—it *does* hurt. I move my face closer to his. I want to comfort him, but I don't know how.

"Simon . . ." he says.

"Yes."

There's a soft thrum in his breath. "You should really wash your hands."

"Oh." I pull my hand away. Covered in vampire blood. "Right."


When Baz gets out of the shower, he's wearing his fresh jeans and no shirt. His chest is covered with blotches and cuts, and there's a dark grey bruise on his side.

Shepard is back with the pizza, and even though he says it's the cheapest possible, it's better than any pizza I've had back home.

He was surprised when he came back to the hotel room and we were still here. But he doesn't ask us any more questions, and none of us bother keeping watch tonight. Penny and Baz take one bed, and Shepard takes the other. I take the extra pillow and a bedspread, and fall asleep on the floor.

# 37

## BAZ

I know that I heal faster than other people. (More proof that I'm not a person.) But I've never really tested my limits. No one's ever emptied a shotgun into my chest or kicked me in the gut with steel-toed cowboy boots. . . .

The worst I've been injured before this was when the numpties took me. I *think* my leg healed right away even then—but it healed *wrong* because I was stuck in that coffin.

Before that, there were fights with Simon. A few black eyes over the years, a split lip. I healed fast from those injuries, but so did he. I think Simon's magic used to heal him, even when he couldn't cast the spells to heal himself.

Not anymore—there's something wrong with his wing, it won't close all the way. I'm going to try to spell it better as soon as he gets up.

I woke up before everyone else, feeling livelier than I have in days. The rest of the buckshot scrubbed out last night in the shower, and my chest has completely stopped burning. It's covered in glossy white scars now—but those will heal, too, I think. All my other scars have.


Breakfast is cold pizza.

We pool our money on the bed. We have a few hundred dollars between us. I have my credit card, but I'm still nervous about using it.

"This isn't even enough for gas," Shepard says, looking at the pile.

"We'll cast spells for gas," Bunce says. "And we'll make this stretch." She holds her ring over the bills. **"A penny saved is a penny earned!"** The pile doubles. Bunce smiles. "I've always wanted to try that. . . ."

Shepard's mouth drops open. "You can *make* money?"

"Looks like it."

"You can't keep casting American phrases," I say to her. "It's too unpredictable."

"Needs must." Bunce shrugs. "We need food and clothes. And this one"—she points at Shepard—"needs to tell us where we'll find the NowNext."

"I don't know *exactly*," he says.

Simon is eating the last of the pizza. "Tell us what you do know."

Shepard pushes up his glasses. "That they're a new group of vampires. Any vamps we get around here tend to be loners. Or part of a family that keeps to their own. But the Next Blood . . . they're not a family. They're more like corporate raiders. They don't sneak around, snagging spare Normals— they just take what they want. And they're ambitious. Even I know they're trying to obtain magic."

"What about the magicians?" Bunce says. "How are they letting this happen?"

Magicians don't tolerate vampires. The fact that the Mage made a deal with the vampires was the biggest hit to his reputation back home. It's the reason he was buried without a marker. Even the Mage's Men, his little band of minions, spit on his memory now.

"The magicians could probably stop them," Shepard says, "but they'd have to get organized. I don't know what it's like where you come from, but Speakers over here don't really . . . *talk* to each other."

I don't feel like volunteering anything about where we come from. "You said these vampires were trying to learn how to speak with magic," I say. "They can't. You're either born a magician or you're not."

Simon clears his throat.

"Is it genetic then?" Shepard asks. "I've always wondered. . . . Does that mean, if I married a Speaker, we could have a magickal baby?"

Bunce guffaws.

"How do you know that these new vampires want magic?" I ask. "If you know so little about them?"

"They've sent out feelers all over the country, looking for tricks and lore. They've contacted some of the magic enthusiasts in my network."

"This is why!" Bunce points at him. "This is why we keep secrets! Are you going to share what you learn from us with upstart vampires?"

"No!" Shepard is adamant. "I've already sworn on my life."

"Where are they?" I ask.

"I don't know where the Next Blood is," he says. "But I know where most of America's vampires are. Vegas."

"Las Vegas . . ." Bunce looks vaguely disapproving.

I look over at Snow. He's grinning.

———

Before we leave, Simon decides we should try calling Agatha.

"But what if the NowNext track the call back to us?" Bunce worries.

"If they find *us*," he says, "we won't have to find *them*."

"Let's call," I say, "just in case Wellbelove picks up and tells us she's at a wellness camp, having her pores extracted."

"You don't really believe that," Bunce says.

She's right. I don't.

Bunce and I spell her phone secret, or try, and call Agatha's number. It goes straight to an automated voicemail. Agatha's never recorded a personal message. (I wouldn't have been surprised if it had been, *"Penelope, stop calling me."*) Bunce immediately hangs up.

"Right," Simon says after a moment. "We press on."

When we open the hotel room door to leave, most of my socks and three of my shirts fly in. I'm so happy, I actually hug them. (I was going to have to magick up a shirt. Or let Shepard run into a Walmart to buy me something. Without a shirt, I wouldn't even be allowed *into* a Walmart.) One of my socks is covered in feathers, but the shirts are clean. I put one on straightaway—a good print, aubergine with navy leaves—and tuck the rest into a plastic bag. (I regret leaving my suitcase in that creek, but there's no going back for it now.)

Bunce has spelled Simon's wings away again. He insists I squeeze into the cab of the truck with Penny, instead of riding in back with him. "You're already sunburnt," he says. "And you know what the wind does to your hair."

Shepard tells Simon he has to lie down in the truck bed; apparently riding back there is dangerous and illegal. "Both my middle names," Simon says.

"You don't have a middle name," I say. Which seems to hurt his feelings, which I immediately regret. I'm just *worried* about him. I grab his hand, trying to make up for it. "Just be careful," I say. "Plenty of time for derring-do when we're fighting vampires."

"What's 'derring-do'?" he asks.

"Your middle name."

He tugs on my hand. Crowley, we're bad at this. I can't ever tell what Simon wants. Does that tug mean *"I like you"*? Or is it *"Take care"*? Or *"Give me my hand back"*? I swear what it feels most like is *"I'm sorry."* We can't even hold hands without exchanging apologies. If we knew how to talk to each other, it'd be over, wouldn't it? If either of us ever found the words . . .

"Basil, get in." Penelope's holding the door open. She's making me sit between her and Shepard.

I squeeze Simon's hand, then do as I'm told.

# 38

## SHEPARD

Yes, yes, *yes*.

I am *in*. I am more in than I've ever been in before—and I've midwifed a centaur foal! I've helped an unfairy with his taxes!

But *nobody* gets to hang out with Speakers and vampires. Speakers don't hang out with anyone! And if they do, they don't let on. I've heard that sometimes Speakers marry Talkers and *still* never tell them about their magic.

It'll be hard keeping all this a secret. I'd love to drop it on the message boards. It's the *get* of all *gets*. But I've kept secrets before—I never told anyone about Maggie until yesterday. (She told them first, I think.)

Knowing is better than telling.

And maybe, if I help these three get their friend back, they'll keep me around. I could be their Normal friend! (Simon calls himself a Normal—but he has dragon wings.)

"I feel like we still haven't really met," I say, when we're back on the highway. "You know that I'm Shepard. . . . And you're Baz, right?"

The vampire nods.

"And you're Penelope?"

"I suppose," Penelope says. The first time I saw her, her hair was pulled back in a ponytail. Now it's mostly falling out of a ponytail, hanging in wild and frizzy brown curls around her face. She doesn't seem to care. She hasn't complained about her clothes either, though she's been wearing the same plaid skirt and knee socks since we met. I like her shoes—shiny black Doc Martens Mary Janes with silver buckles.

My pickup isn't really meant for three passengers; Baz and I are elbow to elbow.

"You really don't bite people?" I ask.

"Not yet," he says.

"I didn't think you could help it."

He glances over at me without turning his head, then rolls his eyes.

"Then why don't more vampires do that?" I ask him. "Not bite people?"

"I'm not sure. . . ." he says. "But I suspect it's because people taste really good."

Penelope huffs and leans around him to look at me. "Do you even know where we're going?"

"Well, I figured we'd head to Vegas—"

"And then what? *Excuse me, sir or madam, could you direct to us to the vampires? Not the old, bad vampires. The new, worse ones.*'"

"We can cast a spell to find them, if we're close enough." Baz has turned to her, closing me off.

"I've got a friend in the area," I throw in. I need them to keep on needing me. "She's got connections. She'll help us if she can."

# 39

## SIMON

You've never seen sky so blue.

I'm lying on my back in the bed of the truck, using Shepard's sleeping bag for a pillow. Baz fixed my wing up with magic. He bought me a pair of knock-off Ray-Bans and a case of bottled water at the last service station. And every once in a while, I see him cranking his head around to check on me.

I'm fine.

I'm so fine.

I can almost believe, under this sky—you've never seen sky so wide—that he and I will be fine, too. Him and me. We're getting by, aren't we? Mostly? Even with people tying us up and shooting at us.

We're getting by. He keeps touching me, and I keep letting him. And I haven't felt, I don't know, that static that I usually feel, like what's happening between us is a building I have to run out of before it collapses on me.

Baz is touching me, and it's good.

(Touching *Baz* is always good; it'd be easier if I could just touch *him* all the time. And kiss him. And not have to *be* kissed.) (I can't explain how it's different. Why kissing is easy, and *being* kissed is like being suffocated.) (Except it *hasn't* been like that this week. It's been fine. This sky is so big. There's so much air.)

Shepard stays off the big motorways. We have the road to ourselves most of the time. I sit up and lean on the side of the truck, watching the land change from green to grey to red.

America changes every time you look away from it.

It spills out in every direction.

I can't even believe that Utah is in the same country as Iowa. I can't believe they're on the same planet. That's how I feel, like the first man on Mars. I'm half glad Baz isn't out here with me, to see my mouth hanging open.

Plus it's too hot out here for him, too bright. And the constant wind and rattle is merciless. I feel half-baked and scrubbed raw.

I feel fine.

# BAZ

We've been in the car for four hours, and Shepard says it will be at least eight more. Bunce wants to cast spells to make the truck go faster, but I'm worried we'll need all our reserves when we get to wherever we're going.

Shepard keeps trying to draw us out. To no avail. I've never been drawn out in my life, and Bunce especially has taken against him.

There's nothing to do but look out at the increasingly depressing scenery. Green isn't green in America. We've driven through every kind of field, and none of them are as saturated as the fields back home.

Presently there's little green at all. The whole country's gone sharp and red.

I turn back to check on Simon. I gave him sunblock—

He's not there.

"Pull over." My hand is clenched on Shepard's arm. "Snow is gone."

Bunce turns to look. "Where'd he go?"

"He must have fallen out," I say. "Turn back."

Penny unbuckles her seat belt and rolls down her window, climbing partly out to look.

"He's fine!" Shepard shouts. "Get back in the truck!" He elbows me. "She's going to fall out."

I grab Bunce by the waist.

"Your friend's just there," Shepard says, pointing through the front window. "He's flying."

I see the shadow on the pavement ahead of us—Simon, with his wings spread, his arrow of a tail stretched out behind him.

"That lunatic," I whisper.

# 40

## PENELOPE

"I'm going to need your help with this part," Shepard says.

"Which part?" I say. "Why?" I have to lean around Baz to argue with the Normal, and it's getting tiresome. We've been in this truck for eleven hours, at least. Simon has been in the back—or above our heads—exposed to the desert, the whole time. I've pumped him full of protective spells, and I know Baz has, too, but *really*, this is getting excessive. I want to save Agatha, but not at the cost of microwaving Simon.

I suppose he seemed fine at the last stop. If anything, he seemed exhilarated—perhaps dangerously so. "I can't believe we're coming this close to the Grand Canyon and just driving by!" he lamented. "And Route 66! And Joshua Tree!"

"We have trees back home, Snow," Baz said. "Snap out of it."

Baz has fared much better on this leg of the trip, with a roof over his head. That black ash on his nose is mostly gone, though he still looks too grey for my liking.

He drank a snake after lunch, and it left him sour and tetchy.

"There you go," Shepard said, when Baz got back in the

truck. "A snake for breakfast, a snake for lunch, and a sensible dinner."

I ignored him. I've tried to ignore the Normal as much as possible. We've said he can stay with us and help us, but we didn't promise him explanations or—entertainment.

But he never stops trying. He never stops *talking*.

When we don't answer his questions about our families, he tells us all about his own. His mother, a teacher; his older sister, a journalist. His parents are divorced, and his dad, a flight attendant, lives in Atlanta, and that's all right, because it's someplace warm to visit at Christmastime, and sometimes Shepard gets to fly for free—and for the love of magic, I even know that he played football in primary school, but now he prefers role-playing games. There's really nothing too small for him to mention.

What he *really* loves to talk about is magic. It's almost as if he thinks telling us about all the magickal creatures he's met will tempt us to reply in kind.

It doesn't. Besides, magicians don't fraternize with magickal creatures, even the non-evil variety. We went to school with a few pixies and brownies, there was a centaur the year ahead of us—but they were all at least *part* magician. (How does a magician fall in love with a centaur? What do they even have in common?) (*"The top half,"* Simon said, when I tried to discuss this with him.)

Shepard, however, has never met a magickal creature he didn't strike up a friendship with. If he can be believed.

"You have *not* gone backpacking with a sasquatch," I said after five or six hours of this nonsense.

"Well, I told you, he doesn't carry a backpack. He's got this pouch, and all that's in it is a comb and a carving knife. I gave him my toothbrush, and he was pleased as punch with it. I need to get back up there, get him another toothbrush. . . ."

"How could you even have *time* for all these adventures? You're no older than us. Don't you have university?"

"I'm twenty-two. How old are you?"

"None of your business."

"Right, well, I put off school for a while. I'm going to go back when I know what I want to study. In the meantime, the road is my teacher."

"The road. The road is your distraction, I'd wager. You'd learn more *from* the world if you knew more *about* the world."

"Ha, that's what my mom says."

"Your mum is clearly cleverer than you."

"No argument here. What's your mom like?"

"Pfft."

We're in Arizona, I think, on a dark road. We've been staying off the main motorway, but we're never far from towns and people.

"What we're about to attempt," the Normal says, "isn't exactly legal."

"I thought you were Mr. Law and Order."

"I'm Mr. Don't Steal Cars, Counterfeit Money, or Commit Other Acts of Grand Larceny. But this won't hurt anybody. We need to get in to see my friend, but it's sorta after visiting hours—"

"Just tell us what you need," Baz cuts in.

"A few 'Open Sesame's should do it."

"Aghh," I groan. "Don't name spells. You shouldn't *know* any spells."

"I heard you use it back at the motel! And besides, everyone knows 'Open Sesame' is a spell. It's probably a spell *because* everyone knows it. Have you ever thought about that?"

I'm hiding my face. I want to cover my ears. "*Who* explained the nature of our magic to you? Please tell me, so I can make sure they face an international tribunal." There's no such thing as an international tribunal, but I like the idea of muddying Shepard up with false information.

"Fine," Baz says. "Just get on with it. We don't have time to argue."

We turn onto a larger road, following signs towards something called the Hoover Dam. I think I've heard of it.

I glance out the back window. Simon is sitting up, leaning eagerly on the wall of the truck bed. There doesn't seem to be any part of this trip that he doesn't relish. (Aside from the times when we've almost died.) (And, honestly, he seemed to enjoy those, too.)

"Maybe you could make us harder to see," Shepard says. "There are cameras."

Baz casts, ***"Through a glass, darkly!"*** on the truck.

Shepard nods. "Cool. Now those gates . . ."

***"Open Sesame!"*** I say. It comes out flat and sarcastic, so I have to cast it again.

"There might be guards," Shepard says, squinting into the darkness ahead of us.

"I'll take care of it." Baz is all business. "Should I put them to sleep?"

"Whoa." Shepard holds out his arm. "I don't want anyone to accidentally fall asleep on their control panel and blow up the whole dam. . . ."

"I doubt there's a *'BLOW UP THE DAM'* button," I say.

Baz is getting impatient. "I'll take care of it."

We park, and Simon hops over the side of the truck. "What's the plan? Are we going to see the dam? Wicked. Did we sneak in?"

Baz grabs Simon's T-shirt and pulls him close, inspecting him for damage. "Are you all right? Are you thirsty? Are you dying of exposure?"

"I'm fine," Simon says. "You should ride back there with me when we leave. Now that the sun's down. You've never seen so many stars." Simon spreads his wings like he's stretching. Baz brushes some dust off Simon's shoulders. Baz seems timid, like he isn't sure he's permitted this much tenderness. It's hard to watch, so I look at Shepard. He's watching them, too. I shove his arm. "So what's the plan?"

Shepard takes a bottled water from the back of the truck. "My friend lives in the water," he says. "Well, more or less. We just have to walk out onto the dam, and see if she feels like talking."

"So Agatha's life depends on someone wanting to talk to you? Brilliant."

"Fortunately for you, most people actually like talking to me. You're a notable exception."

We follow a pathway out onto the dam.

Baz and I make sure the guards don't notice us, with a combination of "Through a glass" and "Nothing to see here."

Shepard watches our every move. I'm sure he's going to write down all these spells in one of the notebooks he has stacked on his dashboard, just as soon as he has a moment. Well . . . we didn't promise not to destroy any evidence.

Simon flies along behind us. I think he's enjoying having his wings out in the open. When we get home, we need to find a way for Simon to exercise his wings. (If we're not in magickal prison.) (At least if we're in *magickal* prison, Simon won't have to hide his wings.)

The dam is enormous—and rather beautiful, I think—a curved wall of concrete, holding back the river. When we get out to the middle of the wall, Shepard leans as far as he can over the water. If I actually cared about him, I'd pull him back. It would be a long fall from here—the river must be at a low

**214 RAINBOW ROWELL**

point. You can see the waterline on the rock around the reservoir, like a ring around a bath.

"Blue . . ." Shepard calls out in a low voice. He tips his bottle of water over the rail and spills some. Nothing immediately answers him.

He keeps hanging out over the wall, emptying the bottle. *"Blue . . ."*

There's a rushing noise below us—a rushing, slurring voice.

"Shhhhep," the voice says.

A pillar of water shoots up in front of us. I jump back. Simon puts his hand on my shoulder to steady me. He's landed.

The water falls.

A few more jets spurt up, then fall.

Then a larger column of water surges up and holds. It looks like a woman for a moment. Like a melting ice sculpture.

"Tassshhtes like plashtic," the voice rumbles. It's a feminine rumble.

"I know," Shepard says, "sorry."

A stream-like hand reaches out to touch his cheek. "Ogallala Aquiferrr," she babbles, caressing him. "Rocky Mountain shhhhhnow."

"Yeah," Shepard says, "I'm on a road trip."

"More like a rescue mission," I say.

The water turns to me, then backs away. Recedes. "Shhtrangerrssh," it says. She says. She rushes.

"Friends," Shepard says.

"You'rrre too trussshhhting, Shhep."

"Maybe," he says. "But I'm usually a good judge of character."

"Magic," she says. "Dangerrr. Let me take them, you shhtay clean."

The water level is getting higher in the reservoir. The column thickens, more decisively taking a woman's shape. I resist the urge to cast a spell. Simon squeezes my shoulder.

"They mean us no harm!" Shepard insists. "They're looking for their friend. We think she was kidnapped by vampires."

The water—some sort of river spirit? Is she the river itself?—hisses. "Bad company," she splatters. My shoes and socks are wet. Baz steps away from the wall.

"The worst," Shepard says. "We think she's with the Next Blood."

The entire lake is disturbed. We can hear it pounding against the concrete.

"We thought maybe you could tell us where they are," Shepard says. "*You're* everywhere."

"Not anymorrre," she sobs. "I am dammed and diminishh-hed and loshht to the mishht."

"You're still grand," he says, "from where I'm standing."

The water laps at his face. It makes a noise like, *Pssssssht.*

Shepard leans out farther—too far, his feet are off the ground. His face and hair are dripping.

"The New Blood taste dishhtilled," she grumbles. "Chemi-calshh, vitamin shupplemntshhh."

I'm getting impatient. "Where are they?"

I get soaked in answer.

Shepard flashes me a *"shut up"* face. Oh, *now* he wants me to shut up. "We'd be so grateful for your help," he says entreatingly.

"Weshhht," she says.

"Just west?"

"On the shhhoresh. Shaltwaterr. Irrigashhion. Golf cour-shesshhh."

"That could be anywhere in California," Shepard says to himself.

"I tashte them closherrr shometimeshh."

"Yeah?"

"Vegashh."

"They're mixing with the others? That can't be."

The water seems to shhrug. I mean shrug. "They all find theirrr way to the Katherrrine eventually."

"The Katherine," Shepard says. "Like, the hotel?"

"No." She shakes her head back and forth, splashing in every direction. "Dangerrr. You shhhould let them go alone."

"Blue. I've promised them my help."

"You'rrrre *too* helpful."

"That reminds me." He smiles and slides to the ground, taking off his rucksack. "Brought you some good news." He pulls a novel out of his bag. "I liked this one. Kind of sad. Good jokes though."

"Is it ficchhhion?"

"Of course," he says, dropping it in the water. He reaches back into the rucksack. "This one takes itself too seriously, but I know you're a sucker for Westerns." He pitches another book over the rail. "I would have brought more, but I didn't know I was coming. I did get this, though, on the way." He holds up a radio. "Waterproof."

"No shhuchh thing," she drips.

"Well, water-resistant," he says, dropping it in. The water gushes up to catch it. "I'll be back when I can to change the batteries."

"Thankshhhep. You'rre a good frriend."

Simon has wandered down the walkway a bit, now that we have as much as we're going to get about Agatha. He's flapping his wings to look farther over the rail.

A wall of water rises up in front of him, and the woman's

shape seems to walk through it, reaching for Simon's chin. "I know you," she says, daubing at him.

Simon lands on the pavement, standing very still.

"You werrre the drrrain."

He nods. "Yeah. . . . Sorry. Did I take your magic?"

"Not mine. The worrrrld'sh, yeshhh?"

"I'm sorry," Simon says again. "I didn't know."

She smooths his hair back, sopping it. "Shhookay," she burbles. "You put it back. And morrre."

He bows his head and lets her hand fall over him.

Baz and I are transfixed. So is the security guard a few feet away.

I hold up my amethyst. ***"These aren't the droids you're looking for!"***

"These aren't the droids I'm looking for," the man says, turning away. "Why was I looking for droids. . . ."

"We have to go," Baz says. He looks at the river. "Thank you."

"She wasn't that much help," I mutter. Baz elbows me.

The water has returned to Shepard to say good-bye. He's promising to come back as soon as he can. To visit her headwaters at La Poudre Pass. "Shhhep," she implores of him, "won't you blow up the dam forrr me?"

"Not this time," he says. "But I'll continue to think about it."

"It would be betterrr for everryone."

"Everyone but me," he says. "But I've got it on my list of long-term goals."

"That would be terrorism!" I say.

"Liberrrashhion," the river disagrees.

"Magic save us from radicals," I say, sounding, to my dismay, pretty much exactly like my mother.

# 41

## BAZ

Sometimes Bunce's boldness is just arrogance. She harangues Shepard all the way back to the truck. As if there's no way the guards will see through our magic, and like the river definitely won't change its mind and sweep us all off the top of the dam.

"Why did you throw litter into the water?" Bunce asks at full volume.

"Because she gets bored," Shepard says. "People used to drop all sorts of things into her. Newspapers, matchbooks, divorce papers. Now all she gets is chemical runoff and iPhones that break as soon as they touch her."

"How does one even *meet* a river?"

"By introducing oneself."

"Is that right, *Shep.*"

Simon is flying just above us, still taking advantage of being unnoticeable.

"You should fly more," I say, when he touches down near the truck.

"Sure," he says. "Up Regent Street, through Piccadilly Circus."

"We could go to the country. There's still my family estate."

"I'd probably show up on Google Maps. . . ."

"I'd magic you before we got there."

Simon shrugs.

Penny is waiting for me to get in the cab. "Come on, Baz, let's go."

Simon takes my elbow. "Ride with me," he says, looking at the place where his hand is touching my arm. "There are stars."

His hair is hanging between us in wet ringlets. I lean forward and bump his head with mine. "Yeah," I say. "Okay."

I can't see him smile, but I think it's there.

He swings up into the back of the truck, and I follow. Penny sighs and gets in the cab. She'll have to argue with Shepard without leaning over me. (I'm not worried about her safety; I've cast three intention spells on the Normal—he means us no direct harm.)

There's a sleeping bag spread out back here, and Simon lies down in it, carefully leaving room for me. I'm still crouching, looking around. The truck starts, and I lose my balance.

"Come here," Simon says.

I really hate riding back here. I feel like a cup of tea left on top of a moving car. "This is so dangerous," I say, kneeling. "What if we hit a bump?"

"You'll be fine, you're Kevlar."

"What about you?"

"Wings."

I look down at him. The truck has already picked up speed.

"Baz," he says, reaching out to me. "Come here."

# SIMON

*Come here.*
*Come on.*
*Please.*
*Give us this.*

# BAZ

I lie down next to Simon, and his left arm slides under my waist. The truck is hard beneath us, and you can feel every piece of gravel under the wheels—but it's better lying down, letting the wind blow over you, not through.

Even though the day was scorching, it's cool now, almost cold. Simon tightens his arm around me. He's not as hot as he used to be. (Literally. He's a less combustible combustion engine.) But, Crowley, he's still so warm.

I try not to think about how long it's been since I felt him like this. Against me, shoulder to knee. I'm afraid if I do, I'll hold on too tight. I'll do whatever I did in the first place to scare him away.

He points to the sky above us, black as pitch here in the desert and filled with twinkling stars. *I see them, Snow, I'm not blind.*

When his right arm drops, he winds that one around me, too. I close my eyes.

What is this? Why is he letting me this close?

Is this a real change? Or just a middle-of-the-night, middle-of-the-desert exception?

Am I only allowed to hold him when we're on the run?

# SIMON

Baz's hands finally come to me. Up the back of my shirt. Familiar and cold.

You'd never think you could crave someone cold, that you'd find yourself always moving closer to them because of it. But Baz is the kind of cold I want to cover.

(His hands are feather light on my back. Feather light and chilled through.)

I want to warm him by hand. By heat, by cheek, by stomach.

I bring my wings up around us and press him into the truck bed, pressing myself into every grey inch.

When was the last time . . .

*No. Don't think about the last time.*

*Don't think it might be now.*

*Don't think.*

I'm wet from the river spirit. My nose is the same temperature as Baz's chin.

I knock my face into his. I hang over him.

This is the point, the proximity, where I usually pull away.

"Can I?" I say, pressing in. I'm not sure he'll hear me, over everything.

# BAZ

His hair is sticky with dust. His face is cold and damp. He's clumsy like this. Hitting me with his chest. Shouldering me. Butting my head back into the metal of the truck.

I touch Simon Snow like he's made of glass. Like he'll explode if I cross the wrong wires.

He touches me like he can't decide whether to push or pull me, and he's settled on both.

I go where he wants. I take what I can get.

"Can I?" he asks.

*Can you what, Simon? Kiss me? Kill me? Break my heart?*

I touch him like he's made of butterfly wings.

"You don't have to ask." I say it loud enough that he'll hear me, over everything.


# SIMON

Cold lips, cold mouth.

I've never heard Baz's heartbeat.

And I've lain all night with my head on his chest.


# BAZ

My favourite part of kissing Simon when he's cold is the way he goes warm in my hands. Like *I'm* the living campfire. Like I'm the one who lives. I warm him in my arms, and then he warms me in his. He gives it all back to me.

## SIMON

I'd give him all that I am.
   I'd give him all that I was.
   I'd open up a vein.


I'd tie our hearts together, chamber by chamber.


## BAZ

It's good, it's good, it's so good.
   And I resist demanding an explanation.
   *Why now, what's the key? How do I get back here tomor-row? Promise to let me back in.*
   Sometimes Simon kisses me like it's the end of the world, and I worry he might believe that it is.


The truck stops too soon. Shepard doesn't want to drive into Vegas at night. "We're less likely to get noticed in the morning," he says.
   He pulls into a campground, and all four of us bed down in the back of the truck, Penny between Simon and me, for safety. There's only one sleeping bag, but I spell the truck soft with ***"Cushion the blow!"***
   Shepard can't get over it. He keeps jumping up and down like a kid in a bounce house.

"So," Bunce says, "what do you know about this hotel we're headed to?"

"The Katherine?" he says. "It's one of the vampire hotels. The oldest, I think. The parties there are infamous—every night in the penthouse suite."

"There are vampire hotels?" Simon asks.

"There are vampire everything in Vegas," Shepard says. "There are probably vampire dry cleaners. Vampire taxis. Vampire accountants . . ."

"I thought you said you've never met a vampire," I say.

"I haven't. I hadn't."

"So how do you know where they party?"

"I know people who know," Shepard says. "Well. Not exactly *people* . . ."

Bunce huffs. "So we're going to crash a vampire party and hope your charm attack works on them? *'Hi, I'm Shepard, and I just want to be friends. Please tell me all your vampire secrets.'*"

"God, no," Shepard says. "I'd get drained. Vampires are notoriously tight-lipped. They keep to their own."

"So?" Bunce asks.

"So I'm not going to do any of that. Baz is."

# 42

## AGATHA

I'm awake. I'm not sure if I'm still in my room.

I think I'm waiting for Braden.

He came yesterday while I was still eating breakfast, and he looked so happy to see me that I found myself smiling back at him. For a moment I felt so ridiculous. Why was I worrying? I'd been given my own room at a luxury retreat. I was being courted by the sort of guy who shows up in *Vanity Fair*, under "Vanities."

He sat on my bed. "Good morning."

"Good morning," I said. "What's on the docket today? I think Ginger and I were supposed to meditate. Or possibly mediate . . . I'm game for either."

"Agatha . . ." Braden said. "I want to really *talk* to you."

"Haven't we been really talking? It's felt like so much talking."

"I want to be honest," he said.

I heroically resisted rolling my eyes. "Of course."

"Agatha, you're a perfect specimen."

"Braden, I know you're in health care, but girls don't like being called a 'specimen.' "

He laughed. "You're so funny."

"I thought we were being honest."

He laughed louder and took my hand. "Agatha . . . I know what you are." He was still smiling at me.

Not a single muscle moved in my face. "I told you everything I am."

"Come on." His voice was gentle. "You can drop the artifice. There are no secrets between us."

There bloody well *are*.

I waited for him to elaborate.

"I saw you," he said. "In the library. I saw you light your cigarette."

"I thought you'd forgiven me for smoking in the house."

His smile faltered for the first time. "Agatha, *come on*. I thought we could really do this—that we could just *have* this conversation."

I smiled exactly the way my mother does when she doesn't want to hear something. It's the look she gave me when I said I didn't want to go to Watford, and when I asked for another horse.

"*Agatha.*"

"Braden . . ."

"I know you have the mutation."

"The mutation?"

"It must be a mutation," he said. "We've ruled out anything communicable."

I genuinely didn't know what the hell he was talking about.

"I know you can do magic!"

There's a protocol for this. It starts with avoidance. Then comes denial. "I don't think I follow—"

"We've got it on video, Agatha! I don't know what spell you cast—you barely moved your lips. Is that something you're taught?"

Next comes flight. I stood up, I headed for the door. "You're being silly." That's also something my mother would say. "I really need to catch up with Ginger. Do you want to come with?" I reached for the doorknob. It wouldn't budge.

Avoid, deny, flee, *fight*. "Braden, what's the meaning of this?"

He stood up, too, cornering me against the door. "You don't have to keep this secret from me. I know about you. I know about your kind."

What options did I have left? I didn't have my wand. I could have started a small fire in my palm, I suppose, but then he'd have the proof he wanted. And a Bic lighter wasn't going to get me out of this. "This is completely unacceptable," I said. "I am a guest in your home, and I demand to be treated as such."

"You can talk to me, Agatha!" Somehow he was still smiling. "We're both part of humanity's next stage."

"Humanity's next stage? Braden, I'm a freshman at San Diego State. I'm probably not going to get into vet school. I'm—"

"Stop. *Bullshitting*. Me." He very nearly raised his voice. "I thought we could do this together. I thought you'd want to do this together. You came here of your own volition—you *want* to level up. You want more from life."

"No. I don't. I was just being a good friend."

"You've gotten to know us, you know we're here to evolve. We're moving mankind forward."

"For fuck's sake, Braden, you're very rich and very good at Ashtanga—"

"*We are the next stage of human life!*" he snarled, baring his teeth at me. Baring his . . . fangs.

My breath caught.

"We are pushing past every single limitation, Agatha! We've already conquered sickness and decay, and next we'll conquer the impossible!"

I walked past him, sitting primly on the bed.

He followed, standing over me, still ranting: "We know all about your people. We're mapping your genome right now. *In these labs.* I'm building an entire facility for more research. We know about your wands and your spells—'Sticks and stones,' right? That's one? And 'Free at last'?"

I folded my hands in my lap.

"We're going to know everything soon, and you could help us—you could make it so much more efficient. And it would benefit you, too. You'd be one of us. Strong. Well. Ageless."

I stared at the wall. "If you're quite finished—"

"Agatha."

"If you're quite finished, I think I'd like to—"

"It's an invitation. But it isn't a request."

"Ginger will be looking for me."

He touched my arm then. Probably with one of his infinitesimal needles. "I hope you consider it," he said. By the end of his sentence, my head felt heavy.


But I'm awake now. My eyes are open.

I can't open my mouth.

I can't remember why not.

I think I'm waiting for Braden.

# 43

## SIMON

Baz is standing in front of a full-length mirror, wearing—I swear to Merlin—a flowered suit. It's some slick material, dark blue with bloodred roses. With a white shirt. No—a light *pink* shirt. When did he start wearing all these flowers? When did his hair get so long? He's put stuff in it, and it's hanging over his collar in thick, black waves.

"You can't be serious," I say.

He cocks an eyebrow at me in the mirror.

"It's perfect," Shepard says. "Vampires are always *way* over the top."

Baz shifts his evil eye over to Shepard. "No, it's perfect because it's perfect."

If Shepard could see Baz's house, he'd know that it isn't just vampires living the goth life; it's also stupidly rich magicians.

Baz didn't blink when we walked into this hotel, the theme of which seems to be *What if Dracula opened a hotel and didn't care whether everyone guessed he was Dracula?*

Everything is black. The walls, the furniture. Everything

but the carpet, which is the colour of spilled wine. Or spilled blood, I reckon.

Penelope walked in and nearly walked right out: The centrepiece of the lobby is a bunch of hanging birdcages. At least a dozen of them, all painted black, with *only* black birds inside. Black parrots and black—I don't know—cockatoos or something.

"Do you think they *dye* them?" Penny asked, walking along the wall to avoid the cages. (She's hated birds ever since fourth year, when the Humdrum sent cravens after us, and they tried to peck out our eyes.)

We all kept our distance from the front desk while Baz secured our room. I'm not sure if he had to use money or magic, or if the employees just recognized him as one of their own. Everyone who works here is pale and incredibly good-looking. The men wear black suits, and the women wear black leather dresses cut into lace. (Leather *and* lace.) (Are they vampires? Is everyone a vampire here? You'd think I'd know, from living with one. But it took me years of very close study to figure him out.)

Our suite is slightly more cheerful, at least. It's only *mostly* black. The walls are the colour of Baz's new shirt (maybe vampires love pink?), and the beds are grey. Everything that could be leather is.

We got here this morning, and spent the rest of the day washing the sand out of our hair, taking naps, and ordering room service. Baz went out for a while and came back with this suit and a change of clothes for Penelope and me. He was the only person Shepard would allow to leave the room.

"Las Vegas can't be *that* dangerous," Penny says. "Some of the most famous magicians in the world live here." She's lying on one of the beds, wearing a pretty yellow sundress—Baz should pick out her clothes more often. (And he should never pick out mine. He brought me back a shirt with buttons. Like I work in a bank.) Penelope sighs. "I can't believe I came all the way to Las Vegas, and I'm not gonna see Penn and Teller."

"Please," Baz mutters. "Sellouts."

Shepard's eyes light up. *"Penn and Teller?"*

Baz finishes adjusting his cuffs and collar, and turns away from the mirror. He really does look perfect. Whatever strange look he's going for—Gothic pop star—it works for him.

Penelope sits up, looking serious. "Right then, Basil, we'll be here listening, and your phone—"

"Will be in my pocket, Bunce," Baz says. "I'll call you before I leave. You'll hear the whole thing." He's all set up for international calling now.

Thinking about him in a room full of vampires makes me itch all over.

"If they start asking too many questions—" Penny says.

Shepard takes over: "Be as honest as possible. *You're not from around here, you're on holiday, you heard there was a party."*

"That's . . . actually a decent plan," Penny says. "And if they don't buy it—"

"You set them all on fire," I cut in, "and we get the hell out of here."

Baz smiles at me. His eyes are soft. I think they're still soft from last night. From whatever spell we cast in the back of the truck.

"On second thought"—I step between him and the door—"let's just set this place on fire and get the hell out of here immediately."

Baz lowers his eyebrows, like he can't tell whether I'm being serious. "What about Agatha?"

I think I *am* being serious. "These vampires might not even know about Agatha. You might be risking your life for nothing."

"I'll be fine, Snow. Have a little faith in me." He adjusts his cuffs again. (What is even the *point* of cuffs that need constant adjusting?) Then he takes out his phone and dials a number.

Penny's mobile rings. She answers it without saying anything.

Baz slips his phone back into his jacket pocket. He steps around me, opens the door, and holds out his hand: I give him the room key.

Then he's gone.

Penny puts her arm on my shoulder. "He'll be fine, Simon." She pulls me over to one of the beds, and lays her phone down right in the middle, switched to speaker.

We hear Baz's phone rubbing against his pocket as he walks. . . .

Then the ping of the lift arriving. . . .

Doors opening. People talking, laughing.

After a few seconds, another ping, and the people get off.

Then we hear the lift whooshing to the top of the building. *"Have a little faith,"* Baz whispers.

The lift pings. The doors open.

He's moving again. The hallway is quiet.

He knocks three times on something solid.

# 44

## BAZ

I knock on the door. Which was apparently a mistake—because
the woman who answers it is scowling. I start to say hello, but
she leans in and sniffs me, then walks away, waving me in. I
suppose I pass her test.

I step inside. It's the penthouse suite, much larger than ours,
and crowded with people.

Not people—vampires. People like me. I worried that I'd
be overdressed, but Shepard was right: Everyone here has gone
a bit over the top. Men in suits, women in gowns and capes.
Everyone dripping jewels and gold chains and feathers. . . .

It's nothing like the club that Simon and I visited in London.
Those vampires were lying low. These vampires *want* to be
seen—and admired. They aren't especially beautiful. (Though
some are.) That's a myth, I think—vampire beauty. What they
are is especially rich. And especially . . . liquid. They move like
oil, like shadows. Like cats.

Is this what I look like? Like I don't have any parts that stick?

Everyone is drinking. So I look for the bar and find it along the wall. I pour myself something golden, just to have something to do with my hands.

I told Simon I'd be fine here, and I will be. I've been to a hundred of my parents' parties—I know how to stand around wealthy people and look bored. Though these people don't look bored. . . .

A few of them are dancing. There isn't a dance floor; they're just dancing wherever they happen to be standing. Two women are kissing very passionately in one of the window seats.

There are Normals here, too. At least a few. I smell their heartbeats. If Penelope and Simon were here, that'd be it—they'd do whatever they had to do to save the Normals.

But I want to save Agatha.

And I want to crush these NowNext people before they take hold. The dragon was right, vampires mustn't learn to Speak—no one should be allowed to be both.

I walk up to a group of four or five people, hoping to introduce myself, but they break up shortly after I join them. I stand there for a moment staring down at my drink, pretending I intended it to go that way.

A very beautiful woman—a girl my age—stumbles past me, laughing. There's blood streaked down her neck, and she isn't wearing shoes. My nostrils burn. A few of the other vampires turn away from their conversations to glance at her. Four hands catch her by the waist and pull her into the crowd.

"Hello," someone says over my shoulder. I turn away from the girl's scent.

It's a man. Well, it's a vampire. Like me. Though not exactly like me. . . . Shorter, slighter, a different shade of pale. His eyes are sparkling, like I've already done something to amuse him. "Can I get you something to drink?" he asks.

I hold up my still-full glass.

The vampire tilts his head and smiles. "You're . . . not from around here, are you?"

I try to sparkle back. "Is it that obvious?"

He smiles, but there's a flash of something else. "It is now. London?"

"By way of Hampshire."

"I know it well." He holds out his hand. "Lamb."

I take it. "Chaz." (Bunce thought I should use something that sounds like my real name, so I'd still turn my head if I heard it.) His hand strikes me as cold, but it isn't really—it's only as cold as mine. I clear my throat. "You've been to Hampshire?"

He feigns heartbreak. "Have I been gone so long? Do I pass as an American now?"

"I'm so sorry," I say. "I take it back." He seems utterly American to me. Or maybe I just mean utterly vampire—with his periwinkle shirt and his unfashionably extravagant auburn hair. It's cut all at one length, loose and shiny, just below the tips of his ears. He pushes it out of his face, and it falls silkily back. He's clearly one of those vampires contributing to the myth of beauty.

"I can already tell you're going to be good for me, Chaz. Round out my vowels, firm up my *t*'s. . . . What brings you so far from home?"

"I'm here on holiday. I've always wanted to see Las Vegas."

"That's a long flight," Lamb says. "Did you fill your shampoo bottles with O-negative—or make intimate friends with the person sitting next to you on the plane?"

I laugh, hoping it's at least partly a joke. "I fasted. It helps with the jet lag."

To my relief, he laughs, too.

"You must have made the trip yourself," I say.

"Indeed. Though it was a long boat ride then." He takes a

drink. "Next time"—he nods at the door—"wrangle an invitation before you drop into a party. You know how we are, no one around here trusts a new face. And you're 'new' for at least the first hundred years. . . ."

"Shame that I've only got two weeks before I'm due home." I take a drink, first trying hard not to gape. (*Hundred years? Boats? Did he come over on the* Titanic?) and then trying harder not to gag (*What the devil am I drinking, lamp oil?*).

I mean, I've wondered, of course I've wondered—do vampires grow old? Can they live forever?

How old *is* this Lamb? He looks older than me—30, maybe 35. Could he be *one hundred* and thirty-five?

I try to steady myself. *Keep it light, Basilton. Keep it casual.*

"So why did *you* decide to talk to me?" I ask him, not ready to look up from my drink. "Was it pity? Or is it your job to send me on my way?"

"Not at all," he says. "I appreciate a new face. . . ."

I look up and meet his eyes.

He's waiting for that—he smiles. "So. You have two weeks to sample our famous Las Vegas charm."

I nod.

"Honestly, Chaz, I don't know why you'd ever go home. I haven't."

"Is it so good here?"

"It is, in fact." He rolls his wrist, idly watching the ice bob in his drink, and watching me, too. "But what I meant was—it's so very bad there."

"When did you leave?"

Lamb shakes his head. His hair follows half a second behind. "A long time ago, when the magicians were just getting organized, before they'd decided our kind couldn't be tolerated."

He looks pained. "I remember hearing, back in the fifties, that there wasn't a single one of us left in the UK—that Old Man Pitch had driven us out, like Saint Patrick driving the snakes from Ireland. More than a few Brits washed ashore in those days. I met a man from Liverpool who hitched a ride on a frigate and swigged down the whole crew, one by one, across the Atlantic."

My chin has finally dropped. I struggle and fail to lift it.

Lamb flips his hair out of his blue eyes. "Imagine the discipline and forethought that required—the timing!"

"Well," I say, "now I feel much less heroic about my eight-hour red-eye." It's very hard to be droll when your head is exploding. *Old Man Pitch*—that's my great-grandfather, it must be. I've never met him, but—

"I've heard that it's eased up since then," Lamb says. "We get more news these days. You know, the Internet. . . ."

"It's eased a bit," I say, "yes."

He draws nearer to me. "But the mages still have you under their thumb, don't they? The stories we hear . . ." He looks stricken. "Underground clubs, raids, *fires*."

"It's not so bad. If you keep your head down."

Lamb looks sad for another moment, then leans in a bit more, tipping his head up to meet my eyes. "Well. Lift that chin, my friend. You're in America now."

I laugh and use it as an excuse to step back. "How different can it be?"

He laughs with me, standing straight again and waving his arm. "Look around. Las Vegas is *ours*. And you'll find our brethren in all the major American cities."

"The mages don't mind?"

"Our mages stick to themselves. They might get involved, individually, if we start affecting population numbers. But this is a big country, full of Bleeders. Frankly, the Bleeders—do you still call them Normals?"

I nod.

"The Normals are more of a threat to themselves. The magicians here are more worried about guns than they are about vampires." He looks at my face again. "Are you sure you're not thirsty?" Lamb's face is almost pink, his lips are nearly red. He must be sloshed.

"You act like the taps run red." My voice is light—thank Crowley. "Do you keep Normals in the minifridge?"

"This *city* is a minifridge. It's like nothing I imagined in the old country. A city of our own, Chaz, can you believe it? A capital!"

"The whole city?"

Lamb nods, his face glowing with satisfaction. "Though we stick to the Strip mostly. Why would we leave? These four miles are overrun with tourists, three hundred sixty-five days a year. Most of them *come* here to lose their mind and do terrible things—bachelor parties, sales conventions—we practically provide a service."

"And the locals don't notice?" I ask.

"Notice what?"

"The . . . bodies."

"If they do, they blame other things. *Organized crime.*" He raises his eyebrows. "*The opioid crisis.* But most of us are more careful than that. No need to leave a corpse when you can leave a satisfied customer, you know?"

I must look like I don't. (I don't.) Lamb narrows his eyes at me. "Chaz," he chides. "Surely in London, you don't drain them *all* dry."

I still don't know what he means. *Is something else possible?*

*Can these vampires drink—and stop? Do they Turn everyone
they touch?*

I shrug. Nonchalantly, I hope. "We can't afford witnesses."

"No. I suppose you can't. . . ." His face is long. His small
mouth is pursed. He looks haunted.

"I apologize," I say. "I've offended you."

"*No.*" He rests his hand on my arm. "I forget myself. I forget what it's like to live in fear and shame. It's been so long since
I've walked in the shadows." He squeezes. "I hope you get a
taste of freedom here, Chaz. This is a place where you can ex-
ult in who you are, not fear it."

He lifts an eyebrow. "Take a walk with me?"

If a vampire invites you to a second, darker, lonelier location,
don't go. That's just common sense. . . .

. . . unless you're already a vampire.

What's the worst that can happen? Lamb could kill me, I
suppose. He probably knows all the ways a vampire can die.

But I need information, and he's the only one talking to me.

The heat was unbearable when we arrived in Las Vegas this
morning, and the sky was so bright, I couldn't open both eyes
at the same time. But now that the sun is down, the night is
warm and pleasant. I'm perfectly comfortable in my jacket.
And Lamb seems fine in his cream-coloured suit. He seems
more at ease than I've ever felt around Normals.

He's giving me an insider's tour of the Strip, pointing out
each casino. Telling me what used to be there and what replaced it. Running down the highlights. The architecture. The
infamy.

"All right, just about . . . here," he says, and stops in front of yet another grand façade, this one with a dark reflecting pool. "Some people miss the old days, before the tourists and Cirque du Soleil and celebrity chefs. Ring-a-ding-ding, et cetera. But Vegas only gets better for me."

"How long have you been here?" I ask.

"Since the beginning."

"When was the beginning?"

"Oh eight," he says. "Nineteen oh eight. It took me almost three hundred years to make my way here from Virginia." He's smiling at me, face wide open.

I shake my head. I'm sure I look as dumbfounded as I feel. "But you're so—"

Lamb stops. His hands are in his trouser pockets, and his head is tilted. He keeps looking at me like I'm something that needs to be examined—and smiled at—from all directions. "I'm so what, Mr.—what's your last name?"

I can't tell him my last name, and I can't think of anything that rhymes. "Watford," I say.

"Charles Watford. Even your name makes me homesick. Go on though, I'm so what—impressive?" He smiles. "Learned?"

*Alive,* I think.

"Open," I say. "About . . . well, your history. Your . . ." I shrug again. "You don't know me."

"But I know what you are," he says. "And you know what I am. I have plenty to hide—but not that."

I nod. "I suppose that's true."

"And *you* have plenty to hide, Chaz. Obviously. But not . . . *that.*"

He's right. I've given him a fake name and false pretenses, but he knows the truth about me. The truth even my immediate family won't look in the eye.

"I keep waiting for you to notice," he says.

"Notice what?"

He touches my shoulder and gently spins me around, so I'm facing the pavement. There are people everywhere, even though it's well after midnight. Everyone dressed up in after-midnight clothes. Everyone a little tipsy. Everyone . . .

It takes my breath away when it hits me:

In every group of people, there's someone moving too smoothly, someone's face shining pearl-white in the spinning lights. With Normals. Without Normals. In twos and threes. In their element. A man looks down at me from a Cadillac Escalade and flashes a bloodless grin.

Lamb's voice is just behind my ear. "Our town," he says. "Yours."

I turn to face him. His eyes are wide and playful, and his tongue is pressed behind his front teeth, as if he's waiting for something. Still waiting for me to catch on.

Suddenly, there's the sound of a violin playing, hot and sweet, all around us. A hundred jets of water erupt behind him. And then a hundred more. It's spectacular!

Lamb is watching the show on my face. He laughs again, as easily and as openly as he's done everything so far.

We're drinking milkshakes, and I'm feeling wobbly. "Is there alcohol in this ice cream?"

"There's alcohol in everything," Lamb says. "And you are the only one of us I've ever met who can't hold his drink." He's giggling so much, he's blowing bubbles in his milkshake.

I start giggling, too, sliding off my stool. (It's covered in fur. Most impractical.) I fall into the Normal sitting next to me. (He smells delicious. Milk-fed.)

Lamb takes my arm. "Come on, Prince Charles, you need a

drink." He drags me out of the ice-cream bar—but it isn't really dragging because I'm happy to go along. This is the best night out I've had in America.

This is the best night out I've *had*.

I don't really go out back home. Simon and I don't. (The wings, you see. And the fact that I hate drunk people.) (I really do. If I were sober, I'd hate myself right now. What a bore.)

Lamb's got me by the hand. And then he's got another man by the hand. A Normal bloke wearing a hockey-themed base-ball cap and a football shirt. He's drunk, too—boring!—and we're all dancing. There's music playing wherever you go on the Strip. Outside feels like inside. Lit up like a ballroom, speak-ers hidden in the trees.

The song is about a place called Margaritaville. I've never had a margarita. I should get one in a milkshake. Lamb pulls the man—and me—into a nook, not quite an alleyway, between two bars. The Normal struggles for just a second, then Lamb's not-so-small-now mouth is on his throat.

The man's neck goes limp. His head droops back, his hat falls off. His eyes immediately glaze over. I've seen that face on a deer before.

Lamb swallows deeply. He's still holding my hand. "Chaz," he says, stopping to take a breath, "come on." He pulls me closer, the man sandwiched between us—the fragrance is irre-sistible. My fangs have dropped. There's no room in my mouth for my tongue.

"I—I can't," I say.

"You can."

"We're in public."

"I promise it doesn't matter." He tugs the man's head back, exposing even more of his neck to me.

I turn away from them both, dropping Lamb's hand. "I can't."

Then Lamb's on me—he's let the man go—pinning me against a wall, his hands on my shoulders. His hair is covering one of his eyes completely and tickling my nose. All I can think about is the blood on his breath. *"Who are you?!"* he demands.

"I told you." My wand is in my jacket. I might be able to cast a spell. Maybe I could overpower him—

"What's your name?" he spits. Maybe spitting blood. I don't lick my lips. I don't. He presses his forehead into mine, crushing my head against the stone wall. "What's. Your. Name."

"Baz," I growl, wrenching my head away from his, to the side. "What's *yours*."

"Lamb will do." A flicker of fire appears at my shoulder. He's holding a lighter. "Now tell me why you're here."

"I already told you, I'm on holiday."

He brings the lighter closer to my hair.

*"I'm looking for the Next Blood!"* I say. It comes out too loud.

Lamb lets go of me, stepping back. His hand and the lighter are hanging at his side. "Oh, Chaz. Not you, too."

"What does that mean?"

He starts to walk away.

"Lamb!"

"You won't find them here," he says over his shoulder. "Not anymore."

"But you know where they are!" I'm running to catch up with him.

"Everyone knows where they are."

I grab his arm. I'm still a little drunk, to be honest. "I don't. I don't know where they are. And they have my friend."

He stops and looks at me, pouting thoughtfully. "That's true," he says.

"It *is* true."

"It's the first true thing you've said to me."

"Lamb—help me. *Please.*"

He studies my face for another beat, without a hint of sympathy, then cuts his eyes to the side. "Not here." He pushes my hand off his sleeve. "Tomorrow. Two o'clock. Lotus of Siam." He's already walking away, barely glancing back at me. "Now go get something to drink." And then he's disappeared into the crowd.

I stumble around for a minute, trying to remember which way we came from. I'm surrounded by landmarks, but they all feel the same. Lamb's right. I need a drink. Something. Rats. I haven't seen any rats. . . . I've seen a lot of little dogs riding around in handbags. . . .

I lean forward with my hands on my knees. *Get a grip, Basil. Breathe.* I close my eyes and inhale. The world smells like blood and alcohol, like milkshakes and burnt popcorn—

My head jerks up:

Simon Snow is standing a half block away from me. His wings are gone, and his hands are stuffed in his hip pockets. He isn't smiling.

I pull my mobile out of my jacket. It's dead.

# 45

## SIMON

The first ten minutes of surveillance were endless. After Baz got into the party. He wasn't talking, no one was talking. What if he'd already been twigged? What if they'd already snapped his neck?

But then there was a voice—*"Hello"*—and a name—*"Lamb."* And wasn't Baz being so slick? I grinned at Penny. "He's good," I said.

"He's going to be fine," she agreed.

"We should have gotten him an invitation," Shepard said. "Or faked one."

Penny rolled her eyes. "Next time we infiltrate a vampire enclave, I'll remember that."

Shepard frowned. "Isn't that exactly what we're planning next?"

"Shhh," I said. The vampire was talking to Baz about England. Raids and fires.

Penny sneered at the phone. "Oh, come off it. It's not genocide. *You're* the genocide."

I shushed her again.

"Baz should bring up the Next Blood now," Shepard said. "While they're talking about American vampires."

But Baz didn't bring it up.

He kept the conversation dancing—and then he left. He left *with* the vampire.

"No," I said to the phone.

Penny groaned. "For fuck's sake, Basilton."

Even Shepard was shocked. "Never go to a second location with an untrustworthy Maybe—that's rule number one! Or maybe rule number two. It's a top-five rule!"

"We have to trust him," I said. "He's there, and we're not. He's reading the room."

"Maybe he left because he didn't want to be in a room with fifty vampires," Penny said.

"Yeah." I nodded. "The odds are better if he leaves."

"The odds aren't good anywhere in this city," Shepard said.

*"Going down?"* we heard Baz say.

"Good man." I punched the bed. "Keep telling us where you're going."

*"Going out,"* Lamb replied.

After that, Baz didn't have to tell us where he was going— because his new friend Lamb narrated every step.

Two hours later, Penelope was lying down on the bed, eating champagne-flavoured jelly babies from the minibar. "Welcome to the Vampire History Walking Tour," she said. "Would you like an audio guide?"

Shepard was taking notes on a hotel notepad. "What?" he'd said when Penny tried to take it away. "These aren't your secrets. They're his."

I was pacing. I couldn't really process any of the interesting facts about the Luxor Casino or how vampires were key to desegregating the Strip in 1960. All I could hear was the constant *flirting.* The *"Chaz, this"* and the *"Chaz, that."* Lamb's voice was getting louder—closer—by the minute. And Baz was just letting it happen! Baz was playing along! He wasn't saying much, but I could hear him laughing.

Penny threw a jelly baby at me. "Relax, Simon. We have to trust him, remember?"

Lamb showed Baz fountains and lights. They went up in a Ferris wheel. They had burgers and milkshakes.

"If nothing else," Shepard said, "this is a great first date."

Penny kicked him in the side.

Baz's voice had got softer and mushier over the last hour, harder to hear over the music that was always playing in the background. He was on at least his third drink. (Baz never drinks with me. He says it's boring.)

*"They all smell so delicious,"* he said. *"Fermented. Like warm bread."* I was pretty sure he was talking about Normals.

Lamb laughed. Closer than ever. *"Come on, Prince Charles, you need a drink."*

Penelope sat up.

Shepard bit his lip.

We heard people laughing, doors opening, music shifting from doo-wop to twang—then, suddenly, nothing at all.

"What's that?" I looked at Penny's phone. "What happened?"

"He hung up," she said.

"Or his phone died," Shepard said.

I stood in front of Penelope. "Spell my wings off," I commanded.

She looked in my eyes, and I could see her deciding not to argue with me. ***"Every time a bell rings, an angel . . ."***

———

It isn't hard to find the ice-cream parlor—Lamb practically drew us a map—but he and Baz aren't here anymore. And I can't find them outside. They could be in any of these buildings, they could be in a car—I need Penelope and her "Lost and found" magic.

Then I see them: Lamb is pale, smaller than Baz, and nearly as vampire-handsome. (*Nearly* nearly.) He's got one of those *Downton Abbey* faces. Like he's just home from the Western Front.

Baz is holding on to his arm—clinging, really—and Lamb is leaning into him as if they're going to kiss.

Oh . . .

Right . . .

*Well* . . .

I clench my jaw and my fists. I guess this *is* what happens on first dates.

But then—Lamb seems to change his mind. He walks away.

Baz looks gutted.

I reckon I should walk away, too. . . .

Though maybe it will be easier in the end if Baz knows I'm here, that I saw them. Then he won't have to tell me.

# 46

## SIMON

Baz sees me and immediately turns away.

He tries to walk past me, as if we're strangers. "Go back," he says under his breath. "You aren't safe here—you're *surrounded* by vampires."

I catch his arm. "So are you."

He still won't look at me. "*Go back.* I'll meet you later. I have to hunt."

"I'll go with you."

"For Crowley's sake, Snow."

I squeeze his arm. I must look just as desperate as he did, when he was hanging on to that vampire. "You're drunk, Baz."

He shakes me off. "I'm just thirsty."

That's when I notice them—a man and a woman, both pale as paper, leaning against a black limousine, watching us. "We're being watched," I say. "Vampires."

He rubs his forehead. "Of course we are." Then he wraps his arm around my waist, and presses his head into my neck. "Act like I've just picked you up. Act like you're enchanted by me. Literally." (Ha—*act*. Someday I'll laugh about this. Someday maybe I'll laugh about my whole awful life.) He pulls away, taking me by the hand and leading me forward.

"Our hotel is the other way," I say.

He swings around and pulls me in the right direction. He's eyeing me like I'm his fifth drink. (He's pretending.) I'm looking like I'd follow him anywhere. (I'm not.)

Penny lets us into the hotel room. "Thank Morgana!"

"We've got a problem," I say.

Baz is holding his nose in his fist. "Not a problem, I just won't breathe."

"He's drunk and thirsty."

Shepard backs away from us. "I didn't think vampires could get drunk."

"Who died and made you queen of the vampires?" Baz honks, still holding his nose.

Penny has her tongue in her cheek, like she's plotting. "That's not a problem." She turns to the door—it's closed—and holds out her hand. The purple gem is in her palm. ***"Come home to roost!"***

After a moment, she opens the door. There's a cacophony in the hallway, flapping and squawking. Dozens of black birds fly into our room.

When the last one has trailed in, Penny steps into the doorway and casts one of her favourite spells—***"There's nothing to see here!"***—out into the hall. She closes the door and locks it.

The birds have settled on the bed. And the lamp. And the headboard. Baz plucks a parrot from the chandelier and twists its neck like it's a bottle of lager. He starts drinking it then and there.

"For snake's sake, Basil." Penny's swatting birds off the bed. "Do it over the bath."

Baz stumbles drunkenly into the bathroom. I've never seen him feed so messily. (I've rarely seen him feed at all, and never up close.) He leans over the bath, and I try to help him out of his fancy jacket. I know he won't want it ruined. "Here," I say, twisting him a bit. "You're getting blood on it." Once I have the jacket off, I start on his pink shirt.

Baz takes a long pull on the bird, then drops it in the bath, letting me unbutton him. "Go away," he says. "I don't want you to see."

"Too late for that, mate."

He has blood smeared on his bottom lip. There's another bird flapping around the bathroom (which was already a mirrored black nightmare, before the blood and the birds). Baz grabs it out of the air, and thwacks it against the sink. "Stop," he says. "Stop watching."

"Fine," I say, turning. "I'll round up the rest."

Shepard and I catch them—mostly in pillowcases and towels—while Penny hides under the duvet. (I might genuinely laugh about that part later.)

Baz drains every bird. The bath is a mass grave.

I stand in the doorway when he's done. He's facing the carnage, leaning against a wall, his bare back swelling with each breath.

"Better?" I ask.

"Better," he says. "Sorry."

"I can help you clean up—"

"No. I'll spell them. Thank you. Just . . . give me a moment?"

I do as he asks, closing the door.

"Clean up these feathers," Penny says. "I'm ordering room service."

# 47

## BAZ

This . . .

Is a new low.

I spell the birds away. Then the blood. And draw myself a bath.

I reheat the water twice just to avoid facing anyone. They've all seen me now. Even the Normal. Sucking down tropical birds. More like a mongoose than a man. At least real vampires look *cool* when they feed on people.

I know that now. I watched Lamb. (Is that his real name?) I watched him, and I didn't interfere. (My mother had that view once; she set herself on fire to stop it.)

I watched him drink from a man's neck, and I did nothing. Is that man a vampire now? *What have I become?*

Lamb talked to me about vampires for hours tonight, and I lapped up every word. To be honest—part of me wishes he were here right now, still talking.

I mean, I wouldn't want him here *right* now. Not in my current, undressed situation. Not that Lamb seems interested in me in that way—and not that I'm interested in him! I'm not attracted to *vampires*. Crowley.

I hold my breath and let my head sink beneath the bathwater.

There's a no-nonsense rap on the door. Bunce. "Come on out, Baz. The food's here."

I didn't bring fresh clothes into the bathroom, so I put my suit back on. (The shirt was ruined. I burned it.)

Bunce is sitting on one end of the bed with half a dozen covered dishes laid out in front of her. The Normal is sitting at the other end. Snow has pulled two leather chairs over. I take the empty one, and he hands me a small, open bottle of Coke.

Penelope starts uncovering the dishes: tiny cheeseburgers, fried chicken strips, mashed potatoes and gravy. I reach for a plate with steak and chips. My fangs are already dropping. (Because the humiliation never ends.)

Bunce hands me some cutlery wrapped in a cloth napkin and gives me a stern look. "Just eat, Baz. It's been a long day in a series of long days, and we've all already seen it all."

I sigh and fish my dead mobile out of my pocket. "How much did you hear?"

Bunce takes the phone and plugs it into a charger. "Enough to write a book called *Vampires of the West*."

"The last thing we heard was you ordering a strawberry milkshake," Shepard offers. "Then you cut out."

"We did *not* hear you ask about the Next Blood. . . ." Simon says, studying his miniature cheeseburger. He opens his mouth and shoves it in whole.

"I kept waiting for an opening," I say. My extra teeth make

me sound like a 12-year-old with braces. I set the steak plate back down on the bed. "I wanted him to trust me."

"Did he?" Bunce asks.

I feel like a fool. "No. He kept trying to get me to drink . . . someone. They treat this street like a twenty-four-hour buffet. And I kept saying, '*No, no, thank you*'—well, you heard me. It felt exceedingly rude to say no to the blood *and* the alcohol. Everything started to get blurry. When we left the ice-cream shop, he grabbed a Normal and pulled us both into a shadow, demanding that I drink with him—it was a test, I think."

Snow swallows fiercely. "He killed someone? Right in front of you?"

I meet his eyes. "No. He drank. And then he let the man go."

"He *Turned* someone right in front of you?"

"I—" I look down at my lap.

"Oh, I doubt he Turned him," Shepard says, smothering his chips in ketchup. "Vampires *hate* to Turn people. They either take a sip and let you go—or drain you dry and leave you dead."

When Shepard looks up, we're all staring at him. You could hear a gnome whisper.

"Which you already knew . . ." he says to me, "because you *are* a vampire. . . ."

Simon and Penelope turn back to me, speechless.

This is too much to digest. (This specific thing. Plus everything else. Plus two dozen tropical birds.) I shake my head. I shake it again. "I wouldn't drink," I say, picking up the thread. "I told him that I couldn't. In public. But he didn't believe me. He pinned me to the wall and demanded to know who I really was—what I wanted."

"What did you say?" Bunce asks.

"I told him the truth."

"Oh no," she says—while Shephard is saying, "Good plan, always for the best."

I rub my eyes. "I told him my first name, my real first name. And that I was looking for the Next Blood because they have my friend."

"Not slick," Bunce groans. "Not slick at all."

"So, what'd *he* say?" Simon asks.

"He told me to meet him at the Lotus of Siam. Tomorrow at two o'clock."

# SIMON

He's sitting there on a black leather armchair. He's sitting there in blue silk with red roses, shotgun scars shining on his pale chest. His hair is wet. His teeth are sharp. His feet are bare.

He used to be mine.

Maybe he still is. A little bit. Enough that I'm allowed to look at him.

But he's less mine than he was three hours ago, that's for bloody sure. He's less mine every minute we spend in this town.

"Lotus of Siam," Shepard says. "It sounds like a temple."

"It might be code," Baz says.

Penny's on her phone. "It's a Thai restaurant . . . in a strip mall."

"But not on the Strip?" Baz asks.

"No," she says. "A few miles away. We'll have to drive."

"Well, he did say that vampires usually stick to the Strip. . . ." Baz leans back in the chair. "Maybe he wants privacy."

I reach for another cheeseburger and the plate of mash. "We'll all go."

Baz shakes his head. "No. Then he *really* won't trust me. He can't know I'm a magician."

"He won't know you're a magician," Shepard says. "He'll just know you have friends."

Baz looks up at the ceiling, not having it. "Abso*lute*ly not."

"We'll go and sit at a different table," I say. "Just in case."

"You won't be able to hear anything! You're better off waiting outside and listening on the phone again."

"I want to go in," Penelope says, still looking at her mobile. "This says they have the best Thai food in North America."

Shepard is slapping the bottom of a miniature bottle of ketchup, even though his chips are already swimming it. "What are you going to ask Mr. Lamb when you get him alone?"

"About the Next Blood," Baz says. "We're starting at zero. So any information he shares is good information."

"Why would he tell you anything?" I ask.

"Well," Penny says, "the man does love to talk about vampires. . . ."

"We'll wait outside," I say, "and watch the door. But you *can't* leave with him this time." I want to add, *"And you can't flirt."*

Baz looks at me and nods. He looks sorry. "I won't."

Then he stands up and takes his steak over to the sofa by the window.

# 48

## PENELOPE

As much as I don't like hiding in a hotel room from a city full of vampires, I very much *do* like room service. My mother never lets us order it on holiday. Too expensive. But I figure we're in for a penny, in for a pound, re magickal credit-card fraud; I spend a king's ransom on breakfast. "Just leave it by the door," I shout when it arrives.

"You have to sign for it, Mrs. Pitch!"

I make a disgusted face, but the hotel employee can't see me.

"I'll get it," Shepard says. "You do the thing."

I stand back, with my amethyst clenched in my fist and a spell on my lips.

Shepard opens the door, and a man pushes a cart inside. He's wearing a black apron over a black suit and his skin is chalky grey. "You have to sign for it," he says flatly.

"I've got it," Shepard says, reaching for the folder.

I hold my stance until the grey man is gone and the door is closed. "Why would a vampire work as a bellhop?" I whisper, tucking my gem back into my bra. (I'm dead afraid of losing it. Magickal heirlooms are scarce enough in my family. My parents had to buy my sister's wand from a *shop*—it's so new, it squeaks—and my brother got stuck with a *monocle*.)

Shepard bolts the door. "Maybe he's new here."

I shudder at the implications.

We lay the food out on the bed. "Were you planning on feeding an army?" Shepard asks.

"I was planning on feeding *Simon*."

But Simon took off into Vampire-opolis this morning as soon as he woke up and realized that Baz was already gone. I tried to stop him from leaving. I stood in the doorway and forbade it.

"I'll be fine, Penelope. Move."

"The vampire risk is untenable, Simon."

"How is that different from the rest of my life?"

"You know damned well."

"I need some fresh air."

"You won't find it in the casino downstairs."

"Then I'll find it somewhere else. *Move*."

"Simon, I'm *begging* you, as the person who will cry the most at your funeral, *please* don't."

"Penny, if I don't get out of this room, I'm going to go off."

I should have said, *"You can't go off, Simon. You don't have anything left that goes. And I don't really care if you feel crazy— because crazy isn't dead."*

Instead I spelled his wings away and stood aside.

I'm still worried about him. And Baz. And Agatha. I start to cry. I can't help it.

Shepard is sitting at the other end of the bed. "What do you think?" His voice is gentle. "Denver omelette? Eggs Benedict? Corned beef hash?"

I point at the plate of eggs Benedict, and he hands it to me.

"I can leave," he says. "If you'd like to have some space to yourself."

"I am not letting anyone *else* walk out into that bloodbath!"

"Penelope. I didn't know you cared."

I roll my eyes, trying to keep myself from crying. "How does this place even *exist*? Where are the mages? If my mother were here, she'd burn this entire city down."

"Maybe we should call her," Shepard says.

"Ha!" I poke my fork into my poached egg and watch the yolk spill out. "She'd murder me first, then destroy Las Vegas."

"Nah, I'm sure she wouldn't."

"You've never met her. She's a force to be reckoned with, she's a—what do you call them—tornado."

Shepard laughs. He's eating the corned beef hash I ordered for Simon. "Then I'd love her," he says. "I used to be a storm chaser, you know."

"What's that, someone who chases older women?"

"No, someone who chases *storms*. Tornadoes, specifically."

"How do you chase a tornado?" My mouth is full, but I don't care. I have no one to impress here. I'm still going to try to erase Shepard's memory when all this is over. "Do you use magic?"

"You use meteorology. And your own senses. When a storm rolls in, you get into a car with your friends and you see if you can find it."

"To what end?"

"Because it's cool! To be close to all that power, to see the storm in action. The air changes. The hair on your arms stands up. It's like nothing else."

"It sounds like something else. . . ." I'm remembering Simon. I shake it off. "It sounds dangerous."

"Incredibly dangerous," Shepard grins.

"You said you *used* to be a storm chaser. Did it get too risky?"

"Nah, I just got more excited about chasing magic. It's a bigger rush."

Ah. Of course. I make a *hmmph* sound in my nose, and it comes out just as judgmental as I intended.

"What was that?" Shepard asks.

"Nothing," I say.

"That was you reaffirming your disapproval over my interest in magic."

"You can't just *chase* us," I say. "We're not storms. Or stories. We're people."

"I don't chase *people*."

I clear my throat and raise my eyebrows.

"I *usually* don't chase people," he says. "I just pursue . . . their acquaintance."

"And their secrets."

Shepard's dumping ketchup on his potatoes. (They send up a tiny bottle of ketchup no matter what we order, and Shepard practically drinks it with a straw.) "People *offer* up their secrets," he says. "You don't have to chase them. There's nothing people—and nixies and trolls and giants—would rather tell you than their secrets."

"Well, *I* don't feel like telling you anything."

"*You* are exceptional." He takes a bite. "This hash is also exceptional."

"Why would a magickal creature volunteer secrets to a Normal? The risk is absurd."

"They're not telling 'a Normal.' They're telling *me*—Shep! Their friend!"

"But you're preying on them! You're only their friend because you want to pin them in your weird scrapbook!"

He looks insulted. "I never take samples."

"*Blechch.* Listen to you!"

He leans towards me, over his breakfast. "Yes, okay, I strategically seek out and befriend magickal beings. But my friendship is sincere!"

"Sincerely manipulative."

"I object—"

"I can't decide if you're more like a starfucker or more like a big-game hunter."

"Neither! I'm a scientist, like . . . an explorer."

"Oh, good, that always turns out well for the explored."

"What can I do to convince you that I don't mean any harm?"

"What can I do to show you that you *do* harm even if you don't mean to? There isn't a magickal being or creature who can trust Normals. We keep magic secret for a reason. Because Normals would grind us into sausage if they thought they could extract our magic that way. Normals have annihilated elephants and rhinoceroses because you *believe* they're magic. They're not, by the way. They're just going extinct." I'm getting more upset as I talk. I drop my fork on my plate with a loud clatter and hide my face in my hands.

"Penelope," Shepard says, "nobody's going to grind your friend into sausage."

"How do you know?"

"Because," he says, "that doesn't work."

"I can't believe we're just sitting here, eating staggeringly expensive eggs, while Agatha is somewhere having the magic fracked out of her."

"Is there something else we could do to find her?"

"I don't know—there are spells. But we'd have to know where she is, generally speaking. And I'd need a lock of her hair. Or a photo. I didn't exactly pack for a séance."

"I'm sure you have a photo of Agatha."

"I'm sure I don't."

"On your phone."

I look up at him. "Merlin, you're right!" I take out my phone and open Agatha's Instagram account. "I have thousands of photos of her. . . ."

Shepard scoots closer to me, still eating his eggs and hash browns. He looks at my phone. "She's pretty."

"I know," I say glumly. "That just makes me worry *more* about her. She stands out."

"What do we do next?" he asks.

"Right," I say. "We'll need a candle."

"There's one in the bathroom."

"And I'll need your help."

"Me? I'm not even a lay-witch."

"As long as you have a soul, we're fine."

He looks a bit worried.

"Shepard, it's fine—this isn't dangerous."

He smiles. "My soul is at your disposal."


We clear away the breakfast dishes and I sit back down on the bed, motioning for Shepard to sit across from me. I set the phone between us and take Shepard's hands. He has objectively nice hands. I notice this because mine are objectively subpar. My palm-to-finger ratio is too high, and my fingers are chubby. There's nothing for it. We had to have Grandmother's ring enlarged to fit me.

But Shepard's hands are perfectly balanced with long, even fingers. He'd look dashing with a magic ring.

We sit with our legs crossed, and I levitate the candle over my phone. I've pulled up a nice photo of Agatha, a selfie on the beach. She looks happy. (Happier than I ever saw her at Watford.)

"Who are we contacting?" Shepard asks.

"Any spirits who can help us."

He twists his mouth like he's thinking. "Maybe we should specify 'friendly' spirits."

"Close your eyes," I say. I close mine, too, and whisper the spell—*"Kindred spirits!"*

# 49

## AGATHA

"Agatha . . . heyyyy, good morning. There you are. . . . How're
you feeling?"

"Aren't you going to tape my mouth shut?"

"That was actually a bio-glue. It's taking the place of stitches
in smaller surgeries. We're really excited about it. . . ."

"I want to leave."

"I was hoping we could talk."

"I don't want to talk. I want to leave."

"Well. I can't let you. I mean, you get that, right?"

"*No.*"

"What you have, Agatha . . . it's more important than you,
you know?"

"What's more important than *you*, Braden? Anything?"

"I have a role to play. I'm a participant in history. I've known
since I was a kid that I was born for big things. Some people
just are. You are, in your way. I think you might be the one who
unlocks it for us."

"I don't consent to this, to any of it."

"Agatha, this is bigger than one person's freedom. It's like eminent domain."

"*I. Am not. Eminent. Domain.*"

"Why are you fighting this? What are you fighting *for*? Do you even know?"

# 50

## BAZ

I almost called my father this morning.

I woke up in the bath (Penny and Simon took the bed, Shepard slept on the sofa), thinking of the Normal from last night, and how close I came to biting him—probably killing him.

I kill everything I drink.

I always thought it was safer that way. If I let the animals live, they might end up like me. (Can a vampire Turn a rat? Or a deer? Or a dog? I'd rather not find out.)

When I'm thirsty, this isn't really a decision. I just drink till there's no more to drink. I haven't ever tried to stop.

I've *never* tasted human blood before. I've had low-risk opportunities, of course; in football, there's blood everywhere— plus, I smashed Simon's nose with my forehead once, and he practically bled into my mouth.

But I've never wanted to cross that threshold. Like, you can say you've never tasted human blood or you can say that you have. And once you have, what does it matter whether it's one person or fifty?

And what if one taste wasn't *enough*? What if I couldn't stop thinking about it? (I already never stop thinking about it.)

What then? What options would that leave me? The way I understood it, mass murder or mass conversion.

But maybe I haven't understood *anything*.

Vampires hate to Turn people, Shepard says. Vampires are capable of "sips."

*I could call my father*, I thought to myself, while I was lying there in the empty bath. *And my father would pretend I'm not a vampire at all. And then I could pretend, too. And that would be such a relief.*

But then Bunce was at the door again. She came into the bath and made it rain magickally counterfeited hundred-dollar bills over my head. "Go buy something to wear on your vampire date," she said. "Hurry. I have to pee."

So now I'm walking up the Strip, dipping in and out of casinos to see what's on offer. There are luxury boutiques in nearly every one. I'm not sure who shops at these places—none of the tourists are wearing Gucci. Perhaps this whole street caters to vampires. . . .

I buy myself a few more suits. Plus clothes for the drive. A few changes for Simon. I see a dress that would look lovely on Bunce, but they don't carry her size. I buy it anyway. We can alter it with a spell.

I'm stealing.

We haven't paid for anything in a real way since Omaha.

Will the bills fade away in the register? Or on the way to the bank? Will this very nice shop assistant be fired? Will they trace any of it back to me, to us? Does it matter?

My father would be so ashamed.

Wouldn't he? Or would he perhaps understand? What would he say if I called him right now? Would he swoop in to help us?

No.

He'd summon me home.

*"Let Agatha Wellbelove's parents worry about whatever nonsense she's got herself into. You can't be tangled up in this sort of thing, Basilton—with these sort of people. You're—well, you're vulnerable. It's bad enough that Nicodemus Ebb has shown his face again. We don't need anyone asking questions about you."*

Aunt Fiona might listen. . . .

I call her instead, on impulse. Standing outside of a Prada. Standing next to a giant ornamental vase.

She doesn't pick up.

It doesn't matter. What could Fiona do? She couldn't get here before 2 P.M.

I walk back to the Katherine Hotel, laden with bags. A pale young man holds the door for me. I'm about to step in when I see something blue tumbling towards me on the wind—my mother's scarf.

I drop my bags to catch it.


When I get back to the room, Bunce and the Normal are having a séance. Holding hands on the bed, with a candle floating between them.

"Sorry to interrupt," I say.

Bunce falls back on the pillows, frustrated. Shepard catches the candle before it hits the bed.

"It's fine," she says. "It's not working. Wherever Agatha is, she's too far away for my spells to snag."

Bunce doesn't mention the other possibility, so I don't either. "Where's Snow?" I ask. He was still asleep when I left this morning.

She picks up her mobile. "He said he needed some fresh air. I told him he'd have to leave the state to find some—"

"You let him leave the room by himself?"

"I'm not his keeper, Baz."

"You bloody well are! It's your one job, Bunce."

"I couldn't stop him!"

"This city is literally crawling with vampires, Penelope. It's not safe for anything that bleeds."

"Which is why I've spent the last twenty-four hours in this hotel room. But you know Simon—he still acts like he's got an A-bomb strapped to his chest."

"Next time, spell him to the bed. Use a 'Stay put.' "

"Keep your sexual habits to yourself, Basil."

The door to the hallway opens. I whip out my wand. Bunce holds up her fist.

It's Simon.

He's cut his hair. . . .

He comes in, self-conscious, looking at the floor. His hair is cut short on the sides, the way he's always worn it—but the stylist left most of his new length on top. It's an extra generous spill of curls. More golden than ever from all these days in the sun.

That haircut cost more than his entire wardrobe.

"Look at you," Bunce says. "You're a brand-new man."

He shrugs. "Are we ready?" To me: "Is your phone charged?"


I take a cab to the restaurant, and they follow in Shepard's truck. I don't want to be seen driving up with anyone.

I changed into one of my new suits before we left. Black this time, with a heather-and-gold flowered shirt. (I suppose Bunce isn't the only one who can't let go of Watford purple.) "You're going to a strip mall," Simon said. "Won't you be overdressed?"

"Good choice," Shepard said, sizing me up.

He's right again: When I walk into the restaurant, Lamb is waiting in the lobby, wearing sunglasses and a three-piece suit. Tiffany blue. Which sounds vulgar, but very much isn't. He looks trim and fresh.

"There's a wait," Lamb says, "there's always a wait." He lifts his sunglasses. "Don't you look rosy. . . ."

I raise an eyebrow, which is my go-to move when I want to look cool but don't have anything cool to say.

Lamb's wariness from last night is gone. He seems to have reset himself to the easy charm from when we first met. So I reset, too. (I can be droll, I can pretend that nothing matters—it's practically my neutral state.)

A hostess takes us to our table. The restaurant is as unassuming inside as out. "Let me order," Lamb says, opening his menu. "The thum ka noon is superb."

He orders half a dozen things without bothering to translate for me. And then he sits back in his chair and smiles. Last night, I took that smile at face value.

"So . . ." he says, *"Baz."* He lets my name hang in the air. "What's that short for?"

"Barry," I say. Which is true. For some people. (I promised Bunce I'd do my best to lie today.)

"Baz suits you." Lamb's eyes are sparkling again; he must be able to turn it off and on. I can still feel it working on me. "Tell me why you want to know about the Next Blood, Baz."

"I told you—they have my friend."

"Where?"

"I don't know."

"Why?"

"I don't know that either."

"What *do* you know?" he asks. His sunglasses are pushed up above his forehead, and a lock of slippery hair falls into his eyes.

"That she was on a retreat with the Next Blood. She didn't know what they were. And then she disappeared."

"So you're not looking for them because you're interested in signing up. . . ."

I sit back. I hadn't realized I was leaning forward. "What? No."

"Because they are our enemy, Baz." Lamb's eyes are still smiling, but it's a sad smile, pulled down at the corners.

"Whose enemy?" I say. "The Vampires of Las Vegas?"

He licks his bottom lip and winces. "*Please* stop using that word. And none of that nonsense about 'reclaiming' it—it draws attention."

"Whose enemy?" I ask again. More quietly.

"*Ours,*" he says. "Our entire brotherhood, here and everywhere."

"Lamb. I don't understand. . . ."

He narrows his eyes. "I'm beginning to think you really don't. You're lying to me about—about *nearly everything*—but you really don't know what you're asking."

"Things are different in England, we're cut off—I thought you understood."

"I do."

We're interrupted then. A waiter has brought our first dish, some sort of crispy pork, still sizzling.

It happens immediately, and I don't know why I wasn't expecting it (pork is the *worst,* sometimes I'd have to leave the Watford dining hall on days they served bacon)—my fangs slide down into place.

Lamb is spooning some of the pork onto a dish for me. "The Next Blood," he says. "They call *themselves* that, by the way—" He glances up at me and stops speaking. His face falls. "*Baz.*"

He's noticed, of course he's noticed. I keep my mouth closed. (Haven't *his* fangs popped? Are they about to?) He looks shocked. And concerned.

"Take a deep breath," he says softly.

I do. That makes it worse. My sinuses are burning, and my mouth is full of saliva. It's all I can do not to bare my teeth.

Lamb moves the dish away from me, casually, like he's making room between us.

"Look at me." His voice is low.

I look at him. I lock my eyes on his.

"Breathe," he says.

I do.

"This is an animal response," Lamb says. "And you are not an animal."

He hasn't blinked. I nod.

"You are a man, Baz. *You* are in control, not the thirst. You don't just take what you want when you want it. I've seen that— you weren't even tempted last night."

A waiter sets another dish between us. Chicken. Coconut milk. Curry.

"How do you control yourself?" Lamb asks. "When you're thirsty, and there's a beating heart laid before you?"

"I—"

"Do *not* open your mouth."

I close my mouth tight.

"Think about it. . . ." he says. "Think of that control."

I nod.

"Now *take* control, Baz. You know how they feel when they break through your gums."

I nod again. I'm getting tearful.

"Imagine pulling them back. *Feel* them pulling back."

I close my eyes and let my head drop forward. It's hard to imagine my fangs retracting when they're filling up my whole mouth. I've never once kept them from popping. Have I ever once tried? My usual strategy is subterfuge and avoidance: Don't let anyone watch me eat. Ever.

Lamb lays his cool hand over mine on the table. "Pull them back. Tuck them in. You can do this."

I try then, I *really* try. I inhale. I pull my tongue into my throat. I suck in my stomach and hollow my cheeks. I pull my fingers into fists.

And then—my fangs jerk.

I try again, and they hitch back into my gums. (I don't know where they go; I'll bet Lamb could tell me.) I look up at him. My eyes must be wild.

He smiles at me, showing his perfectly normal—if a little too white—teeth.

He pulls his hand away then, and resumes dishing up a plate for me. There are now three steaming platters on the table. "You can do this," he says calmly, looking at the food instead of me.

He sets the full plate in front of me. I take a deep breath, thinking, *Stay, stay, stay.* My fangs start to slide down, and I pull them back in.

I keep doing it. I manage the whole meal. Chewing like I haven't since I was a child, with nothing extra in my way. Nothing accidentally cutting the inside of my cheeks. My jaw is trembling from the effort.

Neither of us talk. It doesn't seem like Lamb is even paying attention to me. But then the waiter takes my empty plate, and I meet Lamb's eyes again. I think I might be beaming. He's smiling, but his eyes are sad.

"Baz," he says, "how old are you?"

I don't have a lie ready. "Twenty."

"Right. And I'm thirty-four. How old are you really?"

I look up at the lights, at the acoustic tile ceiling. "Twenty."

I hear him exhale.

"*Right*," he says. "Let's talk about the Next Blood."

The restaurant is nearly empty. The waiter has brought us coffee with cardamom and evaporated milk. Lamb has shifted again, into a brand-new persona. He's not the charming Las Vegas enthusiast I met at the party. And not the terrifying vampire I met in the shadows. He's quieter now and so serious, he seems almost gentle.

"Power down your phone," he says. "And set it on the table."

I reach into my pocket—praying that Simon isn't presently going ballistic. I push the power button and set my mobile on the table. Lamb barely glances at it. I don't know if he suspects something or if he's just taking precautions. He sets his own phone next to mine.

"The Next Blood," he says, "are physically like us, but they're culturally something very different. They're a group of wealthy men and women, mostly men, who discovered our way of life. . . . Well"—he can't help but roll his eyes—"they *act* like they discovered it. And then decided to acquire it. They sought out our brethren, demanding to be Turned.

"It's not our way to Turn someone on request." He looks in my eyes. "As you know. But someone of our kind must have been blackmailed or seduced. They Turned one of the infidels, and that one Turned the others. And on and on . . ."

Lamb looks disgusted. "The Next Blood treats being one of us like being in a social club. Like the Rotary. They even have a board of directors that reviews new members." He waves his hand, like he can't believe any of this. His voice gets a bit higher. "It's like getting approved by the condo board. They see our lifestyle as an extension of their success—as if they have *earned* the undying, and earned the right to share it. They've doubled our numbers in San Francisco, just in the last year."

I'm horrified. Which Lamb approves of.

"Not a one of them pays any attention to social mores or tradition. They don't wonder why we've spent *millennia* building a different path. No, they're the next wave, the Next Blood. They don't care about history—they're too busy curing cancer and reinventing the Internet."

He takes his sunglasses off his head and sets them on the table.

"They threaten our safety and our freedom, Baz. What happens when the Bleeders realize that no one in Silicon Valley is ageing? By that time, will there *be* any Bleeders left to notice?"

"What—" I stammer. "What about the mages?"

"Those magicians are really under your skin, aren't they?"

I shrug.

"Well, it's like I told you, the Speakers largely ignore us. They seem to ignore each other, too; I'm not sure they even know what's happening—though they'll find out if the Next Blood get their way. They're intent on acquiring magic next."

"You can't acquire magic," I say. "You have to be born with it."

He rolls his eyes again. "The members of the Next Blood see it as a genetic challenge. These people are craven, they're already injecting themselves with placental blood—they were doing it before they were Turned!"

He leans in. "That's the worst of it for me. They don't even *drink*, Baz—they *transfuse*. They won't touch anything that hasn't been tested, frozen, and stored. I've heard they've started *pasteurizing.* . . ." Lamb's voice has got less gentle. His eyes have taken on a steely glint. He's sneering at me like—

"Nicks and Slick," I swear. (Bunce is a terrible influence.) "You think I'm one of them!"

Lamb lowers his chin. It's a challenge.

I start laughing. I can't stop. "Seven snakes!" I choke out. "Eight snakes and a dragon!"

"What is this," he asks, "are you stalling? Or hysterical? You know the terms of our treaty, the punishment is severe—"

"Lamb, no! I am hapless and ignorant and out of my depth, but I am not *that.*"

He narrows his eyes to slits.

I stand up. "Take a walk with me?"

I saw it on my way in. A pet shop, in the same strip mall as the restaurant. I know that Simon and Penny must be watching me. I hope they notice that I'm holding my hand in the thumbs-up position at my side. (That's their idiot sign for "all's well.")

I buy a rabbit. I tell the shop owner that I have one at home, and I'm familiar with them. And then I walk with Lamb around the corner, behind a skip.

"Anyone could be watching," he says. "It's broad daylight." Lamb caught on to my game as soon as we walked into the pet shop. He looks disgusted with me—but also a little curious. I used to share a room with that look.

"Block me," I say.

He stands closer.

I break the rabbit's neck in my hands and suck it completely dry. (I don't spill a drop on its white fur or my cuffs.) Then I drop it into the skip.

Lamb looks utterly put off. "Oh, Baz," he says in dismay. "No wonder you're so pale. You're malnourished."

I laugh. "But I'm not one of them."

"No," he says, eyeing me with one brow aloft. "You're a starving child from an oppressed nation who has barely met himself. But you are not one of them."

Lamb's still blocking me from view. Crowding me against the wall and the bin. I feel the rabbit's blood rising in my cheeks. My fangs haven't quite retracted.

He's close enough to make me feel my height advantage.

"Help me," I whisper. "Tell me where to find them. They have my friend."

# 51

## SIMON

"He's getting in the vampire's car," I say. "We have to stop this."

Penny grabs my arm. "He gave us the thumbs-up signal, Simon. We have to let him go."

"I wouldn't expect a vampire to drive a Prius," Shepard says. Like we have time for aimless musing.

I open the truck door and jump out. "Give me my wings back!"

"*Simon*"—Penny's being fierce—"get back in. We'll follow them."

The Prius is leaving the parking lot. I suppose I don't need wings. I start running after it.

After a few seconds, my wings burst out of my back. And then—I *disappear.*

I mean, I'm still here. I'm flying above the Prius, I can see it below me. But I can't see my own hands.

I wonder what spell Penny has cast, and when it will wear off. I don't take my eyes off Lamb's car.

# 52

## BAZ

I know I promised Snow that I wouldn't leave with Lamb. But I think I might have finally broken through with him. (Lamb.) What was I supposed to do—insist that we continue our conversation next to the skip?

I assume Simon and Penelope are right behind me. I'll call them again as soon as I get a chance.

Lamb's got his sunglasses back on. He cuts his eyes towards me without turning away from the road. "Have you always been . . ."

I raise an eyebrow. "A picky eater?"

He laughs. "Yes."

"Yes," I answer.

He grimaces. "But *why*?"

*Because I didn't want to kill anyone,* I think. But that argument won't work with him. Instead I say, "Because I didn't enjoy being bitten."

He glances over at me, turning his head this time. "Then someone was doing it wrong."

I shuffle in my seat. "It just feels barbaric to me. Why should I turn on humanity? I was born one of them."

"It's the natural way of things," he says. "It's the circle of life."

"There's no circle," I say. "We don't die. We aren't born. We don't reproduce."

"We do," Lamb insists. "We were. We can."

It's my turn to be put off. "Vampires have children?"

"Someone made you."

"My parents made me. A vampire killed me."

He sighs. "Then allow me to say how much I enjoy the company of your ghost."

I look out the window. I don't see Shepard's truck in the mirror.

"It might not be the circle of life," Lamb says. "But it is the food chain. I didn't see you feeling sorry for that pig we had for lunch. Or the rabbit you had for dessert. Everything eats something else."

I swing my head towards him. "What eats you?"

He raises an eyebrow, giving me a taste of my own medicine. "Existential despair."

I laugh out loud.

His eyes rest on me for a moment before turning back to the road. And when he speaks again, his voice is soft. "You won't feel so close to them, the Normals, once you've outlived your ties to mortality. . . . Someday, your parents will be gone. Your lovers will be gone. Everything left from the time when you bled will fade . . . and fall . . . and disappear. And then you'll realize that you're something different. There's no unbecoming, Baz. There's no sidestepping your true identity. All the rabbits in the world won't change you back. They'll just leave you thirsty."

Neither of us talk for a moment. I'm grateful he's driving. It keeps him from watching me.

Finally I say, "You must be very lucky."

Lamb tilts his head, waiting.

"To have found the only vampire in Las Vegas who'll listen to your speeches."

He bursts into laughter.

Lamb *lives* at the Katherine. He has a flat near the top, clearly decorated with his own furniture. (There's no black leather. And no black cockatiels.) There's a sitting area at one end and what looks like a bedroom behind a cloudy glass wall.

I sit on an antique sofa covered in turquoise jacquard. Lamb sits near me in a chair built of elaborately carved wood. It looks very old; everything here does. He's taken off his jacket. "So," he says, "I gather you weren't given a choice. . . ."

I know what he means. "It doesn't matter."

"It matters to me, as your new friend."

"I was *not* given a choice," I say, brushing a white rabbit hair off my trousers. "Were you?"

"I predate choice," he says, pushing his hair out of his face with both hands.

"How so?"

He lets his hair fall. "I predate everything. All my people understood was war and hunger, and demons who came in the dark."

"Is that what happened to you? Did a demon come in the dark?" I'm not used to thinking of vampires like this, as fellow victims.

"It's what happened to my brother," he says. "Then my brother came for me."

"Because he wanted a comrade?"

"Because he was *thirsty*. Because he'd already killed our

parents. I put a table leg through his heart before he could finish me off, too."

We're both quiet.

"I'm sorry," I say finally.

"It wasn't his fault—he had no one to teach him. He had no community." Lamb leans forward, his forearms on his thighs. "The culture that we've built here is hundreds of years in the making. We've lifted ourselves up. What happened to you—what happened to me—that isn't our way anymore."

"So you don't Turn people?"

"Rarely. Most of us don't want the chaos and competition. Almost no one wants the responsibility."

"Then why don't you stop the Next Blood?"

"There's been talk. . . ."

"Just talk?"

"It's difficult to persuade our kind into a war," he says. "The longer you live, the more you value your life. You start treating yourself like a precious antiquity."

"Are you sure you're not just sitting back, waiting to see if the Next Blood can figure out how to steal magic?"

Lamb smiles, grimly. "If I thought they'd share it, I'd consider it. But they have no interest in us or our history. They don't even identify as our brethren."

"They don't identify as vampires?"

"Oh no, they're the next stage of *humanity*. Go on, tell me—why do they have your friend?"

"I'm not sure."

"What's his name?"

"Agatha."

Lamb's eyebrow twitches. "Ah."

I stop myself from saying, *"It's not like that."*

"What do they want from her?"

He's going to find this out anyway, if he helps me—"She's a magician."

His hands drop between his knees, and his blue eyes are wide. "Talk about starcross'd lovers!"

"I'd rather not."

Lamb rubs his chin. "So . . . your girlfriend is one of their Speaker guinea pigs. . . ."

"There are others?"

He shrugs. "Well, there must be."

I feel sick to my stomach. I scoot to the edge of the sofa. "Lamb, please, I'm not asking you to get involved. Just point me in the right direction."

"You wouldn't get anywhere *near* them," he says. "They have guards, guns, archers. . . ."

"Just tell me what you know."

"You'll be killed, Bazza."

"I'm not a precious antiquity, remember?"

"You are certainly not an antiquity."

Suddenly—from one breath to the next—Lamb is sitting next to me on the sofa. Before I can even react, his lips are by my ear. I wait for him to bite me—can you be Turned twice?

"There's something in the room," he says, voice so low only a vampire sitting right next to him could pick it up. "Can you hear its heartbeat?"

I close my eyes. Can I? I hear my own heart, faint and always a few beats slow. I hear Lamb's, a similar dirge. Ah . . . there. I *can* hear it—and I recognize it.

"Simon," I say, my eyes flying open.

In that moment, Lamb's empty chair lifts up and slams down into the floor. One of the wooden legs seems to tear itself off and fly towards Lamb's chest. His fangs are out. He grabs the leg midair and raises it like a club—

"No!" I shout, catching Lamb's arm.

Just as the door to his flat flies off its hinges.

Bunce is standing there, with the Normal, holding out her purple gem.

"Hands in the air, bloodsucker, or I'll burn this whole city to the ground."

# 53

## SHEPARD

The vampire holds the stake in the air, giving Penelope some thousand-year-old stink eye. She doesn't budge. He drops it.

I can hear Simon flapping around.

Baz dodges in front of Lamb, holding his hands out to the room. "Snow, I swear I'll throttle you."

"What is this, Baz?" Lamb sounds more confused than threatened. "Are you in league with these mages?"

"No." Baz is still blocking Lamb from an invisible Simon. "Not 'in league.' They're my friends, they're trying to protect me—*which I do not require*. What part of 'thumbs-up' don't you people understand?"

Simon shouts back: "What part of 'Don't leave with him' don't you understand?"

"I'm fine!"

"You're in a vampire's bedroom!"

"I *am* a vampire!" Baz says. "And this is a studio!"

"A vampire," Lamb says, then looks at Penelope. "A mage . . ." He looks at me. "A . . ."

"Bleeder," I say, waving. "Name's Shepard."

Lamb nods and looks over Baz's shoulder, where Simon is disturbing the atmosphere. "And what is this?"

"His boyfriend!" Simon snarls.

*Huh.* I wasn't sure. I mean, I *wondered.* . . .

Baz covers his face.

"Boyfriend?" Lamb repeats. "What about *Agatha*?"

"There isn't a simple explanation for any of this," I cut in, smiling. "But there is an entertaining one. And I swear, no one here means you any harm."

A vase topples off a table near the spot where Simon is flapping.

I keep smiling. "Maybe we could all sit down and talk?"


Fifteen minutes later, we're all sitting on Lamb's couches. Well, except for Simon, but that seems fair. He did break the only other chair. Lamb keeps looking over at the pieces and frowning, like he'd really rather fix his fancy chair than deal with any of us.

Lamb's *much* less vampirey-looking than Baz. (I've been thinking that Baz must come from a long line of vampires—a Transylvania original, with that long black hair and widow's peak. But I guess that isn't how vampirism works. . . .) Lamb's got a soft face and a head full of soft, shiny hair. He looks exactly like you'd expect an English person to look if you'd only seen them in Jane Austen movies—sort of pencil-drawn and pretty. He's pale, of course, and gray around the eyes. But he's not as gray all over as Baz. Not as drained and ghostly.

If this is what a vampire is supposed to look like, then maybe Baz is a vampire with an iron deficiency.

Lamb's definitely not scared of us. Even though we have

magic and numbers on our side. He's treating us like four kids who just confessed to throwing a baseball through his window.

Baz is making our case: "I was telling you the truth. Agatha *is* my friend. We're just trying to find her."

Lamb frowns some more. "How can you be friends with mages? They hate us."

"We grew up together," Penelope explains. "We didn't know Baz was a vampire for years."

"*I* knew," Simon says.

Baz shakes his head, rolling his eyes. "Literally nothing you say is helpful."

Lamb looks right through Simon. "Did you grow up with them, too, invisible boy?"

"He's not usually invisible," Baz mutters.

"A vampire, *two* mages, and a Bleeder." Lamb sighs and stands up. Every one of us flinches. "I'm going to need a cup of tea."

"Oh, thank magic," Penelope says at the same time as Simon says, "Tea?" and Baz says, "Crowley below, please let us have some."

I always accept food and drink from Maybes, though it can be a risky business. (My mother would be horrified if I ever turned down food as a guest in someone else's home.) But I'm surprised to see *this* bunch being so polite. I turn to Penelope, sitting next to me on an antique loveseat. "You're not worried about being poisoned? Or scalded?"

"I'll worry after I have my tea," she replies.

Lamb brings out a tray. Simon gets a plastic casino mug. The rest of us get china.

"I've been thinking," Lamb says, pouring Penelope's tea, "and I can't come up with a single reason to help you. Or even to keep listening."

"Common decency," Penelope suggests—and the vampire actually laughs. His whole face crinkles up when he does.

"We'd be in your debt," Baz adds.

Simon scoffs. "We would not!"

"You're already in my debt," Lamb says. "You're still alive."

"We could say the same of you," Penelope counters.

The vampire chuckles. "You're really quite funny," he says to her. "I know you don't mean to be."

I hold out my still-empty cup, leaning a bit in front of her. "The reason to help them," I say, "is that you share an enemy."

Lamb looks at me and starts to pour. He's listening.

I nod toward Penelope and Baz and (probably) Simon. "They're not stupid. They know they don't stand much of a chance against the Next Blood, even if you help them. But they're going to try anyway. And I promise you this—they won't go down without a fight."

I sit back with my teacup. "These Silicon Valley vampires have never tangled with Speakers before. They don't know what it's like to be hunted and cornered with wands. They've never taken significant losses. Well . . . *they'll learn.* Even our worst-case scenario benefits you—we'll cause chaos for the Next Blood, we'll get in their way."

Lamb is sitting again, next to Baz. He narrows his eyes at me. "How do you know that I consider the Next Blood an enemy?"

"Everyone knows that Las Vegas is at war with the Next Blood," I say. "And you're the king of Las Vegas."

"The Vampire King?!" Penelope shouts at me, as soon as we're in the elevator. "When were you going to tell us he was the fucking Vampire King?"

"I wasn't sure!" I really wasn't—not till I said it out loud, and Lamb smiled and bared his fangs at me.

"You needed to be *sure*? 'I *think* he *might* be the Vampire King,' you could have said to us. Or, 'Hey, guys, did you know there's a Vampire King? There is! And this could be him!' "

"I'd only heard him described once," I say, "and it was from a drunken ditch imp."

"What was the description?" she asks.

"Baby-faced and beautiful, and slick as oil on ice."

Simon huffs. Penelope punches me hard. "That's obviously him, Shepard! For snake's sake!"

The elevator doors open.

"We get our things, and we go," she says. "Shepard, you get the truck. We'll meet you out front."

Baz is frowning. "But Lamb might yet help us—"

Penelope looks ready to punch him next. "The jig is *up*, Baz! We can't sleep under the Vampire King's roof! Especially now that he knows what we are."

"He doesn't know what I am," Simon gloats.

"A foolhardy oaf?" Baz says. "I think he got that, actually."

"You wouldn't call me that if I'd rescued you!"

"I didn't *need* rescuing!" Baz hisses. "I was getting to him. He was *listening*."

"More like *you* were listening," Simon says. "While he told you a bunch of fairy tales about vampires saving princesses and slaying dragons."

"For the last time, Simon Snow, only a depraved savage would slay a dragon!"

"I wasn't *trying* to kill it!"

We turn a corner—our room is just up ahead. "Five minutes," Penelope says, typing something into her phone. "Get your stuff and get out."

Baz and I stop walking.

"Guys," she says, getting ahead of us. "Come on."

"Penelope," I say quietly. She finally looks up and sees the two people standing at our door: a man and a woman, both wearing very expensive suits.

# 54

## PENELOPE

The woman, grey and graceful—I'm getting very good at spotting vampires—opens the door to our hotel room. "After you."

"We were just getting our things," I say.

"After. You."

They follow us into the room. I'd set them both on fire right now if I didn't think this entire hotel would go up in flames. "There's no need to see us out," I say, with as much imperiousness as I can muster. "We're actually in a bit of a hurry."

"Have a seat," she says, motioning towards the bed.

Shepard and Baz sit. I can feel Simon hovering beside me. "What is this?" I demand. "We weren't planning to make trouble, but you can tell your king that we won't be threatened!"

"I'm not a king, you know. It's an elected position." Lamb is leaning in the doorway. "There's a council, term limits. A system of checks and balances . . ."

"Lamb—" Baz stands up. "You changed your mind."

The vampire looks at Baz for a second, then steps into the room, walking towards him. "I just needed a few moments to myself to consider the possibilities. Your Bleeder has a point, I think: This is a rare opportunity."

He says all this to Baz. Like the rest of us don't rate eye contact. Baz, fool that he is, looks hopeful. "So you'll help us?"

Lamb nods, stopping just in front of Baz. "And you will help us."

I wonder how Simon is coping with this conversation. I consider casting a paralysis spell on him, just in case he isn't coping *well*—but he might drop out of the air and injure himself.

Lamb turns his head towards Shepard and me, but his eyes stay on Baz. "*I'm* not a king. This city is bigger than me—I'm just its most dedicated public servant. But the Next Blood . . . they have a king. They can't function without him. I don't know where your missing friend is, but you can be sure that Braden Bodmer does. He's the one snatching up spare Speakers and taking them apart to see how they tick."

Simon, somewhere beside Lamb, growls.

Lamb turns to the empty space. "You're going to help me kill him."


Well, at least there's a plan.

The Vampire King sits in one of the leather chairs, his two well-dressed friends flanking him now, and lays it out for us:

Apparently the Next Blood's headquarters (does every vampire cult have headquarters? How many American towns are vampire citadels?) are in San Diego. But they have a facility near Reno.

According to Lamb's intelligence (there are vampire *double agents*), all the NowNext leaders will be there this weekend; they're having some kind of ceremony. "We'll go in as quietly as we can," he says. "Under the radar. But if we can't go quiet, we go loud. The Bleeder—"

"Shepard," Shepard interrupts.

Lamb pauses to smile at him, like he's making a note to eat him later. "*Shepard* was correct: The Next Blood aren't fighters. They're scientists and software engineers. Chaos may very well work in our favour."

Well, there's Simon accounted for.

Merciful Morgana—*Lamb's face* when my spell finally wears off, and Simon appears out of thin air. Lamb is done talking, and he and his minions are leaving to get their own team in order, when *pop*, there's Simon, glowering, between them and the door.

Lamb takes in Simon's wings and tail, then turns to Baz and shakes his head. "Not just a magician, Baz, but a *disfigured* magician."

As soon as they're out the door, Simon throws a lamp at it. "Fuck this!"

Baz sets a pile of clothes on the bed and starts folding a dress shirt.

Simon puts his hands on his hips. "Well, we're not going with him."

"Of course we're going with him," Baz says.

"We are not getting into *a car* with *a vampire* so he can lead us into a vampire *nest!*" Simon shouts.

Baz throws the shirt onto the bed and shouts back: "Isn't that why we came here?! Isn't that precisely what we asked him to do?!"

"We came here to find Agatha!"

"He's taking us to Agatha!"

"Is he?" Simon's standing directly across the bed from

Baz. "Or is he going to dump us in the desert wearing cement shoes?"

"That doesn't even make sense. Why would they put cement on our feet in the desert?"

"You know what I mean!"

"Lamb isn't going to hurt us!"

"How do you *know*?!"

"Because I trust him!"

Simon looks like he was ready to shout some more, but now he doesn't know what to say. He takes a step back. "You trust him."

Baz nods. "I do. I don't—I don't think Lamb would lie to me."

Simon clenches his jaw. If he still had magic, I'd be sheltering in place. "Oh, really. Well, it's a good thing he doesn't know what—"

"I wouldn't assume we have privacy," Shepard cuts in. "Under this roof."

He's right. This is Lamb's hotel. Lamb's city. I've scanned the room for bugs, but not recently.

Simon is boiling with rage.

Baz is simmering. He deliberately picks up his shirt again. "Fine. We don't have to accept his help. We can head off on our own, without any clues or direction. I'm sure Agatha can wait."

"No," I say. "Baz is right, this is our only lead. If Lamb wanted us dead, he'd just kill us here. Or try." I raise my voice for the benefit of anyone who might be listening: "*We can hold our own in a fight.*"

Baz looks at the Normal. "You should leave now, Shepard. There's no reason for you to endanger yourself further."

"I can think of plenty," Shepard says. "You're not getting rid of me yet."

Baz turns to Simon. "Well, Snow?"

Simon knocks over the remaining lamp. Then scrubs his fingers through his hair. "If you really think he's taking us to Agatha, I'll go. But I'm not killing some rival gang leader for him."

"Right," Baz says, "because of your moral objection to slaying vampires."

Simon just huffs.

Lamb told us to be ready to leave when he calls for us. Baz finishes packing, I'm not sure why—we aren't taking luggage on the rescue mission. I change into my old clothes, so I can think. Then I lie on the bed, making a mental list of spells to kill vampires. When Lamb's "people" come for us, I'm up to sixty-three.

# BAZ

I don't know why I trust Lamb.

Maybe because he hasn't lied to me yet.

And because, when he looks at me, I swear I can feel him looking out for me. It could just be that I'm one of his charges. If he's the king, or the mayor, or what have you, that's his job, right? Protecting the interests of his people? I'm one of his people. Or what have you.

I'm sure Snow would love to hear this theory. *"I trust him because of our vampire kinship."* Though that's better than, *"I trust him because of the way he looks at me."*

Simon won't look at me. He's on the bed with Penny, still wearing his filthy shoes, probably thinking about how much he hates me.

I thought we might come to blows just now; the energy felt so like it had when we were still at Watford, screaming at each other over our school beds. (Though there's no Roommate's Anathema to keep us from killing each other here.)

Those fights used to feel so good. It meant getting to look at Snow. Getting his attention. Having a place to hurl all my feelings for him, even if they came out spiked and razor sharp.

Fighting doesn't feel good anymore. It feels like breaking something because you don't know how to fix it.

I tidy my things, and wash my face. I think about changing into something less wrinkled, but we're just piling into another car.

Now isn't the time to be heartbroken. We don't know what we're driving into tonight, but it's surely a battle.

# SIMON

Right, right, right. So we're just trusting vampires now, is that how it is?

Just telling vampires all our secrets, and then waiting for them to do the right thing? Where I come from, you don't tell vampires secrets! You don't *negotiate* with them. You bloody well don't let them drive!

The Mage used to say—

I mean, I reckon the Mage *did* negotiate with vampires— but that's what made him corrupt! It's one of the *major* ways he proved corrupt in the end!

Vampires are *banned*. They're actually forbidden. It's the law.

They're like pitbulls or adders, simply not allowed in the World of Mages. Because you can't trust them not to murder you!

And, yes, I get that Baz is a vampire. I appreciate the irony. But *he* hates vampires more than anyone! Which is the only reason you can trust him!

I mean, not the only reason.

I'm just saying—

I'll be damned if I—

The king of the vampires! We're trusting the *king* of the vampires? Because he asked us to? Because he asked us nicely with his pretty blue suit and his pretty blue eyes. . . .

I'll be good goddamned.

We don't need *his* help to save Agatha. I've saved Agatha literally *dozens* of times without asking *any* vampires for help. (I mean, Baz pitched in once or twice.) (He complained the whole time.)

Bloody—

*Vampires!*

I mean, we've been here thirty-six hours, and now we're Team Vampire? Maybe we should summon a few demons and get their help, too.

I have rescued bloody everyone I know, including Baz, again and again, and I never *teamed up* with the enemy to do it. (Unless you count Baz. There, at the end. I mean . . .)

This isn't how you rescue someone!

We've been here thirty-six hours, and apparently Baz doesn't hate vampires anymore. Now, apparently, he trusts some. At least one, *apparently.* "King" of the vampires—does that include Baz now? Is that what he is? A loyal subject?

You can't just trust the first handsome vampire you meet!

I mean . . .

This isn't how we do this.

This isn't how it's *done*.

I'll be damned if I follow a vampire into the desert!

I mean . . .

# PENELOPE

We leave after dark. Lamb tries to split us between two rugged-looking four-by-fours, but Simon and I refuse to be separated. Me, quietly. Simon, less so.

Simon doesn't want to get in any of the cars. He wants to ride above us, like a winged escort. Lamb won't have it. "I said 'under the radar,' mage. Not literally through it."

Finally, to accommodate us, Lamb borrows an even larger vehicle from one of the other sharply dressed vampires. Baz shoves Simon into the back seat and climbs in after him. Shepard volunteers to ride up front with Lamb. I take the middle row.

It's startling when you leave Las Vegas, the transition from bright lights to black sky.

We'll get to the NowNext facility around dawn, Lamb says. I'm trying to visualize it. "If we're sneaking up on their facility, wouldn't we have better luck at night?"

"*They* would have an advantage at night," Lamb says. "Enhanced senses."

"But wouldn't your lot have that same advantage?"

Lamb is dismissive. "My friends and I have kept ourselves alive through centuries of daylight—we'll be fine. Besides, we're trying to tip the scales in your favour, young mage. You're the ones leading the charge."

"Why are *we* leading the charge?" Simon demands. (If we weren't leading the charge, he'd demand to know why not.)

"Because you have magic wands," Lamb snaps.

We've already been through this, back in the hotel room:

The Vampire King is offering us intelligence and support. There's a fleet of four-by-fours following us into the desert. At least fifty vampires. They'll deliver us to NowNext's back door. But Lamb says we'll have to use magic to break into the facility and make the first strike. "If we could have quashed the Next Blood with brute force, we would have done so already."

"Tell us more about the building," Simon says. "What sort of defences do they have? Is it a home? A barracks?"

Lamb keeps his eyes on the road. "It's a laboratory."

# BAZ

All right. Well. We knew it was bad.

That doesn't affect our odds. If anything, it helps. Better a lab than a fortress.

I've got spells ready. For getting in and staying low. "Open sesame." "Little pig, little pig." "Now you see it, now you don't."

I know Lamb expects us to fight these other vampires, and I'd like to—I'd like to *end* them—but Snow's right: The only thing we *have* to do is find Agatha. I've got spells for that, too. "Show me the way." "Come out, come out, wherever you are." . . . (That's what Fiona used when the numpties had me.)

I may not be a very good vampire, but I'm an excellent magician. First in our class. And Bunce *would* have been first in our class had she stayed in school. And Simon, even a powered-down Simon, is no one you'd want to meet in a dark alley. Or a bright hallway.

I believe we can do this. I believe Lamb believes we can do this. Why would he bring a small army of his own vampires if he didn't think this was a fight we could win?

"So we sneak in first . . ." I say. I'm in the back seat, so I have to shout to be heard over the air-con.

"Not you," Lamb says. His voice carries. "The magicians." He means Simon and Penny.

"But there are only two of them."

Lamb scoffs. "One mage murdered every vampire in Lancashire."

"Beatrix Potter," Bunce supplies.

"Have you been to this facility yourself?" I ask, ignoring her.

"No. They know my face too well. And, besides, only their top-ranked members visit the laboratory. But we know of it. We've been monitoring . . . the situation."

"Can they do it?" Simon asks.

"Do what?" Lamb replies. "Keep us out?"

Simon hunches forward. "Can they take someone's magic?"

Lamb looks irritated, like Simon hasn't been paying attention. "They aren't trying to take it. They're trying to transplant it."

"Whatever—can they do it?"

"I should think not," Lamb says. "If they could, they'd be ruling the world."

"Magicians have magic," Simon argues. "And they don't rule the world." You can tell as he says it that he's not sure it's true. I'm not sure it's true. What do we know of the world?

The World of Mages is a regional clique.

Watford is an isolationist boarding school.

My parents wouldn't even let me use the Internet.

"Magicians live in fear of being discovered," Lamb says. "The Next Blood live in fear of nothing."

# PENELOPE

We drive through the night. Past miles and miles of barren land. I don't understand this part of America. The heat, the sand, the small towns. Why would you live somewhere that seemed to be doing its best to tell you to go away?

None of us feel like talking. We can't really strategize. Not without outing Baz as a mage, anyway. He and I keep exchanging significant looks, but I'm not sure what we're telling each other.

Even Shepard has run out of small talk. He tried to draw Lamb into a conversation when we first set out, but Lamb ignored him, and now I think Shepard has fallen asleep—two feet away from a vampire!

I suppose I've done that loads of times.

I wish Simon would go for a kip. He really needed this fight to start three hours ago. I can tell he doesn't know what to do with himself; he won't stop huffing and fidgeting. And he refused to let me put his wings away, so they're crowded against the side of the car and the roof.

This is the moment—these are the hours—when I would normally come up with a plan. And I'm trying. There's no blackboard, but I've got two columns sketched out in my head: *What We Know* and *What We Don't*.

What do we know in this scenario? (I can practically hear Agatha say, *"Nothing."*)

*1. That vampires have Agatha.*
*1b. Vampires with ambition.*

And what don't we know? Well, that column is endless. . . .

*1. Whether Lamb knows what he's talking about.*
*2. Whether we can trust him.*
*3. Whether Agatha is okay.*
*4. How to get her out.*

I've come up with thirty-four additional spells for killing vampires. But all the really good ones would kill Baz, too.

I'm far less concerned about sparing Lamb and his friends. Really, if we live through this, we should take out Las Vegas next. Maybe that would redeem us with the Coven. *"Yes, we broke every rule in the Book. But we also de-vampired the American West."*

"If we live through this" being the operative clause, unfortunately.

Simon and I have seen plenty of action over the years. We've saved Agatha from more serious threats than this in our sleep. (Literally. Second year. The Humdrum sent counting sheep. It was epic.)

But that was a different version of us. Post-Humdrum Penelope and Simon just barely survived seven drunken Renaissance Faire vampires, even with Baz's help. And without Shepard, we would have lost to a goat and a skunk in western Nebraska. We *did* lose to that dragon.

We are out of our depth and nearly a hemisphere out of our comfort zone. And it occurs to me, three hours north of Las Vegas, that we are very probably going to lose.

Lamb isn't expecting us to *win*. As he heads into the desert, following the speed limit.

We're just the boiling oil he's pouring over the castle wall. He's expecting us to take a few of the other guys down with us. He's using us to create a diversion.

That is in fact *exactly* what Shepard proposed to him. Shepard doesn't think we're going to win, either! He's just hoping for a good show. He's probably going to find a nice safe hill where he can watch and take notes. (That's how the Americans wrote their national anthem.)

Only Simon, Baz, and I care about finding Agatha. And now that I think about it, I'm not sure why I ever thought that was enough. . . .

I'm not sure why I thought we had to do this alone.

My mother is one of the wisest witches in the world. She's one of the most powerful mages in England. And never once did I seriously consider asking her for help.

Pre-Humdrum Penelope never had to. I had the most powerful mage in the world as my best friend. Together we were invincible.

Oh, hell . . . that was never true, was it?

I was never invincible. I was just in the vicinity.

Simon has no power now, and I'm as powerful as I ever was. Which, it turns out, isn't very powerful at all.

# 55

## BAZ

I don't know what I was picturing. Another improbable American city jutting out of the sand. More American suburbs. Office buildings that look like they came flat-packed from Ikea. Not this. . . .

The Next Blood have set up shop far from the edge of any town. It's nearly daybreak when Lamb turns off the road, directly into the desert.

Snow has spent the whole night on the edge of his seat, fidgeting and glaring at the back of Lamb's head, watching his every move. (Lamb has done nothing but drive and adjust the satellite radio.) Every time Simon moves, he clips me with his wing. I keep shrugging him off. And then he pushes back, like *I'm* the one bothering *him*. He won't let us put away his wings—which have spikes, by the way—even for the ride. He's being relentlessly childish, and I ran out of patience for it hours ago, back in Nevada. Are we still in Nevada?

If I'd known I was going to spend all night in a car with three bleeding hearts, I would have drunk more than one pet-store rabbit. And brought more Altoids. (They're very good for blocking out blood smells. Especially the spearmint flavour.) I refuse to ask Lamb to stop for me to hunt—he'd probably offer me a flask instead.

Simon pokes my ear with his wing.

I shrug him off.

He snaps his wing to shove me back.

"For Crowley's sake, Snow! It's like being caged in with a bear!"

"Nearly there," Lamb says coolly.

Simon and I both look out the window. We don't seem to be *nearly* anywhere.

But Lamb is slowing down. He checks the line of cars behind us in the rearview mirror. We park at the edge of a hill—a hill of sand—and the other cars park beside us. "All right," he says, turning in his seat. "Are you ready?"

Bunce nods. Even though she looks less ready than I've ever seen her. She tumbles out of the car, her right hand clenched in a fist. Snow and I follow. Shepard is still asleep, and I can't think of a reason to wake him.

The other vampires are already standing outside their cars, watching us.

Lamb faces us, talking softly. "There's no time to waste. You'll be able to see the laboratory as soon as you crest the dune. It's the only building. Signal to us when you're in."

Snow is popping his knuckles, and cracking the joints in his wings. "Let's go."

"Right," I say to Lamb. "How should we signal you?"

He frowns, clamping his hand around my arm. "Baz, I meant

it. The mages will go in first—they've got the edge. We don't risk our lives senselessly."

"Lamb—" I start to argue.

Simon cuts me off: "It's fine. Penelope and I have this. We'll signal if we need you."

Penelope doesn't look so sure. "I think Baz—"

"It's *fine*," Simon says again, unfurling his wings like whips. The vampires are all watching him. They've never seen anything like him. No one has.

He lifts off, flying up the hill.

Penny keeps looking at me, both of us trying to communicate something big with our eyes. Something like—*"It's all right. I'm right behind you. We've got this."*

She finally turns away, following Simon. He touches down near her, then lifts up again. He's twitching with energy, spoiling for a fight. Penny's wearing her tartan skirt and knee socks again. The backs of her knees are dimpled.

It's all right, I tell myself. They'll be all right. They always are. The two of them are unstoppable.

We watch them climb the hill, none of us moving, no one speaking. When a car door opens, I spin towards the noise. Lamb startles, baring his teeth.

It's just Shepard, getting out of the four-by-four. He looks rumpled and upset, like he's just woken from a nightmare. "Penelope!" he says, too loudly.

"They're on their way," I whisper. "Quiet!"

"On their way," Shepard repeats, looking at me, his face still muzzy, and then at Lamb.

I point towards Penny and Simon, halfway up the sand dune.

*"Penelope!"* Shepard gasps. And he takes off after her.

# PENELOPE

I tried to tell Baz. I tried to signal him with my eyes—"*I have a bad feeling about this. Mayday, Mayday, SOS.*" But I'm not sure what I expected him to do, send for the cavalry? Tell them to bring holy water?

I nearly cast "SOS" right then and there. But who would answer the call in this desolate place? And if someone rescued *us,* then who would rescue Agatha?

This isn't like me. I don't feel like myself.

The old me thought she would always prevail because she was always right. I'd like some of that confidence back now—even if it did come with a heaping helping of ignorance.

I'd like to believe that our rightness is all that's required to get Agatha out of this mess. That our goodness matters. That our power is *rooted* in those things and thus unmatched.

But what has America done but prove otherwise?

I look back at Baz. And ahead at Simon.

There's nowhere to go but forward.

I run to catch up with Simon. He keeps flying in front of me, then circling back. He's been wanting to kill vampires since we arrived in Las Vegas, and I think he's eager to get down to business.

"Simon," I say, when we're nearly to the top of the dune. "Come down for a minute. I can spell some armour for you."

"I don't need armour," he says, "but I'd take a sword."

He lands in front of me, and I take his hand, holding my gem between us, trying to think of a spell.

"Hey," he says, squeezing my fingers, "don't look like that. I know we didn't plan to get here by vampire caravan, but we're here. And if Agatha's on the other side of that hill, we're going to save her."

"What if she isn't?" I whisper.

Simon swallows and takes my other hand, too. "Is that what you think?"

"I don't know what to think. We're so far from home, Simon."

I hold his hands tight. He holds mine tighter. My stone cuts into both of our palms. I close my eyes and whisper a spell, ***"Steel yourself!"***

Nothing happens.

# SHEPARD

*Penelope, Penelope, Penelope.*

I catch up to them just before they hit the top of the hill, knocking Penelope into the sand.

"For snake's sake, Shepard—"

"Penelope! It's a Quiet Zone! The Vampire King tricked us!"

She pushes me off, spitting sand out of her mouth and shaking out her ponytail. "That would have been useful information to have two hours ago, Normal. Hope you enjoyed your nap."

I look from her to Simon, who's hovering in the air, face hard and arms folded. "I tried to tell you!" I say. "Lamb did something to me. Hypnotized me or something."

They're both looking at me like I'm something stuck on the bottom of their shoes. Which I guess I am.

They turn away from me, heading back up the dune.

I scramble after them. "Wait! *You guys.* This is a trap!"

"We know," Penelope says.

"So?" I try to catch her arm.

She turns on me. "*So*, it's a trap if we go, and a trap if we go back." She's looking over my shoulder. I glance back at the line of vampires at the bottom of the hill.

"You can go back," Simon says to me. "We're going to save Agatha."

"Yeah, but *how*?"

"We fight," he says, lifting higher in the air.

Penelope looks less sure.

"Okay." I'm still a little hungover from my vampire thrall, but my brain is racing through all the possible scenarios here. "Okay, okay, okay—maybe we can talk our way out of this."

She rolls her eyes. "*Shepard.* Just go back! Or go sideways. Go away."

I should. I might have a chance with Lamb. I could still make myself useful to him. Or I could try to warn Baz somehow. I could try my luck alone in the desert—I've got a whistle, and if I blow it, it's supposed to summon a giant eagle. (But I'm not sure whether the eagle's meant to save me or eat me.) (A gerrymander gave me the whistle, it's probably fake.)

Penelope is walking away. Simon is flying beside her.

I led them here.

I brought them to Las Vegas, I talked Lamb into helping them. . . .

I run to catch up with them, taking left flank.

# PENELOPE

I don't know what I'm expecting to find when we crest the hill.
But it isn't Agatha herself, standing right there at the bottom,
between two dark green four-by-fours. Her hands are bound,
I think. We're too far away to see her face, but it looks like she's
crying.

"Agatha!" Simon shouts. He's already shooting towards her.

"Wait!" I call. "Simon! We have to stay together!"

"They're baiting us," Shepard says.

Obviously. But we have to take the bait to see what happens
next. We have to take the bait because it's what we came for.
I start running.

Shepard runs after me. "You should really let me handle
this, Penelope!"

This Normal really thinks his voice is the last thing I want
to hear on this earth. "Honestly, Shepard. *Shut up.*"

I'm making plans. And backup plans. I'm thinking of spells.
I'm clutching my stone in my right hand. I'm telling myself we
might catch a break, even though I've never felt so far from
one. Agatha's alive, that's something.

We're close enough to see her face now. She *is* crying. She's
shaking her head no.

I push my gem in my mouth and swallow it.

# AGATHA

I knew it. I knew they'd come for me, they always do—they
can't help themselves.

*Idiots!*

They think they can keep sticking their heads into the lion's mouth, just because they haven't lost their heads so far. It's flawed logic! I've told them it's flawed logic—I've told them so many times!

Surviving monsters doesn't make you monster-proof. Escaping *once* doesn't enhance your odds of escaping *again*.

Penny always argues with me. *"The past is the best predictor of the future."*

Simon refuses to engage on any discussion of logic. What did he say to me seventh year? *"Ease up, Ags, I'll always save you. I'm good at it. And I get better every time."*

*"You think luck makes you lucky,"* I told him. He'd just found me in a well. My hair was still wet. *"But you're just a cat burning through his nine lives. And mine, as well."*

He didn't listen. They never listen.

And now here we are again.

Here we are, finally.

Fresh the fuck out of luck.

# BAZ

Shepard ran after them before I could stop him. Lamb didn't care. I watched them all climb to the top of the dune—Snow flying beside Bunce like her pet dragon. When they got to the top, he turned back and waved at me.

I waved back.

A moment later, there were gunshots.

# PENELOPE

It happens fast.

Simon reaches out for Agatha, and she shakes her head so hard, she falls over.

The vampires step out from behind the cars then. They weren't even hiding, really. Just standing back there, holding automatic weapons.

I want to laugh. We wouldn't have been ready for those guns, even if we still had our magic. Would I have got out a single spell?

Simon fights anyway.

The vampires—youngish men, mostly white, dressed like they're on safari—fire their guns in the air, presumably at Simon.

I don't see it happen—they already have me. They tape my mouth, tie my hands. Throw me into the back of a four-by-four with Agatha. She kicks me in the ear, trying to push them off of us.

That's it. That's all that happens. Then it's over.

Then we're done.

# 56

## AGATHA

The guns keep firing. Like there were more than two people to shoot down.

I thought the guns might be for show—that the NowNext creeps would want to take us all alive. But maybe Penny and I are enough of a score.

She's sitting next to me in the back of Braden's Mercedes.

I look in her eyes, half expecting her to have a plan—is anyone else coming? I wonder if Penny even realizes how bad this situation is. I try to tell her with my glued-closed face:

*It's worse than you think, Penelope. It's worse than we ever thought to fear.*

She looks wildly back at me. There's no plan. There's no hope.

No one comes to throw Simon into the back of the car. But after a few minutes, one of the NowNext guys gets into the front seat, his face flushed with excitement. He grins back at us, like he expects us to celebrate with him. They must all be feeling so tough and clever.

Penny slumps forward, refusing to look at or be seen by him.

I turn to the window. We're parked facing away from the fight, so I can't see what they're doing to Simon. I'm glad of that—does that make me a coward? Well, a leopard can't change its spots.

I stare out at the blank horizon. I pretend I don't notice the vampire in the front seat taking a selfie.

What a fool I've been.

I thought I was the *practical* one.

I honestly thought I could walk away from it all—like magic was a *place*. Like magic was a person. Or a habit I could break.

When Simon first came to Watford, he couldn't make his wand work. He could barely cast a spell. He thought they were going to kick him out, that he wasn't magic enough.

"*You don't* do *magic*," Penelope told him. "*You* are *magic*."

*I* . . . am magic.

Whether I like it or not, whether or not I claim it. Whether or not I carry my wand.

It's in me, somehow. Blood, water, bone.

And Braden is going to get it out.

I should have ended this before he had the chance. That would have been the heroic thing.

I should have thrown myself down a well. Penelope would have.

How have I lived through so many happy endings without ever learning how to save the day?

# 57

## BAZ

When the gunfire starts, Lamb is still holding on to me. "Steady," he says.

I'm anything but.

I drag him up the sand dune, the rest of the vampires forming a V behind us. I've got my hand inside my jacket, ready to cast a spell the moment it's worth spoiling my cover.

The guns quiet, then *rat-a-tat, rat-a-tat,* then settle again.

Lamb stops me at the crest, squeezing my arm. "Steady, lad. I need you to trust me to get you through this."

I'm half mad to get over the hill. "What? I do. I will. We followed you this far."

Lamb pulls me closer, his nose nearly touching my chin, his hair flopping over one eye. "Trust me *now,* Baz. I'll get you through."

I nod, hauling him forward. He won't let go of me. He follows me over the edge.

We look down and see a dozen or so vampires with machine

guns. They've got a gun to Shepard's head—and Simon is lying on the ground.

One of the vampires looks up at us and waves.

Lamb is holding me so tight, I think my arm will snap. He's whispering in my ear. "It was the only way, Baz. There's a treaty."

"*No. . . .*"

"Any mage who comes to Las Vegas gets turned over to them, no exceptions. It's how we keep them out."

I try to shove him away. "*No!*"

"This is going to be better for you in the end!"

I clutch my wand in my pocket and point it at Lamb, hissing, **"*Et tu, Brute!*"**

Nothing happens.

# 58

### · AGATHA

At first, I think it's a mirage.

Because it's exactly what I wish were there.

I was supposed to be at Burning Lad this weekend. Ginger and I had been planning it for months. A weeklong festival in the middle of the desert. A pop-up city. A celebration of life and death in a place where nothing lives, and even death has slim pickings.

I bought body paint, and sewed feathers onto my bikini. I was going to wear it on the last day—to the Grand Parade, the climax of the festival.

I'd pictured it so many times:

All that skin and fire snaking through the desert. I imagined how it would feel to *shine* like that. To be a small, spangled part of something so magickal, without anyone using any magic at all.

I see it now, on the horizon.

That glittering snake.

A mirage, surely. A trick of the sun and the sand.

I'd swear it's getting closer. . . .

I see the line of moving parts, of dancing bodies. I see the figure at their head—a large wooden boy, in flames.

I see it. . . .

It's not a mirage! It's real!

It's here!

And my first thought is, *It's coming for me!*

That's how accustomed I am to being rescued; I see a parade of people coming over the hill, and I assume they're coming to save *me*.

They're not.

They wouldn't even hear me if I could scream.

Which I can't.

And yet . . .

*And yet!*

I was wrong about Burning Lad! It's *full* of magic. Fifty thousand Normals. The third-largest city in Nevada, for one week of the year.

A pop-up city heading my way!

The line on the horizon gets thicker, but the Normals are still so far. . . .

That's okay. I don't need much of their magic for this spell. It's the only one I can cast without a wand, without even moving my lips.

# PENELOPE

I'm worried that they won't kill us. Promptly.

That our bodies might hold *years* of useful information.

The vampires will find what they're looking for, I suspect. Magic is genetic, after all—it must be coded into mages in a way that can be decoded. We should have been the ones to figure it out first.

Mum would call that heresy. Trying to *explain* magic.

But isn't that just . . . science?

I wish I could have this argument with her. . . .

I've read that bodies disappear completely in the desert. Good. I hope Mum never knows my role in this.

The gunshots go on for a while. Simon shouts.

And then he doesn't.

It's— ·

I can't—

I slump forward against the front seat, choking on something that comes out half sob, half vomit. My lips are taped shut. My mouth and nose are full of bile. I see sparks.

*This is it, this is what happens. This is not getting away.*

There are more sparks. . . .

In Agatha's lap, above her bound hands.

I look up at her face. Her chin is tilted back, and her eyelids are heavy. She looks like she's casting a spell.

Magic? Where is Agatha getting *magic*? And how is she casting without a wand? Without speaking?

She sees me watching her. She looks so sorrowful. Her hands spark again.

# AGATHA

Penelope is nodding at me.

Does she think I have a grand plan?

*I'm sorry, Penny. I'm not getting us out of this. I was never a hero. I was never a very good friend—I did try to tell you.*

She shimmies up next to me. The vampire in the front seat isn't paying attention to us; he's still on his phone. I jerk my head towards the window, towards the glittering parade. When Penny's eyes widen, I know for certain that I haven't hallucinated it. She pushes her face against my neck, and I feel my magic snap into focus, almost as if I'm holding my wand—the sparks above my hands catch into a flame.

Penny grunts. I pull back to look in her eyes. She nods again.

I lean forward and hold the flame over the front seat.

It happens so fast. He burns so bright.

I turn back to Penelope. Her face is damp. Her nose is running. She's still nodding at me. I push my forehead against hers and close my eyes.

# PENELOPE

*Agatha, yes—you brilliant girl.*
*You've saved the day in the end.*

# 59

## SHEPARD

"My name is Shepard," I say. "I'm from Omaha, Nebraska."

"I told you to shut up!" the vampire says, pressing the nose of his gun more firmly into my temple.

He did tell me to shut up, but I think he's probably going to kill me whether I shut up or not, so I may as well keep playing till I'm all out of cards.

I put my hands up as soon as I saw the guns. The vampires seemed to know I'm not magic. They taped Penelope's mouth shut, but not mine. They shot Simon out of the air.

He went down like a rabid bat. I don't think the vampire he landed on will ever see again. (Can vampires grow new eyes?) Then Simon grabbed the vampire's rifle and swung it at another one's head—it was like watching a *Mortal Kombat* character.

The vampires shot him again.

He didn't get up.

Baz is coming down the hill now. He looks like he's in shock. Like Lamb is practically holding him up.

"My mother's name is Michele," I say to the man holding

me. "With one *l*. She teaches Spanish. My parents are divorced, what about yours?"

One of the NowNext guys steps forward to meet Lamb. The guy's dressed in brand-new, expensive camping gear—they all are. Space-age nylon pants with zippers. Glacier glasses. One of them even has one of those aluminum hiking poles. It's like getting ambushed by a heavily armed *GQ* spread.

The Next Blood vampire is spitting mad. "For fuck's sake, Lamb, you could have warned us that one of them was feral!"

"I did warn you," Lamb says, cool as ever. "The treaty holds."

"And you brought a rando with a cellphone?!" (That's me, I think.)

"Consider him a bonus." Lamb is trying to turn away, but Baz won't turn. He won't look away from Simon.

"You promised us two mages!" the Next Blood vamp says, still spitting.

"I *brought* you two mages." Lamb's voice cracks, like he can't believe he's got to deal with this nonsense. He gestures at Simon. "It's not my fault you ruined one!"

"Well," the other vampire says, all sullen, "at least take the kid with you. You know we don't like to involve NPCs."

Lamb laughs. A few of the other Vegas vampires snicker.

"Does that mean you won't kill me?" I ask the guy holding the gun to my head. "Because that's really good of you. That's an admirable policy."

Lamb is still smiling. Smiling like he's happy to have someone to hate this much. "You really think you're the superior model, the next step on the evolutionary ladder. . . . And you can't even cope with a teenage Bleeder?" (I'm 22, but I decide not to interrupt him.) "You haven't worked out a *protocol* for this? Give him to us, Braden! We'll show you how a real vampire takes care of business."

The Vegas vampires are leering at me.

The other guy, Braden, rolls his eyes with his whole body. "There's no such thing as a 'real' vampire, Lamb! It's an apocryphal concept!"

"I assure you I'm real!" Lamb roars, letting go of Baz. I get the feeling he and Braden have had this screaming match before.

"We don't have to play by your rules!" Braden shouts back. "We don't have to play into your age-old fallacies!"

"No indeed, you're free to behave like uncultured cowards!"

"We're not cowards!" the one holding me shouts, jabbing me again in the temple.

This is not an encouraging direction.

"Don't listen to Mr. Las Vegas over there," I say, using my just-between-you-and-me voice. "That guy does *not* have your best interests at heart."

"You live in denial!" Lamb says. He's addressing them all. "In fear!"

With Lamb distracted, Baz has taken a step forward. Toward Simon. Baz is swaying on his feet.

The gun drops from my forehead. Two hands close like vise grips around my biceps. "We're not afraid to do things your way!" the man behind me yells.

I close one eye, bracing myself. "My dude . . . *please*, no. I fear this won't go well for either of us."

Braden turns to us. He's a different variety of cool than Lamb, but he's definitely the alpha wolf of this pack. "Josh, no—don't lower yourself."

"Don't do it, Josh," I agree.

"I'm tired of them *mocking* us, Braden! We can be strong when it's required of us!"

"That isn't real strength, Josh!" Braden and I say at once.

Braden waves his gun at me, losing his temper. "Why didn't you glue his mouth shut?!"

The Vegas vampires look bored. Some of them are still laughing. Lamb has got Baz by the arm again—he's trying to keep him away from Simon, but Baz won't be kept. He's leaning over Simon's body, pulling his own hair in his fists.

"I've got this," Josh says, yanking me back into his chest. He takes a heavy breath, and then clamps his fangs into my neck—

And then he falls over, oily smoke spiraling from his mouth.

"Josh," I say, swooning forward. "I told you this wasn't going to be good."

On my way to the ground, I see Baz running for Braden, his arms flying around the other vampire's neck.

# 60

## BAZ

It's a dead spot. We should have—I should have—

Simon's lying on the ground. His wing is bent the wrong way.

Lamb: "Yes, all right, I've betrayed you. Just keep your cool, Baz, and you'll live to hate me for it."

I'll live . . .

Simon.

We heard gunshots. On the other side of the hill. And then we didn't.

Simon's on the ground, his wing is bent the wrong way. Someone should fix it for him. Someone should cast a spell. I'd cast it, but I'm in a dead spot. I'm in a Quiet Zone. I'm keeping my wand a secret, I'm pretending to be a vampire.

"Simon . . ."

*Simon Snow.*

*The way you were. There wasn't a day when I believed we'd both live through it.*

*(Through what, through what, through what?)*

Lamb: "The treaty holds!"

Simon:

Simon is on the ground. There were gunshots, and then there weren't. His wing is bent the wrong way. His hair is a mess. He doesn't have a sword.

I told him it would be all right.

I told him . . .

I didn't tell him, I never told him. Not in a way that he believed. Not in a way that he could let in and hold on to. Everything he was to me. That he was everything.

*Simon, Simon . . .*

*You were the sun, and I was crashing into you.*

*I'd wake up every morning and tell myself . . .*

*I'd tell myself . . .*

"You live in fear! In denial!"

Simon is on the ground. His wing is bent the wrong way. His blood is red and abundant. It smells like brown butter. His hair is a mess, his face is in the sand. He doesn't know how much I love him. He's never really heard it.

*I'd wake up every morning and tell myself . . .*

"Simon . . . love . . . get up. We still have to save Agatha."

Simon is on the ground.

*This will end in flames.*

# 61

## SIMON

I'm going to get up. As soon as my head clears. If my head clears.

I think I've got holes in my wings. . . . Can I bleed out through appendages that didn't originally come with my body?

I'm going to get up. As soon as I can. I'm waiting for the right moment.

The right moment will be the moment when I have a shot at one of these bastards. (I got at least one already. I yanked one of his eyes out.) (Heal that, fucker.)

I'm getting up. So I can go down with a fight.

They took Penelope.

I can't—

I don't think I can—

The vampires are fighting, I think. Maybe they'll kill each other. That would make my job easier.

My job is getting up.

My job is going down.

With a fight.

I saved Agatha from a werewolf once. And from a Pegasus foaming at the mouth. I killed a dragon. By accident. Did you know that, one time, the Humdrum hid Agatha at the bottom of a well? I found her. I hauled her up.

He sent cravens, and I caught them in my bare hands.

Once there was a nar-do-whal. In the moat.

And I . . .

There were so many goblins.

So many trolls.

I killed them.

A gryphon. A diphthong. An aspssasin. And I . . .

They've got Agatha. They took Penelope.

There's no magic here, but that's okay—there's no magic left in me.

I'll take one more when I go. When I get up. And go down.

I'll take at least one more.

For Agatha. And Penelope.

For . . .

"Simon . . ."

*Baz!*

# 62

## SHEPARD

The vampire who bit me is definitely dead. And probably everyone here would be more horked off over that if Baz didn't just grab the leader of the Next Blood by the neck and rip off half his jaw.

The rest of the San Diego vampires are emptying their clips into Baz and Lamb—and, incidentally, each other. Lamb's crew hadn't been taking any of this seriously; a few of them had even headed back up the hill after the Speakers were officially turned over. But now they're running into the mob with their mouths open and their fangs all the way out.

I feel weak as shit and woozy, but I drag myself back behind one of the Mercedes G-Wagens. Penelope's in the other one. I lie on my belly and army-crawl between the SUVs, hoping the guns are pointed in any other direction. I'm halfway to the second Mercedes when it literally bursts into flames. I leap up into a run, yanking one of the back doors open. Smoke pours out. And then the blond girl. Then Penelope. They're alive.

They're . . . surprised, I think. I untie their hands. But their mouths are glued shut, and I can't get them open.

Penelope reaches frantically into my pocket and pulls out my Swiss Army knife, holding it up to her face.

I try to keep my hand steady. I try to ignore the blood.

# 63

## BAZ

Go ahead and shoot me. This isn't my favourite shirt.

These vampires don't know what to do. I'm biting off pieces of their president and CEO. He's very strong. But I'm also very strong, and very angry, and very determined to tear him into pieces, even if he can grow them back like a starfish.

Let's tear each other into pieces and see what grows back. I won't miss this suit.

Lamb is trying to restrain me. *Go away, Lamb. Brutus. Betrayer. Vampire.*

"Baz!" he shouts. "We can still save ourselves!"

Ha! There's no saving me. Everything I am is already gone. My teeth are like knives. I use them.

"Baz! Listen to me!"

One of the vampires jumps on my shoulders. Lamb sighs and pulls him off. "I guess we're doing this. . . ."

Lamb fights like someone who's stayed alive for three hundred years.

Lamb isn't afraid of machine guns.

"Baz!"

That wasn't Lamb. . . .

I let go of Braden (some of him still sticks to me) and spin around—

Simon Snow is getting up on his knees.

Simon Snow is alive. . . .

Somewhat.

"Simon!" I scream. "Stay down!"

Of course he doesn't listen.

# SIMON

Baz is fighting twenty-six vampires, and I'm getting up to help.

I'm probably going to get shot again.

Before I get the opportunity, one of those expensive Land Rovers starts on fire. The vampires scramble away from it. One of them has a metal cane. The telescoping kind. I snatch it and drive it through his heart. It's not a wooden stake, so maybe it won't do the trick. I'm prepared to keep trying.

*Penelope was in that car.* I try my wings. They work. Ish.

I spear another vampire.

*And Agatha.*

I bring the cane down on someone's back. It feels like hitting a brick wall with a lead pipe.

I'm just warming up to avenging their deaths when Penelope and Agatha themselves walk out of the flames, holding hands, both of their mouths bleeding—looking like their own bloody ghosts.

Penelope raises one hand and screams, **"Swords into ploughshares!"**

The machine guns fall into the sand. She's turned them into . . . ploughshares, I reckon. My cane changes, too. Which seems fair given the circumstances.

"Penelope Bunce," Baz says, his eyes lit up with wonder.

The vampires seem confused, on both sides.

I look down. . . .

A ploughshare is basically just a really wide axe head. It takes two hands to swing it.

# BAZ

Penelope Bunce is a fierce magician, I've never minded saying it.

She's just escaped from handcuffs and a flaming car. She's casting spells without her wand in a dead spot. Harry Houdini himself couldn't top it.

And she's got Agatha—alive.

"Basil!" Bunce shouts. "There's magic!"

She's pointing at something in the distance. A line of trees? No, it's moving. Are those *people*?

The vampires have turned on each other again. One of Braden's friends is charging at me. I whip out my wand and point it at him. ***"Off with your head!"***

Nothing happens.

But I feel it. The magic. I feel it stuttering in my wrist and on my tongue. Like an engine trying to catch in my belly. ***"Off with your head!"*** I try again.

That does it. I can't help but grin.

When I turn away, I see that Lamb is watching me, his blue eyes wide. The vampire at his throat is staring at me, too. "You've done it," the man says to me, awestruck. "You've levelled up."

Lamb rams his forehead into the man's nose.

The magic here is a capricious thing. Half my spells fail. So I cast twice as many. And the tide—it wasn't a tide so much as a melee—turns:

The vampires don't have guns anymore. But Simon has some sort of scythe. He looks like the grim reaper. Drenched in blood, his T-shirt as red as his wings. One of his wings is drooping, I don't think he can fly. He doesn't really need to. Unarmed, untrained vampires aren't much of a match for Simon with a blade—any blade will do.

Penelope and Agatha are fighting together, holding hands and using their free hands as flamethrowers. The vampires go up like tinder, any of them who get too close; the girls and the fire aren't discerning. Lamb's vampires are leaving the fight, running up the sand dune or already running down the other side.

I spin around, my wand out, looking for my next bout. There's more fire than foes now.

Lamb is still at my back. (The better to stab me, I suppose.) "Baz!" he hisses. "Come on, let's go!"

"You must be kidding."

He heaves me around by the arm, so I'm facing him. His suit is stained. His hair is disordered. "I'm glad your friends made it," he says, "but that doesn't change reality—*nothing* can change what you are."

"You saw what I am," I say.

He nods grimly. "Yes. You're one of them. I see that. But Baz, you're one of us, too. Blood will out."

"Could I live as a mage in your tower, Lamb?"

"Can you live as you are with them?"

I don't answer him. He's still holding my arm. "Come with me."

I shake myself free. "No."

He runs away then. Maybe I shouldn't have let him.

When I turn back to the fight, there's one last member of the Next Blood running towards me. He's already alight. I hold out my wand. ***"Fuck off and die!"***

The spell doesn't catch.

I try again.

Nothing happens.

Then *something* happens: Simon Snow sweeps me out of the way and into the air.

He's got me by the waist. His wings are pumping hard. I hold on to dear life.

# 64

## SHEPARD

I take shelter in the unburnt Mercedes for the rest of the fight. I'm foolhardy, but I'm not a fool.

The vampires flare up and ash out quickly. Only their clothes keep burning. All that's left in the end are little puddles of fire in the sand.

Agatha took out the last one. She and Penelope are still holding hands. Their mouths are smeared with blood, and sparks are sputtering from Agatha's palm.

Simon hasn't landed yet. His wings are beating unevenly, and he keeps lurching down, then flapping back up, still holding Baz by the waist.

I climb out of the car and kick some sand over a pile of burning clothes. "So," I say, "the keys are still in this Mercedes. Anybody feel like blowing this Popsicle stand?"

Penelope and Agatha just stare at me. They're like something out of a Stephen King movie.

I get in front of them and clap my hands. "Guys!" I clap

again. "Friends! Let's go. Get out while the getting's good, right? Penelope?" I touch her shoulder.

She blinks at me. "Right," she whispers.

She starts pulling Agatha toward the car—"Come on, Agatha. . . ."—and looks up at Simon and Baz. "Simon! We're leaving, Simon!"

Simon keeps flapping.

I open the car door and help Agatha in. "I'm Shepard," I say, taking her hand.

Penelope has run back for Simon, getting under him and catching his ankle. "Simon! Come on! Come down. It's over. . . . *Simon!*" The boys fall more than land. "Merlin," Penelope says. "Watch out for the fire, Simon—he's still flammable. Can you walk, Baz?"

The three of them are holding each other up.

"Yeah," Baz says. "Not to worry."

One of Simon's wings is hanging and mottled a darker red. I weave my way through the fires to them. Up close, it's clear that both of the guys are bleeding badly. Baz looks like he was wearing squibs under his shirt. "Come on," I say, getting my arm around Simon. He leans hard on me.

Penelope pulls Baz's arm over her shoulder, but Simon won't let go of him. He's got his hand fisted in Baz's bloody shirt.

"It's all right," I say, "we're all going to the same place." Simon still won't let go. Penelope and I half drag the two of them to the car. We get Baz in first, in the middle seat, and he hauls Simon in by the waist. Simon loses consciousness as soon as he's off his feet. "We can go straight to the hospital," I say.

Baz sneers at me. "Are you kidding? We'll fix him with magic. We'll fix it all with magic. Just get us out of here if you can."

I can. The key fob is sitting in the console. And the car's

equipped with satellite navigation. I run around and get in the front seat. "How were you guys casting spells at all? In a Quiet Zone?"

"There were Normals in the desert," Penelope says. "Not close—but close enough."

Their magic comes back full force almost immediately. That Quiet Zone was small. The vampires knew exactly what they were doing when they brought us there.

Penelope heals Simon first, leaning over the seat and clutching his wing.

"Where's your gem?" Baz asks.

"I've got it." She closes her eyes. ***Good as new!***

Simon groans, stretching the wing, inadvertently knocking Penelope back into her seat.

She casts the spell three more times—on his head, his heart, his stomach.

I watch them in the rearview mirror. I know I should focus on the road, but this is *spectacular.*

Penelope reaches for Baz next, but he shrugs her off. "I'm full of lead," he says. "I don't know what will happen. I just need a drink."

"We'll be in cattle country soon," I call back.

Baz nods. "I'll wait." He snags her hand. "Come here, Bunce."

"I'm right as rain, Baz."

"Don't make me climb over Simon."

Penelope sighs, leaning over the seat, and Baz holds his wand to her mouth. ***Kiss it better!***

"Basil, that's a family spell!"

"Hush," he says, kissing her cheek. He wipes the blood from her mouth with his sleeve. His arm is shaking. "You okay?"

She's tearful. She nods.

"Do you have anything left for Agatha?"

"Of course."

Penelope sits back in the seat and gently touches Agatha's face. I can't hear the spell.


Baz drinks a cow.

Simon's still asleep.

Agatha hasn't said a word.


It's a ten-hour drive to San Diego. Baz moves up front with me, casting spells on the car, I think. He looks like he took a bloodbath. I run into a Target in Reno to buy him fresh clothes. He cleans up in a gas station bathroom and comes out looking pale and affordable.

I'm nervous about being pulled over, even with his spells. "Will we dump the car? I'm sure we've been clocked somewhere."

"We're going to destroy this car," Agatha says, speaking up for the first time. "And anyone who asks about it."

Baz sighs. "Two thousand and eighteen. G-Class. Jade Green Metallic."

I keep waiting for them to dump me, too. (I hope they wouldn't destroy me at this point, after everything we've been through together. Then again, that's probably *why* they'd destroy me.)

But when we finally get to Agatha's apartment, and I'm standing down on the sidewalk wondering how I'm going to get back to Vegas, Baz holds the door open for me.

# PROLOGUE

## BAZ

We're leaving for the airport in an hour—I should probably get out of the shower. I stretch, and what I hope is the last of the bullets breaks through the skin on my shoulder and clanks against the bottom of the bath.

I never, *ever* want to feel this way again. I don't want to test the limits of this body, even if it might give me a better understanding of what I am.

We've spent the last day sleeping and eating and casting spells on each other. Agatha's stuck to Penny like a little girl clinging to her mother on the tube. She's coming back with us. Agatha. "Just to get my wand," she says. "It doesn't mean I'm staying."

When I get out of the bathroom, Agatha's friend Ginger is here to pick up her dog, that ridiculous little spaniel I stole back in London. Apparently Ginger is the one who introduced Wellbelove to the NowNext vampires, and she's in a full pout that she hasn't heard from them.

"Josh isn't even replying to my texts," Ginger says.

"Would you want him to? He abandoned you in Rancho Santa Fe."

"So did you, Agatha!"

Bunce is standing behind Ginger, holding up her purple stone and silently offering to magickally befuddle her.

Agatha is shaking her head at both of them. "Ginger, I told you it was a drag! And I left as soon as I realized you weren't there."

Ginger looks tearful. She's got a ring of red above her top lip, and it takes me a second to realize she's drinking beet-root juice. "I thought they were going to let me level up," she moans. "And they didn't even invite me to their after-party!"

"They couldn't have invited you," Agatha says, rubbing the girl's arm. "You're too good. You would have seen what they're really about, and made them all feel like hypocrites."

Ginger hangs her head. "I guess. . . ."

"Don't talk to Josh anymore," Agatha says, "even if he calls."

I'm fairly certain he won't.

Ginger sniffs. "I'll think about it."

I look around the living room. "Where's Snow?"

"He walked down to the beach a while ago," Bunce says.

"I'll go get him," I say. "We need to go."

"Freshen up his . . ." She flaps her elbows. "If he needs it."

I nod, touching my wand. It's under my shirt, tucked inside the waistband of my (cheap, horrible) jeans. I'm lucky to still have it. And my mobile. Everything else is gone.

None of us have called home yet. But we'll have to talk to our parents eventually about what happened—about the Next Blood, at least. Lamb said there were more of them. And Agatha thinks they really do have a lab in the desert.

It's telling that not a one of us suggested we go find it. Not even Simon.

He slept all the way to San Diego. I think he had internal injuries after the battle. Bunce thinks she's fixed him, but we're taking him to see Dr. Wellbelove as soon as we get home, just in case.

# PENELOPE

Agatha's friend Ginger is crying because she missed her chance to become a douchebag vampire, and Agatha's being nicer than I've ever seen her be to anyone. Is this why she doesn't reply to my texts? Because they're not idiotic enough?

I find Shepard on the balcony. You can see the ocean from out here. He's looking down at his phone.

"Writing this up for your blog?"

"Nah," he says. "I'll do that when I get home. I can't type on my phone."

"Ha-bloody-ha," I say, glancing down at his screen. He's looking up bus tickets. To Las Vegas. "Shepard, *no!* By no means!"

"I've got to get my truck, Penelope."

"The *vampires* have your truck!"

"It's in short-term parking," he says. "I'm paying forty-three dollars a night."

"There are other trucks, Shepard."

"Yes." He shrugs. "But none that I'm entitled to drive."

I see them when he shrugs—two fang marks under the collar of his jacket. Just as Baz said.

"Hey," I say, fishing my amethyst out of my bra. (Very happy to have it back *outside* my digestive tract. Sweet Circe, that was an unpleasant task.) "Let me see that bite."

"I'm all right," he says. "Save your magic."

"You can't save magic," I say. "It's not like spare change."

"It's not?" There's that infuriating light in his eyes.

"No. Come on. We should have done this yesterday."

He scoots his chair closer to mine, and I pull back his collar. There are two scabbed-over puncture wounds and bruises from the vampire's non-fang teeth. I can't help but shudder. "Are you worried that they might have . . ."

"Turned me?" He finishes my question. "No. I haven't felt especially bloodthirsty. And . . . and anyway, no, I'm not worried."

I hold my gem over his wound and say, ***"Good as new!"***

When I pull my hand away, the scabs are still there. I frown. "Shepard . . . are you immune to magic?"

"No," he says, running his fingers over the wound like he's curious. "Not immune."

I sit back. "Baz said that a vampire bit you, and it made the vampire sick."

He looks out towards the water. "Maybe *the vampire* was allergic."

"Shepard. I thought you believed in straight answers."

He looks over at me like he's hurting somewhere, and it has nothing to do with a vampire bite. "I do."

I sit back a little farther. "What *are* you?"

He turns himself completely towards me. "Penelope, I'm exactly what I look like. I'm a Talker, a Bleeder, a Normal."

"And . . ."

"And I am also slightly . . . a little bit . . ." He swallows. "Cursed."

I wasn't expecting him to say that. I don't even know what that means. "You're *cursed*?"

He rubs his eyes under his glasses. "Yeah, I . . . Josh the tech-bro vampire couldn't claim my soul because, *technically speaking*, it belongs to someone else."

"*Who?*"

"Nobody you'd know. I hope. A demon. Demon-type. I'd tell you his name, but then he might show up. I . . ." He looks embarrassed. Caught out. He slowly takes off his jean jacket. . . .

His arms are covered with twisting black tattoos. Runes and numbers. Thorns.

"*Shepard.*"

"Pretty goth, right? Not the ink I'd choose for myself. I thought about getting a Vonnegut quote, but everybody has those. . . ."

"How did this *happen?*"

He looks down. "Oh, you know—your classic wrong place, wrong time scenario. A summoning circle. Midnight. And then . . . a series of miscommunications and cultural differences."

I'm still looking at the curse markings. I press my gem to his flesh. **"Out, out, damned spot!"**

The spell shoots down through my arm, then seems to double back on me. I pull my hand away like I've been shocked, and my gem drops.

The balcony is made of wood decking, and the gem is resting at the edge of one of the slats. Shepard carefully picks it up and holds it out to me. "Thank you," he says. "But I don't think there's any un-cursing me. Some magic works on me, but nothing that would change my fate—"

I clench my amethyst in my fist and press my hand against his neck.

"Penelope," he says, catching my wrist.

**"Get well soon!"** I say. I feel the spell hook on him. He feels it, too. His head rocks back a bit, and he squeezes my wrist.

I move my hand away. The vampire bite already looks a bit better. Good.

He's still holding my wrist.

"Shepard, you're not going back to Las Vegas."

"But my—"

"If you mention your truck again, I'm going to turn you into a frog." I pull my hand away. "A demon-cursed frog."

"I need to get back home."

"No." I fold my arms. "You're coming back to London with us. I'm taking you to my mother, and she's going to fix you."

"I appreciate the offer, but this situation is beyond ma—"

"*Nothing* is beyond magic!"

Shepard snaps his mouth closed, and I hope that means he's done arguing.

I stand up and make a show of heading back into the flat. Like, *case closed.* "I mean," I say, without turning, "I know you think you know everything there is to know about the magickal world, but I don't even know that, and I'm smarter than you, and I've spent my whole life studying it."

"I can't afford the airfare, Penelope."

"I'll take care of it."

"I don't have a passport."

"Oh ye of little faith."

"Is that a spell?"

I stop at the sliding door, looking at his reflection in the glass. "Come to London and find out."

# SIMON

The Pacific Ocean is warmer than the Atlantic.

This bit of it, anyway.

I'm sitting out on the sand, with my boots off and my jeans

rolled up. The jeans got wet, anyway. Penny will dry them. She's been plastering me with spells since we got out of the dead spot—I came out here partly just to give her a break. And to try to clear my head.

I had this idea about America. . . .

That I'd find myself here.

That's why people get in a convertible and hit the road without a map. That's the promise. That you'll finally see yourself when you don't recognize the scenery.

Maybe it worked.

I fell for the blue sky and sunshine—then this country dragged me behind it, kicking and bleeding. I failed every test. I fell. I fell short. And only someone else's spells got me back on my feet and breathing again.

It's time for me to stop pretending that I'm some sort of superhero. I *was* that—I really was—but I'm not anymore. I don't belong in the same world as sorcerers and vampires. That's not my story.

Dr. Wellbelove said he could remove the wings. And the tail. Whenever I'm ready. I could go back to school then, or get a job—I think I'd rather get a job. Earn something for myself. Pay my own rent.

It feels good to think about.

It feels like—shit, I'm crying. It feels awful, but it feels clean.

There's a wave crashing towards me. Sometimes they start out fierce, then lose their nerve before they get to the beach.

This one doesn't blink.

# BAZ

Simon's sitting on the beach, like a boy in a music video. White T-shirt, rolled-up jeans. Head full of sun.

There's a wave headed for him, he must see it, but he doesn't move until it comes up over his legs. His head falls back. I think he might be smiling.

I take off my socks and shoes and leave them on a rock, then find my way down to him. He looks up when my shadow reaches him, closing one eye against the sun. "Hey."

I smile. "Hey."

Another wave is coming our way. I hop back to avoid it. Simon laughs. The wave breaks a few feet away from him.

I decide to join him on the sand—I can spell myself dry later. I sit a bit behind him, on slightly higher ground.

He glances back at me. "Oh, hey," he says like he's just remembered something. He leans back to reach in his pocket, and takes out a wad of blue silk.

"That's my mother's scarf!" I reach for it.

He opens his hand. The scarf threads through his fingers as I pull it away. "Sorry," he says. "I forgot it was in my pocket."

"I thought I left it in the hotel room."

"You did."

I fold the scarf, gently. Snow watches for a moment, then looks away.

"Well," I say. "Now you can say you drove across America."

"Not really." He folds his arms over his knees. "We started in the middle, and I was in a coma from Nevada to California."

"You didn't miss anything."

He hunches forward, hanging his head. "I wanted to see those ancient trees, the sequoias."

"They'll still be here when you come back."

He shakes his head. "Not coming back. You can send me a postcard."

"Me? I don't think I'm ever leaving Camberwell after this. Possibly to visit my parents at Christmas. I'll decide in December."

He looks back at me. The way he's sitting, his face tilted, he looks like a child. He looks like the Humdrum. "You don't have to leave with us, you know."

"What?"

He turns back to the sea. "I saw you . . . with Lamb. I heard you."

"Snow . . ."

"He'd let you stay there."

"In a glam-rock hotel in Las Vegas? No, thank you." It's the wrong thing to say. But everything Simon's saying is already the wrong thing. This is a wrong conversation.

He raises his hands, frustrated. "Baz, I was there! You—you fit in."

"I was *trying* to fit in."

"You're like them! And he could show you how to be *more* like them; you wouldn't have to go looking for answers in books. Baz, we've read all the books. All mages know about vampires is how to kill them!"

"Knowledge I have very recently put into service."

Simon growls and turns towards me, one leg dropping into the sand. "Baz, you wouldn't have to hide anymore!"

"I'll always have to hide! So will you!"

"Why can't you just admit that you'd be happier here?"

I raise my voice: "Why can't you see that I wouldn't be happy anywhere without you?"

He sits back, like I've slapped him.

"Simon . . ." I whisper.

I wait for him to *get* it. To finally give in to it.

Or maybe to say I've passed the test.

Instead he shakes his head. "Baz . . ." His voice is barely there.

"Baz!" someone shouts.

Penelope's running towards us. She's out of breath. We both stand when we see the look on her face. I catch her by the shoulders. "What? What is it?"

Her brown eyes are lit with horror. "Baz, there's trouble at Watford. We have to go home—*now!*"

# ACKNOWLEDGMENTS

I wrote this book after a hard time and during a hard time. So these acknowledgments come from a more tremulous place than usual.

Thank you first to Thomas Smith, Josh Friedman, Michelle McCaslin, and Mark Goodman, four people who treated me with absolute respect and compassion, and never stopped listening or trying to understand.

Thank you to my editor, Sara Goodman, who could have said, *"Another Simon and Baz book?"* But instead said, *"Another Simon and Baz book!"* Sara has never asked me to be anyone but myself, and I treasure her for it.

I've been very lucky at Wednesday Books and St. Martin's Press, where my books are treated with so much care and enthusiasm. I'm especially grateful for designer Olga Grlic, who is my favorite combination of fearless and committed to great work; and for publicist Jessica Preeg, who has been my rock.

Writing a sequel is surprisingly tricky. . . .

Sincere thanks to Bethany and Troy Gronberg, Margaret Willison, and Joy DeLyria, for helping me detangle multiple knots. To Ashley Christy, Mitali Dave, Tulika Mehrotra, and Christina Tucker, for their keen insight and attention to detail. To Melinda Salisbury, Keris Stainton, and Melissa Cox, for their endless patience and good cheer. And to Elena Yip, whose instincts are second to none.

Thank you to my agent, Christopher Schelling. (You know that your agent has your back when they're there for you, day after day, even when you're not writing at all.)

And thank you to Kai, who tells me it will be okay and means it.

Finally, I know this is sappy, but I want to thank everyone who really *got* what I was doing with *Carry On*. (It was a weird idea; I know it was a weird idea.) Thank you to everyone who read that book and shared it, who made fan art and fanfiction and sour cherry scones on Simon's birthday. And thank you for getting excited about this sequel, even though four years was *obviously too long to wait*.

Simon and Baz walked directly out of my heart, and I'm so glad I get to keep writing their story.